The End of the Line

The End of the Line

Ted Darling crime series

'gripping twisting hunt for justice'

LIVRES
LEMAS

L M Krier

Published by LEMAS LIVRES
www.tottielimejuice.com

© Copyright L.M.K. Tither 2021
Cover design DMR Creative
Cover photo Neil Smith

THE END OF THE LINE

ISBN 978-2-901773-50-4

Contents

Chapter One   1

Chapter Two   11

Chapter Three   21

Chapter Four   31

Chapter Five   40

Chapter Six   49

Chapter Seven   57

Chapter Eight   66

Chapter Nine   75

Chapter Ten   83

Chapter Eleven   92

Chapter Twelve   100

Chapter Thirteen   109

Chapter Fourteen   117

Chapter Fifteen   126

Chapter Sixteen   135

Chapter Seventeen   143

Chapter Eighteen   152

Chapter Nineteen   160

Chapter Twenty   169

Chapter Twenty-one   178

Chapter Twenty-two   187

Chapter Twenty-three   196

Chapter Twenty-four   205

Chapter Twenty-five   214

Chapter Twenty-six   222

Chapter Twenty-seven   230

Chapter Twenty-eight   238

Chapter Twenty-nine   247

Chapter Thirty   255

Chapter Thirty-one   264

Chapter Thirty-two   272

Chapter Thirty-three   280

Chapter Thirty-four   289

About the Author

L M Krier is the pen-name of former journalist (court reporter) and freelance copywriter, Lesley Tither, who also writes travel memoirs under the name Tottie Limejuice. Lesley also worked as a case tracker for the Crown Prosecution Service. Now retired, she lives in Central France and enjoys walking her dogs and going camping.

Contact Details

If you would like to get in touch, please do so at:

https://www.teddarlingcrimeseries.uk/

tottielimejuice@gmail.com

facebook.com/LMKrier

facebook.com/groups/1450797141836111/

twitter.com/tottielimejuice

For a lighter look at Ted and Trev, why not join the fun in the We Love Ted Darling group? on Facebook. FREE 'Ted Darling is billirant' badge for each member.

Discover the
DI Ted Darling series

If you've enjoyed meeting Ted Darling you may like to discover the other books in the series. All books are available as ebooks and in paperback format. The First Time Ever is also now available as an audiobook. Watch out for audiobook versions of other books in the series, coming soon, as well as further books in the series:

The First Time Ever
Baby's Got Blue Eyes
Two Little Boys
When I'm Old and Grey
Shut Up and Drive
Only the Lonely
Wild Thing
Walk On By
Preacher Man
Cry for the Bad Man
Every Game You Play
Where the Girls Are
Down Down Down
The Cuckoo is a Pretty Bird
Dirty Old Town
The End of the Line

The First Time Ever is also available translated into French by Jean Sauvanet, under the title of 'Darling.'

Acknowledgements

I would just like to thank the people who have helped me bring Ted Darling to life.

Alpha and Beta readers: Jill Pennington, Kate Pill, Karen Corcoran, Jo Baines, Jill Evans, Alan Wood, Paul Kemp, Eileen Payne, Valérie Goutte.

Police consultants – The Three Karens.

Medical advisor – Jo Baines

Special thanks to Jane Cassell and Emma Faulkner for their invaluable special help.

And a very special thanks to all Ted's loyal friends in the We Love Ted Darling Facebook group. Always so supportive and full of great ideas to be incorporated into the next Ted book. FREE 'Ted Darling is billirant' badge for all members.

To Robin,

My old friend and sparring partner
Well done, thou good and faithful servant

Author's Note

Thank you for reading the Ted Darling Crime Series. The books are set in Stockport, and Greater Manchester in general, and the characters use local dialect and sayings.

Seemingly incorrect grammar within quotes reflects common speech patterns. For example, 'I'll do it if I get chance', without an article or determiner, is common parlance.

Ted and Trev also have an in joke between them - 'billirant' - which is a deliberate 'typo'.

If you have any queries about words or phrases used, do please feel free to get in touch, using the contact details in the book. I always try to reply promptly to any emails or Facebook messages.

Thank you.

L M Krier

Chapter One

Saturday afternoon

'But we wanted to come straight there, before we go to the B&B. We wanted to take you and Aldwyth out to tea somewhere nice, and we're making good time.'

Trevor Armstrong, in the front passenger seat, was talking into his mobile phone as his partner, Detective Chief Inspector Ted Darling, drove. They were heading towards the Amman Valley, in Wales. The plan was to spend a relaxing few days together, far from criminal enquiries, as well as visiting Ted's mother, Annie.

It was Annie to whom Trev was speaking. He was making a face at Ted as he listened. He didn't have the call on speaker, but he'd been telling Ted for some time that his mother didn't sound her usual self whenever he spoke to her, which was daily, if he could.

'Are you all right, Annie? Really? You don't sound yourself.'

He listened for a few moments then said, 'Well, if you say so. Think of somewhere nice you want us to take you both. We'll see you tomorrow, then. *Dw i'n dy garu di.*'

'So, straight to the B&B, or do you want to stop somewhere for tea on the way, if we're not going to take mam and Aldwyth out?' Ted asked him, changing down approaching traffic lights which had just turned amber.

He'd been listening to the one-sided conversation. He still

struggled to say 'I love you' in any language to the mother who had been missing for a large part of his life. Such spontaneous affection came much more naturally to Trev, though not for his own mother.

'Absolutely not,' his partner told him firmly. 'I only said that. I didn't mean it.

'Something's wrong with Annie and I won't rest until I know what it is. And this is me using my detective skills. She's not sounded herself all week. Longer, really. I've said so before.

'She didn't even show her usual reaction when I told her about how well the court case had gone, and how I'd actually managed a hug with Sir Gethin.'

Trev's feelings for his father had mellowed after the man had finally acknowledged his belief in his son in public. Sir Gethin Armstrong had given evidence in court against a long-standing friend who had been convicted of numerous sex offences against under age boys, including Trevor. They'd shared their first ever hug, but Trev had yet to refer to him as anything other than his title.

'Whatever she says about everything being fine, I don't believe a word of it. We're going straight there to find out what's going on.'

Ted didn't argue. It was what they'd planned to do originally, and he believed Trev when he said he wouldn't settle until they knew all was well.

Annie had moved back to her native Wales after she was mugged when living in Stockport. She'd gone to live with her lifelong best friend, Aldwyth, in a small former mining village on the edge of a national park.

When Ted parked the car outside the house and the two of them walked up the small drive to ring the doorbell, there was the sound of barking from inside.

Trev laughed at the change in Ted's expression, knowing how wary he was of dogs, as he told him, 'Don't worry, that'll be Cariad, Aldwyth's Corgi. She's not had her long, she's just a baby really. At her size, she might just about manage to suck your ankles.'

'You knew there was a dog here and you didn't warn me?'

Trev was about to answer when they heard a voice from inside the door, quietly telling the dog to be quiet, in Welsh, then, more loudly but hesitantly, asking, '*Pwy yw e?*'

Annie's voice, but sounding wary. Not her usual tone at all. Ted hadn't heard her sound so scared since she'd been assaulted up in Stockport, which had precipitated her move back to Wales.

Trev frowned as he said, 'Annie, *fach*, it's Trev and Ted. I was worried about you, so we came straight round, despite what you said. What's wrong? Let us in, please.'

There was the sound of a safety chain rattling, someone fumbling with a lock on the inside. Then the door opened a crack and Annie's tear-stained face peered out at them, looking frightened.

Trev gently pushed the door open wide and stepped inside to wrap his mother-in-law in one of his famous healing hugs. Ted followed him cautiously, keeping a wary eye on the small Corgi, which seemed, at least, to be wiggling its whole rump as well as its tail in a reassuring manner, with no obvious sign of murderous intent.

'Annie, whatever's wrong?'

'I didn't want to worry either of you. You've had such a difficult week. But Aldwyth died. Suddenly. A few days ago. And I'm not allowed to stay in the house. I have to get out. I've got nowhere to go.'

* * *

Ted's sharp eyes didn't miss the fact that once they were inside, Annie not only locked the front door behind them but put the safety chain back on. It was a new one. He'd never seen it

3

before, and he knew that neither Aldwyth nor his mother had ever been in the habit of locking the door when they were at home, despite his repeated warnings that they should.

It had always been a quiet village, where everyone knew everyone else and crime rates were low. Ever the policeman, Ted had told them both that they should at least lock the door. He wondered who had fitted the chain, when, and why.

It was Trev who instantly took charge. In Ted's work role as Head of Serious Crime, he oversaw not just his own team but several others in different divisions. When it came to dealing with his mother in such a state, he was more than happy to leave it to his partner. He went and put the kettle on. Whatever had gone on, tea could only help.

'I'm so sorry to hear about Aldwyth. You should have told us. What happened?'

Trev sat Annie down at the table and pulled up a chair next to her. He took out a clean, neatly-ironed handkerchief from the pocket of his jeans and helped her to dry her tears. Then he took hold of both her hands, gently rubbing the backs of them with his thumbs.

'She had that heart condition, of course. She'd had it for years. She took those little white pills for it, every day, and that seemed to have it under control.

'A couple of months or so ago she started getting a bit breathless again and had little heart flutters. She hadn't had anything like it for a long time, not with the pills, so I made her go to the doctor. These days you're in and out in five minutes, if you can even get an appointment. He put the dose up a bit and told her to go back if things didn't settle down.

'They didn't, though. She tried all sorts of things, as well as the pills. She even gave up taking sugar in her tea and you know she had a sweet tooth to match mine. And yours, Teddy bach. But nothing made any difference. She was clearly getting worse so I made her make another appointment at the doctor. But before she could go, she collapsed, right here in the kitchen.'

She was crying again at the memory. Wordlessly, Trev stood up and moved closer to hug her once more.

'I didn't know what to do. I phoned for an ambulance, of course. It seem to take so long to get here. The lady on the phone was very kind, while I was waiting. She told me things I could try to keep her alive until they got here. But I couldn't. I couldn't.'

Trev was crying too, now, seeing her pain. He looked towards Ted, who had finished making the tea, a plea in his eyes.

Ted put an awkward hand on Annie's shoulder; gave it a gentle squeeze.

'Sometimes even if the paramedics get there fast they can't always save someone. You did your best, mam, don't blame yourself. It must have been hard for you. Here, have some tea.'

It felt inadequate. It was the best he could manage.

Once she was drinking tea with a shaking hand, helped by Trev, Ted asked her, 'But what's this about you having to leave the house and having nowhere to go? I thought all of that was taken care of in Aldwyth's will? Her nephew gets the house and he's agreed you can stay living here as long as you need to.'

'She changed her will, *bach*, and she never said anything to me, or to Bryn. He was as surprised as I was when Gemma told us about it.'

'Who's Gemma?'

Trev was quick to spot the instant difference in Ted's behaviour. This was Ted the detective, not Ted the son.

'She's a young lady who does aromatherapy. Aldwyth met her a few months ago, when she went to visit a friend of hers in a care home. Gemma goes round some of the homes treating the residents. She got very friendly with Aldwyth. She came here a lot.'

'So let me guess. Bryn the nephew is also cut out of the will, so he can't give you permission to carry on living here, and Gemma gets the lot?'

Ted's tone was hard. Cynical. Trev frowned at him as Annie's tears started once more.

'Sorry, mam, none of this is your fault.'

There was a noise from the front door which made the little dog bark once more. A key turning in the lock. The doorbell ringing. Thumping against the wood. A raised voice, shouting half in English, half in Welsh.

'Annie? Open the door. Let me in. This is my house now, you've got no right to lock me out.'

Ted moved noiselessly as he left the kitchen and closed the door behind him.

As soon as he slid back the bolt and undid the chain, there was a determined effort from outside to push the door open. Ted kept his foot against the base to control how wide it could go.

The head of a young woman, mid-twenties, dark hair, flashing dark eyes, cheeks flushed red in fury, pushed its way through the gap. Then the expression changed to one of surprise at the sight of Ted standing there.

He eased the door open just wide enough to allow her to step into the hallway.

'Gemma, is it?' he asked. 'I'm Annie's son. Detective Chief Inspector Darling. I imagine you weren't expecting to find me here.'

He'd slid his photo ID out of his pocket. It went everywhere with him, even on holiday. Her eyes widened at the sight of it.

'Annie didn't say you were coming.'

'There's no reason why she should,' Ted told her, keeping his tone neutral. 'You see, even if Aldwyth had made a new will and left you the house, it doesn't pass to you until probate has been granted. And that can take at least nine months to a year, even with a straightforward will.'

'A year?'

She looked and sounded shocked at his words. He knew

she wouldn't be the first person not to understand how inheritance laws worked in England and Wales.

'At least,' Ted told her. 'But in the meantime, without any court order to the contrary, and with Aldwyth's next of kin, Bryn, in full agreement, there is nothing at all to stop my mother continuing to live here, as Aldwyth had always intended.

'So in that case, I see no reason for you to have a key to the house. If you need access for any reason, you can ring the bell. Like any other visitor.'

He held out his hand to her, waiting. His team members knew all too well the expression he currently had on his face. Even the most rebellious of them, Detective Constable Jezza Vine, could read the signs that said it was pointless to push any further. The boundary had been reached.

Gemma didn't know him. Couldn't read his moods. But something in the unwavering hazel eyes with the odd flash of emerald warned her that she was on the back foot. Annie may not have known her legal rights, so she was easy to walk all over. But this policeman clearly wasn't.

She knew when she was beaten.

With a scowl, she handed over the front door key she had, then tried a defiant parting shot.

'It's only delaying things. Aldwyth left the house to me, so once I take possession, Annie will need to move out. I don't want a sitting tenant.'

She turned and flounced out.

Ted closed the door behind her, saying under his breath, 'Well, we'll see about that, Gemma *fach*.'

He went back to the kitchen where his mother was already looking more cheerful than before from the simple pleasures of hot sweet tea and plenty of hugs and love from Trev.

Ted put the key on the table in front of her.

'I've told Gemma she's not entitled to have a key nor to come and go as she pleases. Not until probate is granted.

'All things considered, I think it's best if you don't stay here tonight, mam. I'm going to need to talk to Bryn about all of this, so why don't you go to the B&B with Trev? See if they have a spare room, or if not, I'm sure you can improvise something. You need a change of scene and some TLC.'

He was looking hard at Trev as he said it, hoping he would understand. He'd promised him a nice relaxing week, with no work getting in the way, as it so often did. At least none of this could have been anticipated. It shouldn't count in the same way as work calling him in unexpectedly.

'That's a good idea,' Trev told him, instantly reassuring. Then his face cracked in a mischievous grin as he said, 'There's one small flaw in your plan, Mr Policeman.'

He pointed to the dog as he continued, 'You know that the B&B is a dog-free zone, so that means Cariad will have to stay here and you'll have to look after her.'

Seeing Ted's expression change, his mother hurried to reassure him.

'You'll be fine with her, Teddy bach. She's very gentle and loving. More like a cat than a dog. You'll need to give her her tea and take her for a walk before bedtime. Keep her on the lead, and don't forget to take the poo bags.'

Despite the seriousness of the situation, the mental image reduced Trev to hysterical laughter.

'Tell me what I have to do and I'll write it all down so I don't get anything wrong,' Ted told his mother. 'And give me Bryn's telephone number. I think it would be a good idea if he and I got together to talk about this.'

Ted grabbed a few things he would need from the car while Trev helped Annie to pack what she wanted to take.

Cariad the Corgi didn't seem in the least concerned to see the two of them drive away whilst Ted waved them off from the doorstep. She simply sat with her rear end planted on Ted's foot, gazing up at him with interest. If she sensed she had been left in the hands of a novice, she showed no concern. Ted had even forgotten to ask how much English the dog knew, and what commands he should use in Welsh, if necessary.

'Well, Cariad, you're stuck with me, so I apologise if I do everything wrong. Come on, then.'

He made to go back in the house, but the dog stayed sitting, studying him with her big brown eyes.

Ted dredged up long-forgotten memories. Snippets of what his mother used to say to him when he was a little boy, before she'd left home.

'*Dere ymlaen*, Cariad.'

He could have sworn the dog smiled at him as it stood up and padded after him on its truncated legs.

Saturday night

He could spot danger a mile off. He was streetwise. He had to be, doing what he did.

He could tell as soon as the two men appeared that whatever their plans were, it wasn't going to be good news for him.

He had no idea who they were, how they had found him or who might have sent them. But he knew without a doubt that it was not going to end well.

They wore dark clothing and moved soundlessly, despite the military boots they had on. They were medium height, compact, and they moved with a fluid purpose which chilled him with sudden terror.

They were adults. Grown men. Not other kids like him, jealous of what he was doing to make a bit of money on the side.

They were advancing on him, keeping a disciplined distance of about a metre between them. A classic pincer movement. Whichever way he tried to run, one of them would be straight after him.

And run was the only thing he could think of to do. Whatever they wanted with him, it was clear that it was not going to be to his advantage.

He couldn't see if they were armed. Something about the way they carried themselves told him they would be. Told him also that they didn't need to be. They would be capable of doing him serious harm without weapons.

He hesitated for a fraction of a second longer, desperately thinking of a survival plan. Then he turned and bolted.

His mind was racing, seeking an escape route. He knew with a dread certainty that he could never outrun these pursuers. His only hope was if his local knowledge was better than theirs.

He sprinted alongside the ever-present looming silhouette of the Stockport viaduct. The sounds of trains rumbling over it almost drowned out the desperate thudding of his heart against his skinny chest.

As he ran he felt for his pocket where the newly-bought knife nestled. Could he get it out in time when he needed to? And would it be of any use to him?

He jinked round a corner and ran into an alleyway, desperately trying to remember where it led. Hoping against fading hope that it was a cut-through.

There were brick walls on either side of him. Red brick, typical of the town's architecture. A dirty, stinking place. Partly a service road to the back of commercial properties.

Then he saw it. Ahead of him. The sight he'd been dreading.

Not the cut-through he'd been hoping for.

Another looming red brick wall.

Solid. No way around it. No hope of getting over it.

The men were hard on his heels now, but this was it.

The end of the line.

Chapter Two

'This is a bad business, Ted,' Aldwyth's nephew, Bryn, told him as the two of them went into the kitchen at the back of the house.

'I mean, it was a shock, of course, auntie dying suddenly like that. We've known about her heart condition for years now but I think we all thought she'd go on forever, as long as she took the pills.

'It's this thing with her will, though. To do something like that, without a word to me or your mam. That wasn't like her at all. It was a cruel thing to do to your mam. Annie has always been a good friend to her. They'd been friends forever. The joke in our family is that they were so close they must have been separated at birth.'

Ted had headed straight for the kettle. His default setting in difficult situations - offer tea.

'D'you want a brew, Bryn? Or there might be something stronger somewhere, if you prefer. You'd know better than me.'

Bryn Evans gave a short chuckle.

'Auntie would never have the demon drink in the house. Proper old-fashioned chapel, she was. I know your mam smuggled in the odd Snowball when she felt like it, because I used to get them for her. But tea's fine, *diolch*. Strong, dark, two sugars.'

Cariad the Corgi had greeted Bryn when he'd first arrived but was now back to shadowing Ted's every move, planting a round rump on his foot whenever he stood still.

'You're a policeman, Ted. Does any of this sound right to you? Is it possible that Gemma somehow made auntie change her will? To leave her everything? Threatened her, or something like that? I don't know. You'd probably have some idea of how it might be done, though.

'Auntie had only known her five minutes and suddenly she leaves her the lot, then dies not long afterwards. It doesn't seem right to me.'

The kettle hadn't long boiled from Ted's last brew. He put mugs of tea on the table and sat down opposite Bryn, who was voicing exactly what had been going through his own head since he'd heard the news.

'Have you seen the will or are you just going off what Gemma told you? By the way, I had the pleasure of meeting her earlier. She came round, trying to let herself in. I presume it was you who put the chain on the door? I made her give me the key, at least.

'Whether or not the will is legal, she has no rights to come round here whenever she feels like it. Not before probate is granted. She's clearly got mam very frightened, so I wanted to put a stop to her letting herself in whenever she feels like it. I hope you agree with that?'

'Good for you, Ted. I'd have done the same if I'd come face to face with her, but she's a sly one. She knows well enough when I'm at work and when I'm likely to come round, so she's never here when I am. I'll have to sort out getting the locks changed next.

'And yes,' he pulled photocopied documents from his jacket pocket and slid them across the table to Ted. 'Here's a copy of the will. She insisted on giving it to your mam when she was telling her to pack her things and get out. I took it and got my own copy made, so I could study it. This one's for you, if it will help at all.

'You'll know better than me if it's genuine enough. I'm not up on such things. What does strike me as strange is auntie's used a different solicitor. The family's always used one in Ammanford, for everything. This time she's gone to a different one in Swansea, someone I've never even heard of. I've no idea how she would even have got there. She still has - had - her little car but she never drives far. She'd never have driven herself off to Swansea, I'm sure. Certainly not without telling anyone. None of this is right.

'Ted, look, I'm trying not to make a drama out of this if there isn't one. I know you're the crime expert, not me. But with anything like this, when you see it on telly, it's always the person who gets everything in the will who's the suspect when there's a sudden death, isn't it?'

Ted got his reading glasses from his jacket pocket and scanned the document. It was brief and to the point. As concise as any testament he'd ever seen. The usual statement about replacing previous wills, then everything left to Gemma unconditionally, with no mention of any other beneficiary.

'Do you know this solicitor, Jonathan Joiner?'

'Never heard of him,' Bryn told him. 'I looked on Google and some of the reviews he has are less than complimentary. Sloppy work, missing documents. All that sort of thing. I've no idea how or why auntie picked him. She didn't know anything about Google, as far as I know, so she can't have found him there.'

'Perhaps she didn't pick him. If you're right in your suspicions and she was coerced into changing her will, perhaps whoever did that picked a solicitor who wasn't likely to ask any difficult questions or put up any obstacles. Possibly even someone they know well, or have connections with.

'And was the death certified as natural causes? Her doctor signed off on it without raising any red flags?'

Bryn's look and tone changed. Explaining something in simple terms to someone who didn't quite get it.

'Ted, I don't know what it's like up where you live. Manchester, is it?'

'Stockport,' Ted corrected him automatically.

'Well, here it's got so hard to get a doctor at all that some people don't see theirs from one year's end to the next. I doubt anyone ever looked at auntie. Her GP will have signed it off because he saw her briefly not all that long ago to change the dose on her tablets. He might perhaps have wondered if she'd forgotten to take the new dose, if he even gave it a second thought, but probably nothing more than that.'

'So the next question is, was she taking them, at the right dose? And if she was, why didn't they have the desired effect? Have you asked anyone about that?'

'You're sounding like a policeman, Ted. Are you really suggesting that someone did something to auntie? Poisoned her, or something? Because that's what I've been wondering, but then I thought I was just overreacting, because of the shock.

'And no, I've not been able to talk to anyone yet. Will there be an inquest or something, and will someone there ask those questions?'

'I don't have enough information to be suggesting anything. You said yourself that something wasn't right and I agree with you, by the sound of things. To change her will without telling anyone, then to die suddenly so soon afterwards is always going to sound suspicious.

'Trev's been saying for a while now that mam hasn't sounded herself when he speaks to her on the phone, but she wouldn't say what was bothering her. And no, with the death certified by her own doctor and nothing to indicate anything suspicious, there wouldn't routinely be an inquest. Nor a post-mortem examination, unless a coroner requests one, for some reason.

'Was she definitely taking her medication, do you have any way of knowing?'

'Oh yes, that was the first thing your mam and I talked about after it happened. She said auntie was always very good about her pills. She knew she relied on them so she was always very careful not to miss a single dose. She had one of those little dispenser things, so she could easily see if she'd missed one.'

Ted paused to drink some of his tea. Almost unconsciously, his hand went down to find the top of Cariad's head and give it a gentle rub, rewarded instantly with a lick from her pink tongue.

Bryn saw the gesture and smiled.

'You seem to be getting on well with Cariad. I thought your mam said you didn't like dogs.'

'I don't dislike them. I'm just very wary of them. I had a scare with one when I was very small, apparently, although I don't remember, so now I'm a bit anxious about all of them and they seem to know it.

'Cariad seems kind, though. Mam said she was quite cat-like and she is. I had to look online when she first lay down with her back legs stuck out behind like she does. I thought I'd broken her.'

Bryn laughed at that.

'*Splootio*, we call it in the family. I think you'd call it splooting? They do that, Corgis.

'But speaking of auntie and her pills, I can't see how she could have missed any, never mind enough to make her go into heart failure. If I called in the evening I sometimes saw her take them. She had that organiser so she could never make a mistake either way. Your mam and I checked and it didn't look as if she'd missed any. And Annie always reminded her. We didn't touch the box though. Afterwards, you know, in case it would need to be checked for fingerprints or anything. I only know about this stuff from the telly so I might have got it all wrong.'

'No, you did exactly the right thing. It's always best to do nothing than to risk doing the wrong thing, in most circumstances.'

'One of the good things about Gemma was she seemed to have taken a big interest in auntie's health. She was always an eggs and bacon for breakfast type of person, but Gemma had got her onto fresh fruit, grapefruit, that sort of thing instead. And persuaded her to stop the sugar and have those little sweetener pills to replace it.

'Everything about that girl makes me suspicious of her, but it's hard to see why she would be so keen on auntie living a healthier lifestyle if she was trying to kill her off to get her hands on this house, isn't it?'

'Bryn, would you mind if I went to see this solicitor, as soon as I can get an appointment? It's not just because this affects mam, but if you've been cheated out of your rightful inheritance, that needs to be addressed. There may be nothing to it, but it at least needs looking at. Especially if there's the slightest chance that Aldwyth's death wasn't natural causes and there was a serious crime involved.

'And while I'm out and about I could do worse than to call at the nearest police station that's big enough to have a CID. Just to sound them out a bit.'

'Not Swansea then, wrong force. You might have to go as far as Carmarthen.'

He said it as if talking about some long trek. Ted knew it was not much more than twenty miles.

'What about the funeral, Bryn? Have you set a date for that?'

'Not yet. It's all been a bit overwhelming, to tell the truth. Not just auntie dying but all this upset for your poor mam. Does that mean you're thinking about perhaps getting a second opinion? Getting auntie's body examined to see what really happened?

'And if you want to talk to anyone, if you think it might do some good, go right ahead, Ted. I wouldn't even know where to begin. I'm happy to leave it to you. I suppose this is what you're trained for, after all.

'This is really going to spoil your holiday though, isn't it? I suppose you were looking forward to some nice quiet time with your mam and Trevor. Now here you are, looking at something which might be a fraud or whatever, with the will. And a possibly suspicious death to investigate.'

* * *

Once Bryn had left, Ted went to find a pair of crime scene gloves in one of his pockets. Something he never went anywhere without. Force of habit.

He wasn't sure what he was looking for, but everything he'd heard so far was setting his senses on full alert.

He started with the kitchen cupboards. He hadn't seen any sign of tablets lying around and didn't expect to, not with a dog in the house.

Gemma's eagerness to take possession of the place might simply have been the naive belief that it was now hers so there was no reason not to. On the other hand, she might be anxious to get rid of anything incriminating left lying around.

He found a colourful pill dispenser in the cupboard above the kettle. Different colours for each day, separate compartments for times of day, just as Bryn had described. The ones for the days leading up to Aldwyth's death were empty. It looked as if she might well have been taking them as prescribed right up to the end.

The packet the pills had come in was also on the same shelf. A cardboard box with a blister-pack strip in it, a few tablets still remaining. Ted carefully eased one out of the pack into the palm of his hand. It looked the same as the others, to the naked eye.

Cariad, sitting by his feet, was gazing up at him, then gave a small woof.

'If you have any theories or any information, Cariad, feel free to share them. Perhaps you saw something. I'd welcome any help, because I'm struggling here to know if there even is a crime.'

The dog barked at him again, several times, until the penny dropped. Ted glanced at the clock on the cooker, surprised at how late it was.

'Sorry, you want your tea, I suppose. I'm a novice at all this. I'll feed you, then have something myself before I take you out. I forgot to ask mam how far I'm supposed to take you, so I'm counting on you to tell me when to turn back.

'Just remember, it's not a good idea to lie to a policeman.'

* * *

Ted and Cariad were heading back to the house after their evening walk when his phone rang. It had taken him longer than anticipated because so many people had stopped him to talk.

In such a close-knit community, the residents seemed to know everyone by sight, or at least know who they were. If Ted was a stranger to some of them, Cariad certainly wasn't.

Ted was glad of the opportunity to sound out what the local gossip was saying. Everyone who spoke to him expressed surprise at Aldwyth's sudden death. Most knew of her pre-existing condition, but all said that up until recently, she had seemed fine. She and Annie had been a regular sight, taking Cariad for her walks three times a day round the village.

'I want to report a crime, Mr Policeman,' Trev told him when he answered his phone.

His voice was as mellow as a contented cat. Trev imagined he'd enjoyed a good dinner at the B&B, with plenty of wine. Ted had had to make do with the uninspiring and seemingly random contents of the fridge. It appeared that his mother had had too much on her mind to do any proper shopping.

'I'm supposed to be on holiday,' Ted reminded him.

'I know, and I shouldn't make light of things, really, in the circumstances. But they didn't have a spare room tonight, although they will have one from tomorrow, if we need it. So instead Annie is tucked up, sleeping like a baby, in that lovely king-sized bed we were meant to be sharing. Meanwhile I have the joys of sleeping in one of those folding abominations with a mattress about an inch thick.'

'And how is mam doing?'

'Bless her, she offered to sleep on the instrument of torture and let me have the bed, but clearly I couldn't do that. She's fast asleep, nicely relaxed. I gave her a glass of wine, and a small port after her meal. I thought she probably needed some complete rest after what she's been through.

'What did Bryn have to say?'

'Pretty much what we were thinking. He's no idea why Aldwyth changed her will like that, without saying anything. And he has no time at all for Gemma. It was him who put the safety chain on the door, to stop her going round bothering mam. He's going to get the locks changed next.

'I thought it might be a good idea if the three of us go out for the day tomorrow. Visit somewhere nice, eat out. Somewhere we can take Cariad. She and I seem to be getting on okay, for now.'

He hesitated for the briefest moment. Trev picked up on it instantly, always finely tuned to his partner's moods and feelings.

'There's a but, isn't there? And I'm not going to like the but, am I?'

'Bryn pointed out that the will was drawn up by a solicitor he's never even heard of, not Aldwyth's usual one. I think it might help if I went to visit him, to see if I can find out what's behind it all. He's in Swansea, so you and mam could go shopping, while I drop in on him. You can use my card.'

He knew that would be a powerful bribe.

'I might also need to go to Carmarthen, to the local police HQ. Just a quiet word, off the record, to see if they know anything. I can't do anything tomorrow, being Sunday, so let's all have a nice day out together.'

Trev gave a theatrical sigh.

'You know there would be consequences, if this was any-one other than your mother, and poor Aldwyth. Of course you should do whatever it takes to sort things out. And before you say it, this isn't something you need to make up for.

'Neither of us saw anything like this coming. Not for one moment.'

Chapter Three

Ted and Cariad were waiting patiently outside the house when Trev drove up, later than promised, with Annie in the front passenger seat. Punctuality was never his strong point and from his description of the bed he'd had to use, he can't have had much sleep. His usual position always filled a large double bed, let alone something the size of a camp bed.

'Where are we going?' Ted asked, as he and Cariad got into the back.

'The seaside!' Trev told him, sounding as excited as a small child. 'Walks along the tideline. Fish and chips from the paper on the seafront, then afternoon tea in a cosy little cafe somewhere. Just what we all need.'

'Are there any dog-friendly beaches?'

Trev laughed at that.

'Careful, Ted, you're starting to sound like a proper dog owner. Yes, Annie knows all the right places to go, as long as we've got poo bags.

'And speaking of Cariad, I have very good news on that score. I spoke to Piet and Lotte, at the guest house, and explained the circumstances. They're happy to let Cariad stay this week, while they're quiet, as long as she promises to behave.

'They have a room vacant for Annie from tonight, too, so you and I can put that nice king-sized bed to good use.'

He made eye contact with Ted in the rear view mirror, a wicked grin on his face. He loved to tease. Annie was looking out of the side window, apparently fascinated at the sight of scenery she must have seen hundreds of times in the past.

'It will be nice for us all to eat together tonight. The food's as good as always,' Trev continued.

'I'm sorry there wasn't much in for you at the house, *bach*,' Annie told him. 'I hadn't really thought much about shopping, after what happened.'

'Oh, don't worry about Ted,' Trev reassured her. 'He's used to surviving on beetles and dead leaves, not to mention sleeping on a clothesline, when he goes off on training sessions with his mysterious Special Forces friend.'

Ted caught his eye in turn and smiled back at him. Trev's joke was nearer to the mark than he realised, on some of the training marches he'd been on with Mr Green, his special skills trainer.

'We'll need to swing by the house on the way back, then, to get my things and stuff for Cariad. I want to lock it up tight. Bryn's going to get the locks changed, in case Gemma had another key cut that we don't know about. But for now, a bit of a blow at the seaside sounds like just the thing for all of us.'

* * *

Annie's cheeks had gained some colour from the stiff sea breeze. She was looking much more like her old self, happy and relaxed in Ted and Trev's company.

Cariad had been run off her little legs, chasing after the endless sticks Trev threw for her. She was outside in the car, sleeping on the old cover Ted had thrown in for her, to help keep sand off the seats.

The three of them were sitting in the bay window of a pleasant cafe not far from the beach where they'd been walking. The car was right outside, so they had it in full view. They'd ordered tea and *bara brith*, with Trev assuring his mother-in-law that there was no way the rich fruit cake was going to equal, let alone exceed, the standard of hers.

When the waitress brought the tray and started putting everything they needed onto the table, Trev automatically pushed the sugar bowl across nearer to Annie.

'*Diolch, bach*, but I suppose I should stick with the sweeteners really. I changed to them to keep Aldwyth company. Not that they helped her, after all.'

She reached in her handbag and took out a small container of sweeteners, the type with a button to press to eject them one at a time. Ted's eyes locked onto it in an instant, a motion not missed by Trev, who could be equally as observant.

'What do they make this stuff from, mam?' Ted asked her, holding out his hand for the container.

'I don't know, Teddy *bach*. Some sort of a plant, I think. Although sugar's a plant, isn't it, but these are supposed to be better for you.'

Ted was clearly only half listening. He carefully tore a piece off one of the paper napkins on the table, put it in the palm of his hand, then pressed the lever to drop one of the small, round, white tablets onto it.

'Have you solved it, Miss Marple? Have you worked out how it could have been done?' Trev asked him.

Ted shook his head.

'I don't know, is the honest answer. I may be looking too hard in the wrong way. But seeing these little white pills, looking so much like the ones Aldwyth was prescribed, makes me wonder why young Gemma is so aggressively keen to get back into the house.

'Mam, have you let her in there at all since Aldwyth died?'

'I haven't, *bach*. I didn't want to do that without Bryn there and she always comes round when she knows he'll be at work. She was very insistent, though. That's what made me afraid. She kept trying to push me back but I managed to shut the door on her each time, and then Bryn came and put the chain on.'

'Good for you,' Ted told her.

Like him, she was small and slight. Deceptively so. She

23

must have been frightened, but she'd stood her ground.

'I think I need to phone Bryn and ask if he can arrange to get the locks changed first thing in the morning. For tonight, we'll just lock the place up as tight as we can, and I'll remove anything which I think Gemma might be anxious to get her hands on.'

'You don't really think Gemma killed Aldwyth do you, *bach*? Murdered her, I mean? Deliberately?'

'I don't know. But the first rule with a crime scene is to preserve any potential evidence, and that's what I'm going to try to do.

'For now, I think we should finish up here and get back to the house. In case housebreaking is another of Gemma's skills and she beats us to it.'

* * *

Bryn managed to pull out all the stops and get a locksmith round to the house first thing in the morning. He worked for the local authority so he knew the right network of trustworthy contractors. It meant Ted had to be up and at Aldwyth's house early to let the man in.

No chance of Trev stirring at such an hour. Certainly not when his body clock was set to holiday mode. Cariad was sleeping with Annie in a small room at the end of the landing. Ted didn't intend to wake either of them. With luck he could be there and back, with the new keys, in time to join them both for breakfast.

He'd certainly feel easier in his mind if he knew the house was as secure as it could be, and if he'd removed the tablets, the sweeteners and anything else which could be indicative of something untoward having gone on.

The locksmith was prompt and seemed efficient. He greeted Ted in Welsh but quickly switched to English when he realised Ted didn't understand him.

While he was fitting new locks to both front and back doors, Ted got more gloves from the car boot, together with a couple of evidence bags, which was all he could find. He'd packed the car in the hopes of a relaxing holiday, rather than a busman's one.

He wanted to take the medication organiser, as it was, any remaining medication, and any sweeteners he could find in the house. It was impossible to tell with the naked eye but the two sets of little white pills looked almost identical to him.

He'd also asked his mother where he could find Aldwyth's original will, or the photocopy of it Annie had. He wanted to read through that carefully before he went to see the solicitor about the more recent one. He'd seen it once before, when Annie showed it to him, but hadn't studied it in detail. He'd been keen to check what the situation would be for his mother should Aldwyth die before she did, from a practical point of view.

He'd enjoyed his taste of holiday the day before, but for now, it looked as if he was going to need to be in work mode. It was possible he was reading too much into things, spending all his time dealing with Serious Crime as he did. All his instincts told him that he wasn't.

He made a phone call before he set off back to the guest house.

'Ted, you're supposed to be on holiday.'

His Detective Inspector, Jo Rodriguez, more informal than he would be if they were both in the workplace.

'How are things going there?' Ted couldn't resist asking him.

'Absolutely fine,' Jo told him, crossing his fingers and promising himself he'd go to confession as soon as he had the time - whenever that was likely to be. 'Stop thinking about work and go and have some fun. That's what holidays are for.'

'I went to the seaside yesterday,' Ted told him with a laugh. 'But you know what us coppers are like - we attract crime wherever we go, and I seem to have stumbled on a suspicious death.

'I need you, please, to find me someone in Dyfed-Powys Police with time to talk to me later today. Probably at HQ in Carmarthen, I imagine would be best. About a suspicious death.'

'And you can't do this because ...?' Jo asked.

'Because if I walk in off the street with the tale I've got to tell I may get arrested for wasting police time. Even with my ID card. So I need someone to pave the way, to let them know I am who I say I am and that despite appearances, I'm relatively sane.'

It was Jo's turn to laugh. A much-needed release of tension.

'I think I can probably tell them that with a straight face and without the need to go to confession for stretching the truth on that one. I'll give them a bell then call you back when I have contact details. But seriously, once you've sorted whatever this is all about, go and have a proper holiday.'

Ted's next phone call was to the office of the solicitor who'd drawn up the will in Gemma's favour. He introduced himself by his rank but was careful not to mention which area he was from. He intimated that his enquiry was pressing so was offered an appointment mid morning.

It at least gave him time for a leisurely breakfast with his mother and Trev before they needed to set off for Swansea. They'd leave Cariad at the house, which they had to pass on the way, then return at lunchtime to see to her. Safer than leaving her in the car in a busy shopping area, with dog thefts becoming more frequent of late.

Ted tried to approach his meeting with the solicitor with an open mind and no preconceptions. His instincts told him he might find some less than meticulous work in evidence. He was shocked by the reality.

The address turned out to be a somewhat cramped set of offices in a dubious backstreet. A small plaque near the door announced the firm as Singleton-Joiner, Solicitors.

Chaos reigned from the moment he walked through the door to announce himself at the reception desk. Files and document boxes were stacked in a haphazard fashion in corners. The waiting area looked in need of a thorough clean and tidy up.

The woman behind the desk was talking on the phone, in Welsh, whilst thumbing through an old-fashioned desk diary and making scribbled jottings in it. Hi-tech, cutting-edge, twenty-first technology was not much in evidence.

Ted waited patiently until she had finished, then held out his photo ID, carefully keeping hold of it so she couldn't study it too closely and see the different police force name.

'Detective Chief Inspector Darling, here to see Mr Joiner,' he told her.

She asked him to wait a moment, indicating the chairs, while she made an internal call, again speaking in Welsh. Ted didn't fancy the look of the seating so remained standing, waiting patiently.

'He can see you now,' she told him, directing him back out into the entry hall to an office doorway at the far end of the corridor.

If the reception area had resembled organised chaos, the interior of the dusty office, gloomy, with little natural daylight filtering through the dirty windows, was like the aftermath of an explosion in an archive. Ted wondered when anyone had last done the filing - assuming any was ever done.

'Mr Joiner? Detective Chief Inspector Darling.'

Ted again held up his card without relinquishing his grip on it.

'Thank you for fitting me in. I'm looking into the recent death of a lady called Aldwyth Evans. You drew up a new will for her shortly before she died, I understand.'

Joiner hadn't moved from his chair, but indicated the one opposite him for Ted to sit on. The solicitor's appearance was

somehow out of keeping with the antiquated clutter of his surroundings. He looked scarcely out of his forties so Ted was
surprised to see so much old-style filing. Perhaps he'd inherited
the practice and it had not yet been digitally updated.

'Oh, she died, did she? I hadn't heard yet. I think we're the
executors of the will?'

He said it as a query.

Ted took the copy from his pocket and put it on a rare
empty space on the cluttered desk.

'That's correct. I should declare an interest at this point. I'm
here not just as a police officer, but as the son of Annie Jones,
who is mentioned in the earlier will, of which I also have a
copy.'

He added the photocopy of the previous will to the desk
and waited while Joiner scan-read it.

'Quite a big difference, as you can see, from the earlier will
to the one which you drew up.'

'Well, yes, but then it's not unusual for people to change
their will. A falling out in the family or something like that is a
frequent reason. It's not my job to go into all of that. I just have
to be satisfied that the person making or changing their will is
doing it without any coercion and knows what they're doing.'

'And you were quite happy there was no sign of anything
like that?'

'Well, yes, of course, otherwise I wouldn't have gone
ahead.'

Joiner was already starting to look flustered at the presence
of this quietly-spoken police officer with the direct gaze in his
office.

'And the witness signatures? Who were they? Did someone
come with Miss Evans?'

The man picked the document up to look at it, then said,
'These are two members of our admin staff here. It's perfectly
normal for them to act as witnesses for client documents, if
they don't have their own witnesses with them.'

'So she came alone, Miss Evans? There was no one with her during the signing and witnessing?'

Joiner's chair creaked as he shifted his weight, his discomfort visibly increasing.

'I see a lot of clients. I don't always remember every detail ...' he began, but Ted cut across him.

His voice was even quieter now. It would have signalled a clear message to any of his team members to hear him in that mode. *Don't mess with the boss any further; you're on thin ice.*

'Mr Joiner, this was comparatively recently, not some years ago. A new client, one you hadn't seen before, coming to change their will. I assume there is at least some sort of risk assessment process you perform for yourself in such circumstances? Even a visual assessment of the situation to ensure there is no question of someone changing their will under duress?'

'Well, the lady seemed quite confident of what she wanted the new will to say. That's why it was all done very quickly ...'

'But was she alone?'

'No, I, er, I seem to remember she'd come with a young lady who'd driven her here. I seem to recall her saying she didn't like driving into Swansea by herself. But the young lady sat quietly in the background. She certainly didn't influence her in any way.'

He looked more sure of himself now. A hint of triumph about his reply.

Ted allowed himself a moment to ensure he stayed in total control of his voice as he said, 'Mr Joiner, what would you say if I told you that the young woman who was with her was, in fact, Gemma Thomas, the primary beneficiary of the new will? Someone who, I believe, according to your profession's code of ethical standards, should not have been anywhere near at the time the will was being signed and witnessed. Certainly not present in the same room.'

Ted had the satisfaction of seeing the man's face drain of

29

all colour as he stood up to leave.

'It's likely the police will need your full, detailed statement in the near future, Mr Joiner. The death is, at present, being treated as suspicious, so any relevant information will form part of ongoing enquiries.'

He was slightly jumping the gun, he knew. But armed with the latest information, he felt confident that if Jo had managed to find him the right person to speak to, there was at least a chance of getting a case file opened on Aldwyth's death and the circumstances surrounding the will.

Chapter Four

Ted had muted his mobile whilst he was with the solicitor. He checked it as he left the office, found a missed call from Jo and phoned him straight back.

'Right, I've spoken to a DS Rhys Morgan, at Headquarters in Carmarthen. He works on Serious Crime and he sounds on the ball. I've told him I can vouch for you being normally sensible and not prone to flights of fancy, but with the caveat that I've no idea what you get up to on your holidays.'

There was a note of humour in his voice as he said it, then he went on, 'I have his mobile number. He said to give him a bell and he'll find time this afternoon to see what it is you want. But seriously, Ted, take a break while you can.'

He had no intention of even hinting to the boss that he would be coming back to plenty to keep him busy, so he really needed to take advantage of his leave.

'I can't let this one go until I know for sure whether or not there's any criminal activity behind it. Anyway, how are things there?'

'At the risk of repeating myself, you're on leave. You don't need to know. But we're fine, honestly. Everything is under control. Go and do something relaxing. Go back to the beach and ride a donkey. Eat candy floss or something.'

Ted was still laughing to himself as he rang off. He knew everything would be fine. Jo was an excellent deputy in his absence and he had the benefit of two first-rate sergeants, Mike Hallam and Rob O'Connell, to support him. It didn't stop the inner control freak in Ted from feeling the insatiable need to stay in touch.

He kept his call to DS Morgan brief and light on detail. He preferred to talk to him face to face. Even with Jo's assurances, what he was going to tell him sounded far-fetched so it might be better dealt with in person. They fixed a time for the afternoon.

He called Trev next for an update.

'We've just bought the cutest little coat for Cariad. Or rather, you did, on your card. She's going to look adorable in it, for the cold weather.'

Trev loved shopping. He sounded in his element. Ted was in no hurry to join them. Not his thing at all, from choice, and it sounded as if they were having enough fun without him.

'I thought you should perhaps buy us the makings of lunch and we'll go back to the house to eat it, to make sure Cariad is all right,' Ted told him, which made his partner laugh.

'Ted, you soft thing, you're starting to sound like a real devoted doggy daddy. But yes, that's a great idea. I'll find a good deli and get us all sorts of toothsome treats. Or rather you and your kind will. Then we'll come and pick you up if you let me know where.'

Ted was walking in search of somewhere to get a cup of tea. He also needed to make another phone call before he went to speak to the DS at Carmarthen. It was a long shot. He knew Monday mornings were often busy for the person he wanted to speak to.

He was in luck. He dialled a saved number as he sat down with his cup of tea and was almost instantly rewarded by the familiar booming tones of Home Office Pathologist, Professor Bizzie Nelson.

'Edwin! How lovely to hear from you, and most unexpected. I heard via the gossip mill that you were on leave.'

'Sorry to bother you, Bizzie. Are you with your students at the moment? I don't want to disturb you, only I could really do with your advice.'

'Unusually I'm not up to my armpits in a cadaver as we speak, while the dear, eager young things have something else on this morning, in connection with their studies. So you have my undivided attention. And you are something of a welcome distraction as I am currently wrestling with the dreaded paper-work and admin which appears to breed in my in-tray as soon as I leave my office. I'm sure you know that feeling all too well.

'So please fire away. I'm delighted to help in any way I can.'

'It's going to sound very far-fetched,' Ted warned her.

'Edwin, most of my life is spent dealing with the far-fetched. If anyone ever says it is impossible for a particular event to cause death, I can tell them of at least one post-mortem examination I have performed where exactly such a set of circumstances was to blame. So please tell me what it is I might be able to help with.'

'You know that my mother lives with her friend in South Wales? We came down to visit them, Trev and I. Only Ald-wyth has died suddenly.'

'I'm sorry to hear that. Please pass on my condolences to your mother,' Bizzie said at once. She'd met Annie previously through Ted.

'Thank you. The thing is, it was all very unexpected. And it might just be my policeman's brain, but something doesn't sit quite right with me about the circumstances. Especially now I've met the solicitor who drew up the new will which Aldwyth made very shortly before she died.'

Bizzie listened in complete silence whilst Ted recounted all the details he had to date, particularly the apparent coincidence of the strong similarity between Aldwyth's medication and the sweeteners she had recently started to take.

Ted was trying to determine the nature of the silence at the other end of the phone as he continued speaking. Polite interest? Total scepticism? Concern for his state of mind? He wouldn't have blamed her at all had it been either of the latter two.

'I'm going to talk to the local police later today, just to flag it up for them as possibly suspicious. The thing which throws me currently is the fact that this Gemma seemed to have been making genuine efforts to help Aldwyth eat more healthily. Grapefruit instead of bacon and eggs for breakfast, for one thing. I can't reconcile that with any intent to do her harm.'

'Ah, but that is because you don't know your pills and potions as I do, Edwin. Otherwise you would know instantly that the particular medication your lady was prescribed is not, under any circumstances, to be taken with grapefruit or any of its derivatives. It's strongly contra-indicated.

'My next question would be, of course, could your young lady be reasonably expected to know that? Posed in tandem with asking why, if Aldwyth has been on this medication for some considerable time, she didn't know, or remember, that fact herself.'

'She's an aromatherapist. Could that be significant?'

'Oh, it could indeed. You might expect a scientific type like me to be sceptical of such things, but the power of plants is ancient and well-studied. If she has done any type of training at all, I would expect her to know something as basic as asking a client what medication they were on before trying any form of therapy on them.

'Substances don't always have to be swallowed to cause an adverse reaction. That can sometimes happen through percutaneous contact - a substance passing through the skin. Which makes this all start to sound cynical in the extreme. As well as eminently plausible.

'And you will know better than I, but perhaps if Aldwyth was somewhat under the spell of this young woman, she might accept some tale of some oil or another she was using on her working to prevent any such interaction, thus rendering it very safe.'

'Bizzie, promise me you will never step over the line into lawbreaking. You would run rings round any poor police officers trying to get the better of you, with ideas like that. I've had my fill of rogue pathologists.'

They both laughed at his words, then began speaking at the same time.

'So what's your next ...'

'What I need to do ...'

'Sorry, Bizzie, after you,' Ted told her.

'I was going to ask you what you're planning to do next. Because if it would help at all, I could have a look to see if there are any Home Office Pathologists of my acquaintance in that neck of the woods. We HOPs are a small and select group so there's the strong possibility that there's someone I either know or know of, if it would be helpful for me to speak to them to assure them of your credentials, excellent track record, and sanity.'

'I'm starting to doubt my own sanity, to be honest, Bizzie. Death by grapefruit sounds far-fetched in the extreme.'

'But substitution of medication is not, by any stretch of the imagination. Without having any of the facts at my disposal, I would say that is a distinct possibility. If you can find the right police officer, and if their budget is not overly constrained, I would say that at the very least, you could profitably begin by requesting an analysis of the pills within that dispenser to see what they actually are. And if they are all sweeteners, you may need to press for a full post-mortem examination. Assuming, hopefully, that the good lady has not yet been laid to rest or cremated.

'Good luck with it all. I'll let you know if I come across a familiar name on the list. Do please keep me posted. It all sounds rather intriguing.'

* * *

Ted was despatched to walk Cariad when they got back to the house while Trev prepared their lunch, helped by Annie. Trev had pushed the boat out with the budget. He'd rightly decided they were all in need of some treats, so the spread was lavish and extravagant.

They took Cariad with them for the afternoon, as Trev and Annie were planning on finding a park with a cafe where they could walk with the dog, then sit and watch the world go by over a pot of tea while Ted went off to, as Trev put it, play policeman.

Ted liked the look of DS Rhys Morgan as soon as he came to find him in the reception area and escorted him to a rest room where they could talk informally over a *paned*, a cuppa. He looked young to be a DS in Serious Crime, so possibly something of a high flyer. He appeared keen, but best of all, he seemed to come at the discussion with no preconceptions. That was encouraging.

'Your DI didn't tell me much other than you seem to have stumbled on a suspicious death while you're supposed to be on leave,' he told him as he put the kettle on and got the makings out of the cupboard above the work surface. 'Bit of a busman's holiday, then?

'He also told me that even if it sounds far-fetched, whatever you want to tell me, I should at least hear you out. I gather you have a good track-record so I'll certainly listen to what you have to say.'

Ted set out all the information he had so far, exactly as he would if briefing his own team. He stuck to facts, of which there weren't many, rather than suppositions. He'd brought the pill dispenser, the prescribed medication and the sweeteners with him, carefully separately bagged and labelled and put together in a carrier bag.

'Well, you'll know better than me, but with any suspicious death we'd be looking for means, motive and opportunity if we're considering it as a possible homicide. It would seem that this Gemma Thomas has all three, from what you say. Certainly becoming the sole beneficiary in a will, even if it's only a fairly modest one, would be a motive.

'If your theory about switching the medication for sweeteners is true, and if that, plus the grapefruit factor, could account for the sudden death, that's the means, right there. And if she had a key to the house, or even if she was being let in with no problem, she had the opportunity.'

He sat back in his chair and studied Ted before he went on, weighing him up.

'I have to say this, though, Ted. By the way, are you all right with Ted? I don't know how formal you are up there in Greater Manchester.'

'Ted's fine,' he assured him. 'After all, I'm supposed to be on leave. I'm not here in any official capacity.'

'I'm going to say something you might not like. But if I didn't say it, I wouldn't be doing my job properly. You know how it works. I've got to make a case to my boss about why we should treat this as a suspicious death, based on your theory about sweeteners, and an elderly lady changing her will shortly before she died. Especially when her GP has signed it off as natural causes.

'That will mean analysis of the pills, to start with, and you know what it's like. It all costs money and has to be justified against the budget.

'So, is it possible that your mam is making something out of nothing here? She's jealous that this Gemma gets what she thought was coming to her? Or at least, she's taking the roof from over her head when she thought she had a home for life?

'If she knew about the new will, is she trying to stir up trouble for Gemma, to stop her getting the house? Or, even more sinister, if she didn't know the will had been changed, did she have a strong enough motive to kill her friend herself, and is she therefore trying to frame Gemma for something she actually did?'

'I'm glad you asked those questions,' Ted told him. 'They're exactly the ones I would have put myself so if you hadn't asked them, I'd be starting to worry.

'And there's more detail I need to give you which is only going to make it sound worse. My mother was absent from my life for a long time when I was growing up. She only came back to tell me that my grandmother, her mother, had been murdered. Poisoned. The work of a serial killer who we couldn't in the end bring to justice because she committed suicide.

'So my mother has been closely linked to two sudden deaths over a comparatively short time.'

Rhys Morgan now leaned right back in his seat, folded his arms and studied Ted closely, frowning.

Then he said, 'Ted, this isn't some sort of elaborate wind-up, is it? An initiative test or something? Because it really is starting to sound beyond credibility and I'm trying to imagine what my boss is going to say when I take it to him.'

Ted smiled at him.

'I'm glad you asked that, too, because again, it's what I would be thinking in your position. But no, all true, all documented.'

'Well, I'll certainly try to get my DI to green light it for further investigation, and let the coroner's office know we're treating it as suspicious in light of further information received.

'One thing that does puzzle me, though. You say neither your mam nor the nephew knew about the new will, and yet it affects both of them in a big way. So why didn't the lady tell either of them that she'd changed it?'

'It was quite recently done, so my guess would be she was planning to sit down with them and explain everything. Possibly when I was there, as she knew I was coming to visit.

'It's only a hunch, but I would think Gemma swore blind that she'd let my mother stay on living in the house until she could find somewhere else, rather than throwing her out on the street, which is what she's been trying to do.'

Morgan stood up and held out a hand to shake Ted's.

'Right, well, I'll go and talk to my boss now and I'll let you know his decision, either way. We'll need statements from you and the others, but there's no point doing all of that now if it's going to stay classified as natural causes.

'In the meantime try and enjoy the rest of your holiday.'

* * *

Ted told Trev and his mother about his interview without too much detail, stressing that it was possible the matter would go no further because of the death certificate and the lack of any concrete evidence to suggest murder.

While he and Trev were walking Cariad last thing before returning to the guest house, Trev turned to him to comment, 'You're quiet this evening, Mr Policeman. Thoughtful.'

'I'm wondering how things are going to work out for mam, whatever happens with this case. Even if Gemma is arrested and the new will is overturned, I don't suppose she'll fancy staying in the house where Aldwyth died.'

'It's more than that. You can't fool me, I know you too well. You're missing it, aren't you? Admit it. It's not just about being on holiday. You're missing the hands-on proper coppering. Actually on the ground, doing the work, now you're more of a desk wallah than anything else.'

He turned to face him in the darkness.

'That's it, isn't it? You like to be closer to the action than you are as Head of Serious Crime, being driven about from meeting to meeting and spending most of your life on the phone.

'I'm right, aren't I?'

Chapter Five

Jo Rodriguez had been pacing round his office whilst talking to Ted on his mobile. The boss would have been shocked at the sight of him. He looked exactly what he was - a man under pressure who had barely slept for the past couple of nights.

His shirt was crumpled, his tie pulled loose and he was in need of a shave around his usually neat beard. There'd been not much time for such niceties since Saturday night's events, and his appearance had been the last thing on his mind.

Jo hadn't wanted any word of the current situation to filter through to the boss. He knew Ted's first instinct would be to abandon his holiday and come racing back if he knew what they were dealing with in his absence.

Jo consoled himself with the old excuse of sin by omission being the lesser of two evils and infinitely preferable to ruining the boss's leave with details of what was actually going on. He'd mention the little white lie at his next confession, to assuage his conscience.

For the moment he was far too busy praying that Trev had lived up to his side of the bargain the two of them had secretly made before Ted had gone off on his leave - Trev would do his best to keep Ted away from news updates while Jo would only phone him in the most dire of circumstances.

It didn't get much more dire than the violent killing of a child on their patch, though. Certainly not that of a young boy, barely into his teens, savagely knifed to death in something which had all the hallmarks of a drugs gang-related killing.

Such a tragic case was always going to be difficult for any police officer. For a devoted father of six such as Jo, it was little short of heartbreaking. It was also potentially the biggest case he'd had to run himself in his career so far. Ted had always been there at the helm, overseeing, if nothing else.

The killing had happened late on Saturday night. The body of the boy, Noah Brooks, had been discovered by someone taking their dog for a last walk before bedtime. Jo had been called in as soon as the seriousness of the situation became clear and had barely been home since.

Even when he had managed to slip back to the house to freshen up, things there had not been easy. His youngest son, Mateo, was recovering from a badly broken leg, a sporting injury which had needed surgery and pinning. He was in a lot of pain still and at the clingy stage.

Jo's wife worked from home, a translator, in high demand for academic work, which eased the situation. But Mateo wanted his dad and kept asking for him. The divided loyalties between home and work were tearing Jo apart.

He'd had a Sunday morning meeting with the station Superintendent, who doubled as Deputy Divisional Commander, Debra Caldwell, known to all as the Ice Queen. She was out of uniform, casually dressed and being as informal as she could ever manage, which didn't say a lot. As soon as she arrived, early, she called Jo down to her office. He was relieved to smell the good coffee she always had on the go.

'Before we begin, I just want to say I have every confidence in your ability to start this investigation. So please don't think it's any reflection on you if I say that if you need an experienced, more senior officer to advise, I'm happy to sign off on asking Detective Superintendent Baker if he is sufficiently bored with his retirement to come in as a consultant as and when needed.'

Jim Baker had been the Big Boss of the team for a good few years, until his new wife had finally persuaded him to retire. He was always looking for an excuse to come back to do some work, to save him from visiting yet more 'bloody fancy houses', as he described his stately home trips.

'Thank you, ma'am. With the boss away, I'd welcome someone I could talk to if and when the need arises. It's early days yet, of course, but what we know so far gives a strong possibility, at the very least, that this is county lines related. It could even be the outfit we're already tracking and haven't yet caught up with. So we may possibly need to liaise with Drugs again.

'We already have a couple of strong markers for county lines. We're a smaller town. Too small for the bigger drugs dealers to be bothering much with in person, on the ground. But that's not to say that they aren't using people to run drugs in for them from outside the town. For these county lines operations, crossing police and county boundaries, we know they're increasingly going to smaller towns, even rural areas, to find their carriers.

'Then there's the victim. Noah Brooks, just turned fourteen. He absolutely fits the profile, from what we've managed to find out about him so far. Not stereotyping, simply stating the facts we've been able to establish. From a single parent home where his mother works all hours to provide for him and his younger brother and sister.

'A bright boy. Possibly too bright for his own good, as he was easily bored and distracted and had a bit of attitude if things weren't holding his attention. For that reason he was currently excluded from school and truanting from his Pupil Referral Unit.

'He's exactly the sort of lad who would have benefited from some sort of organised strenuous activity. Football or basketball, like my sons play. Martial arts or self defence, like the boss teaches. But we both know there have been savage cuts to youth services of late, people to steer a lad like him in the right direction. So that's left him pretty much isolated.'

Jo paused for a quick swallow of his coffee. Hot and strong, which was precisely what he needed.

'Then there's the actual method of killing. Multiple stab wounds, several of which would probably have been fatal on their own. We can't yet rule out a racist motive because Noah was mixed race. His mobile phone hasn't been found, so we don't have that to check for a county lines connection. But given what we know of the victim so far, drugs is a likely possible as the root of it all, I would say.'

'And you think there's a possible link with our ongoing and not yet fully resolved drugs case involving the person of short stature and the cuckooing operation?' the superintendent asked him. 'Or are we talking someone new moving in?'

'Early days to be sure but I would certainly put that as a strong possibility, too. With that in mind, should I liaise with NCA, so we're not stepping on their toes?'

The National Crime Agency would be involved in any type of organised crime, including drug trafficking, which went across regional or international borders.

The Ice Queen sipped her coffee whilst she considered.

'As you say, we could be looking at county lines here, possibly, but perhaps not inter-regional. And we want to avoid bringing in the heavy guns unless we have to. You and the team are more than capable of dealing with things on a smaller scale, as you've proved on countless occasions.'

Jo gave a rueful smile.

'But that was with the boss in the driving seat, ma'am.'

'You're more than up to the task of taking over, inspector.' The sudden formality was a mild rebuke. 'I have every confidence in you, and as I've said, I'm happy to make budgetary provision for Superintendent Baker to act as consultant, as and when you need him to.

'However, I know you are currently one regular team member down, with DC Ellis still on sick leave and then due to return to a desk job at HQ rather than come back here. Again,

I'm happy to allow the expenditure for a replacement for him, and I think I have the perfect candidate in mind.

'I hear that DC Gina Shaw, from Drugs, who was working with you until her cover was blown, is currently driving a desk in a back-room office somewhere, which would appear to be a complete waste of her very considerable talents and knowledge of drugs-related crime.

'I would propose that I put things in motion to second her to the team. Would you agree with that?'

Jo hesitated before replying.

'Normally I would. In fact, I would, to put it mildly, bite your hand off to have someone with her experience join the team. It's just that, you know what the boss is like. He admits to being a control freak and I'm not sure what he'd think about me signing off on Gina joining the team without consulting him.'

The Ice Queen had a reputation for being stiff, starched and formal, devoid of any sense of humour. It was not entirely justified, as she often told Ted.

She drew herself up in her seat to look as formidable as only she could and fixed Jo with her most glacial stare.

'Inspector Rodriguez,' she told him, her tone businesslike, 'as your superior officer,' she stressed the phrase which she would never normally use, 'I hope I don't have to remind you that anything which you and I discuss within these walls remains strictly confidential. There will be aspects of our conversations which you will need to pass on to the team. But I must stress that nothing at all must be shared with anyone not involved in the current operation. And that applies particularly to Chief Inspector Darling, whilst he is on leave.

'Do I make myself clear, inspector?'

Then she stunned him by giving the hint of a tiny wink. It was so fleeting that Jo wasn't sure if he had imagined it or not. He wasn't imagining the small smile playing around her lips, though, so he simply said, 'Quite clear, ma'am, thank you.'

* * *

'If that's work, Ted, remember you're not allowed to answer it,' Trev reminded him, as Ted's phone interrupted their quiet walk through a country park the following afternoon.

'No, it's DS Morgan, from Carmarthen. I'd better take it.'

Trev was strolling arm-in-arm with the mother-in-law he thought the world of. They were admiring the specimen trees in an arboretum. Annie looked better for every moment she spent in their company, away from the house. Trev was already starting to worry about how she would get on by herself when the two of them had to go home.

Ted had Cariad with him, on the lead. As soon as he stopped to answer the call, she sat down on his foot, as she liked to do. The pair were becoming close, against all the odds. The little dog didn't even notice as Annie and Trev continued on their way.

'You've got friends in high places it seems, Ted,' Morgan told him, by way of greeting. 'And it's all to the good, in terms of an enquiry.

'A pathologist up your way, a certain Professor Nelson, phoned one of ours round here who in turn spoke to the coroner. Long story short, the death has been changed from certified natural causes to possible suspicious death and the coroner has initially called for analysis of all the pills and sweeteners you recovered from the scene, and probably a post-mortem examination, unless that analysis shows nothing out of the ordinary.

'My boss has persuaded the purse string holders to allocate some hours to initial enquiries, at least. So with that in mind, sorry to spoil your holiday even further, we're going to need to get full statements, on the record, from you, your mother, the nephew and anyone else with any relevant information at all.

'We could come to the house, if you like, so we disrupt your time as little as possible. It would, in any case, be useful to have a look round the scene, although it's probably contaminated beyond anything useful now.'

'You might usefully pick up something from the pill boxes,' Ted reminded him. 'I did wear gloves to bag them, of course. And you can get plenty of witness testimony about Gemma's visits to the house so you can at least place her at the scene. The nephew saw her there a few times, early on, before she started avoiding him. Not to mention the neighbours, who miss nothing.

'And we're not actually staying at the house at present for a variety of reasons, not least of them the fact that it's a potential scene of crime. We could easily come to the nick if that works better? Just say when and we'll be there.'

They fixed a time for the following morning, then Morgan added, 'We're also going to be taking a closer look at the solicitor who drew up the new will. There's definitely the question of the dodgy ethics of having the main beneficiary in the room without checking who they were - if that's what really happened - for one thing.'

'Are you saying there's more to it than that?' Ted was quick to pounce on the hint.

'He's either breathtakingly incompetent, or he could possibly be in on it. We need to find out which it is, but that's not our main focus, only as a possible factor in motive. I'll keep you posted, as far as possible, but I don't want to spoil your leave. I imagine you're glad of it. I've got my next lot booked for a couple of months' time and I'm counting the days already.

* * *

The DC Gina Shaw who entered the room on Tuesday morning, in plenty of time for briefing at the start of the day, was unrecognisable from her last appearance in the station. There'd been various paperwork to be sorted for her temporary secondment, all of which took time, so she'd missed the first full day of the enquiry into Noah Brooks' death.

The previous occasion when the team members had met her, she'd been working undercover in the best venues in and around Greater Manchester to find high-end leisure drugs and those supplying them. Then she'd been all designer clothes, bling and monogrammed boots. Her chosen attire now was far less distinctive, and her appearance completely changed.

Jo Rodriguez had his eyes on DC Jezza Vine when Gina Shaw came to join them. Jezza could be territorial, on her own admission; prickly with other females who came in to rattle the team's tight dynamics. Jo was relieved to see that her glance towards the incomer looked neutral enough.

It felt good to have the looming bulk of former Detective Superintendent Jim Baker by his side. What Big Jim didn't know about murder enquiries wasn't yet in any training manual. And despite looking like a grizzly bear who wished his hibernation hadn't been interrupted, he was approachable and could, when necessary, do tact and diplomacy to a surprising degree.

'First thing we need to do, after all your legwork yesterday, is to build up a complete picture of how Noah spent his time,' Jo began when everyone had arrived and was sitting ready. 'Where he went, who he saw, who he mixed with. We've made a good start, but we need more. We need everything.

'Maurice,' Jo turned to DC Maurice Brown, the Daddy Hen of the team. The big softy who loved children to such an extent he'd already shed tears over the loss of this one young life. 'Collating everything we have is your job. Build us a picture of where we need to be looking. Where Noah went. Where he might have been meeting to be given the drugs, and where he was going to deliver them. Look for anything that jumps out at you. I know you're good at the detail.

'The next thing I need to sort is who attends the post-mortem. The Professor is doing it tomorrow, early doors. Never a nice thing to attend but especially one like this. So is anyone volunteering?'

The team members went quiet. Eventually the younger of the two Detective Sergeants, Rob O'Connell, spoke up.

'I'll do it, Jo. I don't have kids. Not yet, at least, because we haven't yet got our first foster. It will be hardest of all for those of you with children. Jezza, and for you because of your young brother, I imagine. So I'll do it. I'll go.'

Chapter Six

Trev stayed outside the Police HQ building in Carmarthen to look after Cariad while Ted and Annie went inside to give their statements. There wasn't anything he could usefully add to what the two of them would say.

He'd got up earlier than usual, especially on holiday, to go with Ted when he took Cariad out for her morning walk. It had given him the opportunity to talk to him, away from Annie.

'We can't leave Annie here alone when we go back at the weekend, Ted. I hope you realise that. She's been so much better out of the house and with company, but she clearly can't go back there, and especially not on her own. She's going to have to come back with us.'

'What about Cariad and the cats?' Ted asked.

'You know she's fine with cats. Look how she plays with the one that comes round from next door. Our tribe will sulk, of course. Barcelona will probably decamp to the garden for a couple of days. But we honestly can't leave Annie here by herself. It's all been so traumatic for her.'

'Will she want to come, though? Every time she takes Cariad out and speaks Welsh to her up there she risks getting another thumping from some ignorant racist who thinks she's speaking something Eastern European, or whatever. I wish I could say her last assault was a one-off and could never happen again, but you know as well as I do that's not an assurance I can give.

'I agree that she can't go back to the house by herself.

Especially not while Gemma is still about and capable of doing who knows what. She can't stay on at the B&B either, not being able to drive. She'd be marooned up there, away from her friends.'

'We need to find the time to sit down together to find out what she wants to do. And soon. It's not long before we go back and it needs sorting before we do,' Trev told him.

DS Morgan was waiting in the reception area when Ted and his mother went in. There was a young uniformed female officer with him who greeted Annie in Welsh and took her off to get her statement. Morgan led Ted along a corridor to a spare interview room, inviting him to take a seat while he fiddled with the equipment.

'You're all right with this being recorded, are you?' the DS checked.

When Ted nodded, he introduced himself and Ted, gave the basic details, then posed his first question.

He didn't need to ask many more. Ted knew the form better than most. He set out all the facts he was in possession of as succinctly as possible, including his visit to see the solicitor, Jonathan Joiner. Once he'd finished, Morgan added a timeline then switched off the recording.

'Well, I can see you've done this sort of thing a time or two,' he smiled. 'It would make our job a lot easier if every witness we had to interview was as clued up.

'Have you ever come across anything like this before, Ted? I've had some initial, off-the-record discussion with CPS about it, as it's a completely new one on me.'

'I haven't come across anything similar. But of course, we both know, and I'm sure CPS will have confirmed, that any act or omission intended to cause or hasten death is a criminal act amounting to murder or attempted murder.

'It's the intent to kill which will be hard to prove, of course. If this Gemma is clever, and she might well be to come up with an idea like this, she could simply say she sincerely believed that Aldwyth would be better off not taking the medication she was prescribed and managing her condition through more natural means.

'That would be hard to disprove, and of course it's getting more fashionable, it seems, to do things that way. I'm not telling you how to do your job, but I would be interested in what her internet search history looks like.'

'There's the will, though,' Morgan's tone was hopeful as he said it.

Ted shook his head.

'All Gemma has to do is to deny any prior knowledge of Aldwyth's intentions to change her will and she could plant reasonable doubt in the mind of a few jurors. She could paint a picture of a kind young woman running an older lady to her solicitor's office to sort out some business, to save her from having to drive into a busy town, never knowing she was going to change the will in her favour.

'If that cretin of a solicitor had done his job properly and identified who she was - assuming they don't know one another and he isn't in on it - things might have turned out very differently.'

DS Morgan stood up and gathered his things.

'Shall we go and find how your mam is getting on with Siân? Is she planning on staying down here now her friend has died, or will she move back nearer to you? If you don't mind the personal questions. You should know that people round here have no inhibitions about asking them.'

Ted had to smile at that. It was true. Even his mother could be direct and she'd lived out of the area for years.

'I don't know what her plans are yet. It's something we need to sort out with her before we go back. We're leaving on Sunday but you have my mobile number if you need to speak to me again.'

'So what's it like, being Head of Serious Crime?' the DS asked him.

They'd reached the reception area but there was no sign yet of Ted's mother. Morgan didn't seem in a hurry to get back to his office.

Ted smiled at him.

'The recruiting poster version or the truth?' he asked.

'As bad as that, eh?'

'If you enjoy paperwork, endless conferences and phone calls, budgets and spreadsheets, then I can't recommend it highly enough. Sometimes I do feel a bit detached from proper coppering. It may seem strange, with something like this affecting my own mother, but it's made me realise how much I miss it.'

* * *

Jim Baker joined the team at the end of the day to catch up on progress so far. They were using one of the larger rooms on the ground floor which was slowly filling with the trappings of a major incident. Maurice Brown had been working in there for most of the day, collating all known information on the dead boy, Noah Brooks.

The team numbers would need to be expanded further and Jo was talking to the Ice Queen about who to bring in. Jezza had surprised him by taking Gina Shaw under her wing for part of the day to bring her up to speed. As soon as there was a pause, Jezza spoke up.

'Jo, Gina and I have been talking. She knows more about the drugs scene than any of us here and she highlighted what we've already said. We know we have a growing drugs problem on the patch, and we still haven't managed to track down either the elusive Data from our earlier case, or the mysterious Big Man he could lead us to.

'Data was high end drugs supply, in the expensive clubs, whereas Noah was likely to be trafficking stuff like a bit of skunk for them, at street level. He'd stand out too much mixing with buyers any further up above that.

'So Gina and I need to get our cloaks of invisibility on and get out and about there on the scene to see what we can come up with between us ...'

'Stop right there, DC Vine.'

Big Jim Baker's deep rumble interrupted her.

'You know procedure as well as I do, even if you try to sidestep it sometimes. Anything like this requires thorough discussion with Jo, as your senior officer, and even then he would need to get it signed off from higher authority, either by Superintendent Caldwell, or by myself or probably both.'

'But sir ...' Jezza had her stubborn, rebellious face on, chin lifted in defiance.

'Never mind "but sir", DC Vine. There's another major consideration in this and you must realise that yourself. DC Shaw, you're compromised. Your cover is blown. You know that. As soon as your face appears on the scene again, if it is the same people behind this, they'll know we're on to them and they're simply going to disappear into the ether once more.

'And it could be worse. There could be a real danger to your safety, and that of anyone with you, if you show yourself and are recognised.'

'Sir, Jo, can you at least just listen to my proposal, before dismissing it?'

Jezza was nothing if not tenacious. One of the reasons why she had been flagged as having 'attitude' before she had joined Ted's team and settled down.

Big Jim's eyes rolled heavenward and he looked at Jo. His unspoken message was clear. He was there to advise and oversee. Day to day dealings with team members was down to him as DI.

'Let's hear it, Jezza. If you have an idea which might take us forward, I'll at least hear you out.'

'Thanks, Jo. Right, you all know about my previous drama training. Maurice, you and your wallet will remember that I won a bet against you when I said I could disguise myself so you wouldn't recognise me and you didn't. None of you did. Not even the boss and he takes some fooling.

'Gina's agreed to put herself in my hands for a total make-over. So if she can walk in here tomorrow and you can't all honestly say you wouldn't have known her if you weren't in on it...' she looked straight at the Big Boss as she continued, 'and that includes you, sir. If you can't all say that, then we'll abandon the idea and think of something else. But let us at least try.

'Do we have a deal?'

DS Rob O'Connell spoke before Jo had time to reply. He'd been quiet ever since getting back from the morning's post-mortem on Noah Brooks. He looked paler than usual, too.

'Tread very carefully, Jezza, if you do get the go-ahead. I've seen at first hand what we're dealing with on this one and it's not a pretty sight.

'You should have seen that young lad's body. So many stab and slash wounds. He stood zero chance of survival, even if someone had seen something and called an ambulance straight away.

'The Professor said there were two assailants, at least, and they meant business. But, get this. She also said that not all of the injuries would have meant an instantaneous, or nearly so, death. In other words, they wanted that young boy to suffer. They could easily have finished him off quite quickly but they chose not to. They left him to bleed out in a stinking dark cul-de-sac, where no one could find him until it was too late.

'So think of that, Jezza. I know you're good at changing your appearance, and I know you could do the same for Gina. But don't think even your kick-boxing skills would save you in a situation like that. This killing was a warning, as much as anything else. A distinct "don't mess with us" message, from whoever is behind it all.

'It's up to you, Jo, not me, with clearance from higher up,' he looked at Jo as he spoke, 'but I'm just adding in my views based on what I've seen this morning. We shouldn't underestimate who we're likely to be up against in this. Not for a minute.

'And don't forget, Gina, there's still the outstanding question of who it was who blew your cover and stopped us from getting our hands on the real Data in the last case. Plus your missing colleague, Ian Bradley. Is he still off the radar, or has anyone heard from him? Do we even know for sure he's not gone over to the other side, and is he still getting inside information? The risks are huge.

'This is a difficult enough operation, especially now I've seen what they're capable of. But if we're facing even the slim prospect of a bent copper in the mix, who's feeding information to the gang behind it all, it doesn't bear thinking about.'

* * *

Ted was driving, taking the scenic route, back to the house first then on to the B&B. They stopped off at a small pub with a surprisingly good lunchtime menu.

'Lunch is on me today, I insist,' Annie told them, as they sat down to study the menu. 'Teddy-bach, you've spent enough on me already this week so let this be my treat. No arguments,' she added, as Ted opened his mouth to protest.

'And while we're all sitting down together, there's something I want to discuss with you both,' she went on.

'We wanted to talk to you, too,' Trev cut in. 'Because clearly we want you to come back home with us at the weekend. You know you're always welcome, and we can't possibly leave you alone here after what's happened.'

Annie laid a gentle hand on his and smiled at him.

'Let me finish, *bach*, *plîs*. I know that, and it's very kind of you. But it's not what I want. This is my home. I never realised how much I missed it, all those years living in Stockport. Not until I came back. Now I don't want to leave here again.'

Ted opened his mouth to speak but his mother stopped him,

too, with a gentle touch.

'It's not that I don't like spending time with you both, because I do. Very much. But you have your own lives to lead
and I have mine. Mine is here. But I'm going to need your help,
Teddy *bach*.

'I need to know if I am even allowed to go back to the
house. Because that's what I want to do, for now. Because if I
don't, then she's won, hasn't she? Gemma. However things turn
out in the end.

'I've no idea why Aldwyth did what she did, changing her
will like that. But I know she wouldn't have wanted me to be
driven out, and I know she would have had her reasons for her
actions.

'Now, we'll need to sit down with Bryn and be sure he
would be happy for me to do that, if only on a temporary basis.
And then I need to find my own little place to live. However
things work out with the will and everything in the future.

'But I want to stay here. I still have the money from selling
mam's house, and all the furniture in store. I must be able to
find something small near here for myself. Somewhere I can
feel safe speaking Welsh, and can keep in touch with all my
friends. Aldwyth's friends, too.

'I know it's asking a lot of you, on your holiday, but will
you help me with all of that, the two of you? Before you go
back?'

Chapter Seven

House-hunting showed up as much as anything the contrast between Ted and Trev. Ted was bored rigid and trying not to show it.

Trev was in his element. He looked at everything in detail, opening every cupboard and drawer he came across. Depending on who was showing them round, he couldn't resist camping it up outrageously, bitching about the *décor*, making Annie laugh and earning some disapproving looks from estate agents.

Ted had suggested that his mother also look at some rental options before making the commitment to buy. He was surprised at some of the prices being asked. He knew Annie had enough to buy something in the village, based on what her mother's house in Stockport had sold for. But most of that would be swallowed up by a purchase, leaving her nothing much invested to supplement her meagre pension.

One of the houses Trev had found online, a small mid-terrace, was being sold privately and was priced for a quick sale. The owner agreed to show them round once he'd finished work for the day.

Trev was driving them there. It was impossibly cramped for his long frame in the rear seat but he always insisted on giving up the front seat to his mother-in-law when Ted drove. Ted had to sit behind Annie as Trev had the driver's seat pushed so far back.

It meant Ted could answer his mobile when it rang, and the screen showed him it was DS Morgan, from Carmarthen, calling him once more.

'Sorry to call late in the day, Ted. I hope you're not having your tea, but I thought you might like a bit of an update, as a courtesy. You know, of course, that we took your mam's fingerprints for elimination purposes, which is standard procedure.'

'Again, I would have been worried if you hadn't,' Ted told him.

'Fair play. The good news is that none of her prints were to be found on the items you bagged and brought in. There's nothing to show she ever touched the pill dispenser or the box of medication.

'Now, you and I probably both avoid reading or watching much crime fiction as it's not good for our blood pressure and we might end up throwing things at the TV or dumping a book in the bin.'

Ted laughed at that. He'd been known to hurl a book against a wall in frustration at improbable twists and coincidences in the plot.

'Well, this next bit of news definitely comes into that category. We don't yet have the deceased lady's fingerprints confirmed, although they can hopefully be taken on autopsy. But we ran a match on some stray ones we found on both the pill box and the packet of medication, and they were on file.'

He paused for dramatic effect, milking the moment.

'When she was just sixteen, our Gemma Thomas was arrested, with a bunch of her friends, on suspicion of shoplifting. They were in a clothes shop and one of them grabbed an expensive top, but there was a store detective who challenged them. They all ran off and the top was dropped on the floor outside. They were rounded up, arrested on suspicion of theft and processed, including fingerprinting.

'None of them would say who'd actually snatched the top and they weren't in possession of it when they were arrested, although CCTV showed them leaving the store looking suspicious and huddled in a bunch.

'In the end, with CPS advice, it was decided it wasn't in the public interest to pursue it, so they were all let off with a caution. But it does mean we have her fingerprints on file and they're a match for ones where we wouldn't expect to find them. Gemma was supposed to visit to do the lady's aromatherapy stuff. There was no valid reason for her to touch the medication.'

'I wouldn't be too confident. She could play the helpful card again and say she's simply passed the pill box to Aldwyth to save her getting up to get it herself. And topped it up for her as necessary.'

'Except your mam has nicely pre-empted that for us with her witness testimony. She told us the times of day her friend took her pills, and the times that Gemma came to do her treatments, and they don't coincide. We've also now got the statement from the nephew and he says the same thing. He was often there when his auntie was taking her evening medication, and after the first time he met her, Gemma was never there at the same time as he was. I think we can now take a good guess as to why not.

'Post-mortem is tomorrow and we're not planning on talking to Gemma until we have some news from that. I've been told that it's always hard to prove a negative, in terms of medication, and that with the delay, we may get nothing at all from the analysis. I want to see what, if anything, we do get before I talk to Gemma.'

Trev was just pulling the car up on the small forecourt of the house they'd come to view. Annie was leaning forward in her seat peering at it with evident interest. There was no For Sale sign up outside as it wasn't with an agent.

'Oh, it's this one. We'll have passed it no end of times; it's close to the bus stop. We'd seen the old lady who lived here a few times, just to say hello to. We heard she'd gone into a home.'

'Thanks for calling me, Rhys, but I have to go now. We've brought my mother to look at a house for sale. Keep me posted about the PM, please.'

'It looks really nice from the outside,' Annie was still sounding excited. 'Tidy.'

'Mam, remember what I told you. Don't sound too keen or we'll never get the price down at all. And speak English, please, so I know what you're saying.'

A man got out of a nearby parked car and came over to them. He addressed Annie in Welsh.

'Miss Jones, is it? I'm selling the house.'

As instructed, Annie replied in English, setting the rules for their conversation.

'I'm Miss Jones, yes. This is my son, Ted, who doesn't speak Welsh, and this is his partner, Trevor.'

'Oh right, come in, then, I'll show you round. It's my mam's house. She's had to go into a home. She couldn't manage on her own any more, and we need to sell it to pay the care costs.'

'*Bechod!*' Annie exclaimed, then corrected herself for Ted's benefit. 'There's a shame, but it comes to so many of us in the end, I suppose.'

'The wife and I have given the place a good clean-up and a splash of paint in neutral colours. We've moved the furniture out, too, so it's a blank canvas for someone.'

He opened the front door and moved to one side to let them in. It was certainly clean and bright, especially standing empty, and with the distinctive smell of fresh paint.

Ted could see that his mother wanted the house from the moment she stepped inside, and he had to admit, it appeared to be ideal for her needs. It would be cheap to heat and maintain, and there was a small, well-fenced garden for Cariad. He kept having to catch her eye and give her a warning look not to seem too eager.

When they'd finished the tour and were being shown out, he took the initiative and told the man, 'Thank you for showing us round. It's a possible, but we have several others to look at as well, of course. We'll let you know as soon as we can.'

'Ted Darling, you told a big fat fib,' Trev chided him as they got in the car to drive back to the guest house. 'And you a policeman, too. You know Annie wants it, and I don't blame her. It would be perfect, and it's affordable.'

'I think so, too. But it's too early to let a desperate vendor know that.'

* * *

Most of the team members had previously seen Jezza in character for an undercover role, both looking and sounding totally unlike herself. Big Jim Baker had not yet had that privilege, at close quarters.

He'd come back in at the end of the day to talk to Jo and to catch up with any developments which might need his input. He'd found that most officers were out when he walked through the main office. There was no sign of either Jezza or of Gina Shaw.

Neither of them appeared until last thing, when Jo and Big Jim went downstairs to the room they were now using for a major incident room.

Jo was just getting started when the door opened violently and an apparition appeared. Various of the team members put hands in front of mouths to hide broad grins as Jezza, well into character, swaggered into the middle of the room and glared at the former Big Boss.

She had the ability to look much younger than her age. No one would ever take her for a serving police officer, looking as she did. The neutral Cheshire accent had given way to something much rougher round the edges as she threw at Big Jim, 'Got your eyeful have you? What you staring at, ya perv?'

There was silence, a collective holding of breath, as the team waited to hear if she'd pushed her luck too far.

'All right, DC Vine,' he rumbled. 'Point made. Fifteen-love to you. I wouldn't have recognised you, looking like that, and I doubt anyone would think of you as a copper. You're going to have to go some to keep it up though, now I know what you're capable of. So let's see what you've done with DC Shaw.'

Jezza put her fingers in her mouth and gave a whistle so ear-splitting as to be painful at close quarters, then yelled, 'Oy, Sonja, gerrin'ere.'

There was a palpable air of anticipation as the person they all knew would be Gina Shaw came sauntering in.

Jezza had made her look shorter, with flat-soled shoes. That was the easy part. The rest of her makeover was nothing short of radical and masterfully done.

The long, carefully styled and highlighted hair had been savagely hacked off to leave a spiky cut, dyed black. Coloured contact lenses changed the natural tint of her eyes, with Kohl pencil emphasising the new darkness.

Baggy clothings in sombre colours accentuated bulk, to-tally transforming the previously tall and slim silhouette the team had first seen. No detail had been spared in altering her appearance. Previously long, varnished, and well-manicured fingernails were now short and looked bitten to the quick. She was quite simply unrecognisable.

Maurice was the first to break the stunned silence.

'Bloody hell, bonny lass,' he said. 'Please tell me that's a wig you're wearing.'

Gina smiled at him as she reached up, tugging at the short spikes.

'Not a wig, Maurice. If we're going up against dangerous types I can't afford for my hair to come away in someone's hand when the going gets interesting. And it will grow back, in time.'

Jezza, keeping in character, was looking straight at the Big Boss as she said, 'This is me mate, Sonja,' pronouncing the J.

There was silence again for a long moment, then Big Jim

spoke again.

'All right, DC Vine, I admit it. I wouldn't have known either of you if I'd passed you in the street. Well done. But, and this is a big but, this does not give you the instant green light to go off on your own, the two of you, without a very detailed risk assessment in place, agreed by DI Rodriguez and signed off by me. Clear?'

'Clear, sir,' she said, then gave him a cheeky smile as she added, 'I should have had a bet with you. The drinks would have been on you tonight.'

Even Big Jim managed a smile at her nerve as he told her, 'Once we've finished updating here, you two ladies - I use the term loosely in the circumstances - will sit down with me and Jo and we'll thrash out how best to put you to good use, if you will forgive the phrase.'

'Right, who's got anything new?' Jo asked, as Jezza and Gina found seats next to each other, exchanging a smile and a high five at their success.

'I think I might have a clue as to why the gang made such a clear warning of killing Noah, from talking to my contacts,' DC 'Virgil' Tibbs told them.

Virgil was a popular and respected officer with the black community. They knew he would always listen to any grievances, but that at the same time he showed no favour to anyone and would arrest those who crossed the line too far. It was rare for him not to get any inkling of what was going on on the street.

'We've heard that Noah was a bright lad. He'd also appointed himself head of the family, with no dad there to support them all. He was always trying to find ways to help out his mum, because no matter how many hours she worked, there never seemed to be enough money to go round, to pay rent and utilities, never mind feed them all properly. And by all accounts she did everything she could to make sure those kids were well fed and looked after.

'From what I've been told, Noah was trying to play it clever. Keeping back a small quantity from each delivery he was supposed to be making and selling it for himself on the quiet. Sometimes even dipping carefully into the takings.

'Most of the kids who get sucked into this sort of thing do it because they're being threatened or harmed in some way. Beatings and stabbings are not uncommon as a way to teach them a lesson.

'Another thing these same gangs traffic, as well as the drugs, is young girls, for prostitution. Often very young girls. Noah had a younger sister and the family were a close unit. It doesn't take much to imagine the leverage over him if he was constantly threatened with what might happen to his younger sister if he didn't cooperate.

'So he was siphoning off as much as he dared, which won't have been a lot because these kids get watched all the time, and checked up on. But it seems he liked to boast a bit. Big himself up. Claimed he was actually getting paid to do the runs, which none of the others are, rather than being threatened into it.

'The bosses couldn't afford word of anything like that to be flying about, even if it wasn't true. It would make them look weak and if other kids heard of it, they might start trying the same thing.

'I reckon that's why they took him out, and did it in such a brutal way. Like Rob said, this had "don't mess with us" written all over it and must have put the wind up any of the other kids who got to hear about it. And let's face it, those poor kids are probably running on neat adrenaline as it is.'

'All of that fits in with what I've found out today, talking at length to the boy's mother,' DS Mike Hallam told them.

'She also said that Noah was always trying to play the head of the household. He did anything he could to bring home a little bit of cash. She was struggling so much she never questioned where it came from but she swears she'd no idea he was up to his neck in the serious drugs scene. I'm inclined to believe her.

'She's devastated by his loss, that much is clear, and it also seems she had no reason at all to suspect something like this would happen to him one day. She would surely have done if she'd known he was involved with drugs gangs. You can't turn on the telly these days without seeing something similar.

'So she's either as good an actor as Jezza is, or she genuinely believed he was doing just a bit of petty thieving or something to bring back the few quid he did.

'Whoever killed him and for whatever reason, I think we can be fairly sure that it was related to the drugs gangs. In a sense, we'd better hope it's the same gang we've been looking for. If yet another one has turned up and established themselves on our patch as well as the existing one ... well that really doesn't bear thinking about.'

Chapter Eight

Trev had his arms wrapped round Annie to say his farewells. Cariad was in her customary position, sitting on Ted's feet, gazing up at him with adoring brown eyes.

'I'll phone you, often, and you can always phone me any time you need to. Fingers crossed for the house purchase. If it goes through I'll take some time off and come and help you move in. You know we'll never get Mr Grumpy to come again so soon.'

Once Trev let go of her, Ted leaned in for the briefest touch of cheek against cheek, telling her, 'Sorry to rush off, but we really do need to get going. And I won't be able to get away again for a while, I don't suppose, but I'll sort out getting the furniture moved down here from storage, and anything like that I can help you with.'

'*Diolch*. I better take Cariad inside now, *bach*, she looks as if she might try to follow the car. She's going to miss you.'

Annie didn't tell Ted how much she would miss him, too. That would risk reopening old wounds for both of them, about all the years they'd spent apart. Instead she took the little dog into the house and shut the door firmly behind them.

Trev drove the first leg. They'd stop for a bite and a drink on the way, wine for Trev, so Ted would take over the driving afterwards. They opted for the cross-country route, which was quiet enough on a Sunday.

Even though Ted said nothing, Trev knew his head was already back on the job, wondering what had been going on in his absence.

Trev had been known to compare him to a supposedly retired gun dog who'd suddenly heard the sound of a firearm being cocked. Even on holiday, Ted found it hard to switch off.

'Whatever they've been working on, you'll find out soon
enough tomorrow,' Trev told him with a fond smile. 'Stop
wishing what remains of your holiday away, especially when
it's not really been all that much of a break for you. And you're
going to have some serious explaining to do to the cats when
you get home, with your clothes, and especially your shoes,
smelling of dog.

'Mind you, Mrs Skinner will probably have looked after
them so well they will hardly have noticed we've been gone.
Not to mention polished the kitchen to within an inch of its
life.'

They'd tried to make the most of the week, even with DS
Morgan phoning Ted with frequent updates, for which he was
grateful. They'd taken Annie out every day to visit her favourite places, including the village where she was born.

As anticipated, DS Morgan had told Ted that it would take
some time for all the analysis results to come through after the
post-mortem examination, but the pathologist had found evidence of a catastrophic heart attack, which was what had killed
Aldwyth.

'Lot of big words, Ted, you know how these things go. The
drug she was on has a long half life so should theoretically
show up on analysis. But if you're right and it's been withheld
for some time, there'll be nothing left, of course.'

The pathologist had commented at the time, and had put in
his report, that he had been surprised by the extent of the damage from someone on a high dose of medication. It would be
extremely unusual, though not impossible, to suffer such an
attack when taking the medication as prescribed.

'It basically all boils down to microscopic changes seen at
autopsy which were unexpected in the circumstances. Then

there were clots found in the left atrium which, again, were unexpected, given her medication history.'

That had been all the additional evidence which the coroner, who was present for the autopsy, needed to decide that a full inquest would have to be held to establish all the facts surrounding the death. It was the breakthrough Ted had been hoping to hear about.

DS Morgan was also planning to visit the solicitor who had drawn up the original will, leaving the house to Bryn and with a written clause that Annie could stay there as long as she wished. He'd take the new will with him for advice. For the moment, there was nothing to stop Annie from staying on in the house, with Bryn's permission. In the same way, there was nothing yet to allow Gemma to enter the property. Since encountering Ted, she hadn't even tried to.

Ted had taken his mother and Trev back for a second viewing on the house she liked the day before they left. Annie was even more enthusiastic than the first time, so Ted had tried a cheeky offer and been both surprised and pleased when it had been accepted on the spot. With no chain involved, the sale could go through quite quickly. Annie insisted she would be fine staying alone in Aldwyth's house until it did, and Bryn had promised Ted faithfully that he would check on her every day on his way home from work.

Trev was still studying Ted as he drove. Then he said, 'You've enjoyed all this, in a strange sort of way, haven't you? Well, perhaps not enjoyed,' he went on as Ted made to speak, 'but it's what you do best, isn't it? Solving crime. I know you're good at all the paperwork and the admin, not to mention the people management. But this is what you like best, isn't it?'

Ted gave him a small smile.

'I have to admit it makes me feel more of a proper copper and slightly more useful. But tomorrow it'll be back to the desk job and the spreadsheets once more.'

* * *

Ted had arranged to meet Jo half an hour before morning briefing on the Monday, his first day back, to bring himself up to speed with what had been going on in his absence. When he walked into his office before the appointed hour, he was surprised to get an early morning summons from Superintendent Caldwell.

'I thought I'd sit in on things this morning, so if you would like to come downstairs to my office, DI Rodriguez should be here at any moment.'

Ted wondered what had prompted the move. There was nothing, as he walked through the main office heading for the stairs, to explain why the Super would be involving herself in Jo's return to work briefing with Ted. No signs of anything pinned up or written on white boards to hint at an ongoing enquiry, unless it was big enough to warrant a transfer down to one of the rooms on the ground floor. Had that been the case, he would have expected a quick courtesy call from Jo at some point to keep him in the loop.

Jo arrived moments after Ted had sat down and been offered coffee. Whatever it was all about, he was clearly in on it as he came straight to the Super's office without going upstairs first. The Ice Queen put coffee in front of him then sat down and addressed Ted.

'I'm afraid we've been discussing you in your absence, Chief Inspector,' she told him. 'I hope you won't have heard anything of the reasons why, as we have all been trying to ensure that your well-deserved leave went as uninterrupted as it could.'

Ted smiled at that. 'Thank you for the thought, but I've actually spent a few days working with West Wales Police on a suspicious death, which was not the plan.'

'And you've arrived back to a major incident here, I'm afraid.'

She briefly filled him in on the details they had so far - the killing of Noah Brooks and the likelihood of links to organised drugs gangs, leading to the possibility of it being connected to their earlier, unsolved case.

'Superintendent Baker has been overseeing in your absence, but clearly we need an experienced Senior Investigating Officer to run this. For that reason, I've discussed it with higher authorities and we think that it would be in keeping with your role of Head of Serious Crime for you to take over that position. You already know all the history of the previous cases and linked events. But that would mean you having to abandon the paperwork part of your current role. You won't have time for both.

'All of which fits quite well. You might know Detective Superintendent Sampson, I imagine? Following recent surgery, she's in need of a somewhat more sedentary role than her usual one, on a temporary basis. It's felt that she, with all her experience, could at least maintain the administrative and supervisory side of your usual work for you while you concentrate on this case, which is currently being called Operation Flood.

'We want to deal with these drugs gangs on our patch once and for all. We've been bringing in other officers so you have the resources you need. I've already seconded DC Shaw for you and she has begun some covert operations with DC Vine to see what they can uncover, without putting themselves at risk.

'DI Rodriguez will, of course, continue to assist you, but unfortunately for Superintendent Baker, it means he will have to go back to visiting stately homes. This seems to be the ideal solution all round, especially from a budgetary point of view.

'I can assure you that you can hand over your role to Superintendent Sampson in complete confidence. Her work is, and always has been, exemplary.'

Ted had met the superintendent on a few occasions but never worked closely with her. Her name was Moira but almost everyone called her Sammy. She was short and with a tendency to overweight which would no doubt not be helped by a need to be desk-bound and sedentary. She had a reputation for being able to drink many of her male colleagues under the table and out the other side. She looked the perfect stereotype of everyone's favourite auntie, but Ted knew the image hid a determination to succeed and a razor-sharp mind to ensure she achieved her aim.

Jo saw Ted's gaze on him and help up both hands in mock surrender.

'I know, boss, I know. I should have kept you in the loop. I was under orders not to. And not just from your Trev.'

The Ice Queen added her most frosty look as she said, 'Those orders came directly from me, Chief Inspector. There was absolutely no point in disturbing your leave with anything which was going on here. It sounds as if you had enough on your plate.

'So what do you feel about stepping in as SIO on this case and leaving the admin side of your role in the capable hands of Superintendent Sampson? She's ready to come on board as soon as she receives word, but you'll clearly need some time with her to brief her on what you currently have on your hands.'

Ted was trying to play it cool with his response. He wasn't fooling either of them as he said, 'Sounds all right to me.'

* * *

Ted wasn't remotely surprised to hear that Superintendent Sampson was primed to join him first thing that afternoon for a handover. He'd been presented with a done deal. Fortunately, one he was more than happy with.

He sat in on Jo's morning briefing to bring himself up to speed on the basics. Jim Baker had been stood down now that Ted was back, no doubt grumbling at the loss of his excuse to avoid the sort of trips out his wife Bella enjoyed, which he tolerated at best. Ted's agreement with the new arrangements had clearly been taken for granted.

Jezza Vine and Gina Shaw didn't join them in person, but Jezza gave her input via conference call to update everyone on their progress. They'd be avoiding the station as much as possible for the time being. Anyone spotting them anywhere near it risked blowing their cover out of the water.

'The teens we've spoken to so far are scared,' she told them. 'I'm talking seriously scared. They've all heard about what happened to Noah and it's put the fear of selected deity up them, to put it mildly. They're not saying much to anyone so we're having to tread more than carefully.

'Once again we're hearing mention of a mysterious "Big Man" behind all of this. But like before, whether that is simply an expression, or it's the same person we were tracking before - our vertically-challenged friend with the dark glasses and the white stick - it's far too soon to tell.'

'Be careful, Jezza,' Ted told her. 'You and Gina, both of you, avoid doing anything at all to put yourselves at risk. Watch, listen and feed back, but don't put yourselves in any danger. Either of you.'

'Yes, boss. Nice to see you back, boss. Did you bring me a stick of rock?'

Even on a serious case Jezza could never resist teasing him. Almost immediately, though, she switched back to professional mode as she gave the details they had so far.

'The strongest hint up to now that there might be a connection is from one young lad we talked to who says he saw Noah getting into a black 4x4 a time or two, and being driven off in it. We know our gang suspects have used a black 4x4 before. It's not exactly an unusual vehicle these days and he couldn't give us any more detail, but it's a start. We're working on getting more.'

Mike Hallam was sorting actions for the day, allocating team members to where their skills were best suited. There would be the usual hours of CCTV footage to be trawled through for any sighting of Noah Brooks in his last hours. He made a note of the possible significance of a black four-wheel-drive to their enquiries.

Ted left them to it and headed back to his office. Once he'd handed over to Superintendent Sampson, he'd be free to be back with them, in the thick of the enquiry. The anticipation he felt at the prospect proved Trev's point - he couldn't wait to get back to the front line.

He took the rest of the morning, plus a working lunchtime at his desk with a sandwich, to get things to the point where he was happy to hand over to the new Acting Head of Serious Crime. Superintendent Sampson arrived on the dot of the appointed hour and strode into his office.

Ted rose automatically to his feet to greet her with an, 'Afternoon, ma'am,' as she entered.

She waved a hand at him as she pulled out the chair opposite his and sat down carefully. Ted noticed the slight wince of pain as she did so.

'For goodness sake don't bother with all that old bollocks, unless you want to show off in front of your team. Call me Sammy. Everyone does.

'Now, I'm just here to keep your seat warm, nothing more. And to stop your in tray running amok. Just give me the heads up on any teams I need to keep a closer eye on than usual.'

'Ashton,' Ted told her without hesitation. 'They're doing better than they were but they still need the occasional jerk on the lead as a reminder. Their DI is still off sick and their DS doesn't always assert himself like he should.'

Ted's phone pinged to announce a text message received. He picked it up as he told her, 'I better check it's nothing that needs my immediate attention.'

The message was short. Ted recognised its significance immediately.

'You got a fag, mate? Answer incoming anon call.'

DS Ian Bradley. Gina Shaw's colleague, from Drugs, who had been out of contact with anyone for some time. The first part of the message was how he had approached Ted one time when they needed an arranged meet whilst Bradley was working deep under cover.

'I need to take a call,' Ted told Sampson.

She stood up and motioned him out of the way.

'Shift your arse, then, and I'll make a start. I'm the soul of discretion. Unless you need me to trot off to the powder room while you talk?'

'No, it's fine, thanks.'

His phone was already ringing. A masked number. He picked up the call.

'You got a fag, mate?' Bradley repeated the message.

'Why don't you get yourself a job, then you could buy your own?' Ted remembered his previous response and repeated it back.

Bradley was clearly being wary. He gave a chuckle of satisfaction.

'You know who this is, then. I need to see you, soon. It's urgent. I can't talk much now but I needed to warn you.

'I know some people thought I was the mole on the team who blew the last op. I wasn't, but I'm pretty sure I know who was. I've been waiting for the right moment, and the right person to approach. They're still there. Still in post. They know you've gained a new team member. And if they know, they're not likely to be the only ones.'

Chapter Nine

Ted's first instinct was to try to get hold of Jezza and Gina, urgently, to warn them. They were both currently staying at a safe house as part of their cover. Jezza's live-in partner Nathan was looking after her younger brother Tommy, with the help of the regular carers he knew well who covered any hours Jezza couldn't see to him. Gina lived alone so had no special arrangements to make.

Few people knew which house they were using. It was done that way deliberately, to help protect their cover as far as possible. Ted knew that neither of them would take their work phones with them when they were out and about. They'd be hidden securely at the property and replaced by burners. The best he could do for the moment was to leave a message on Jezza's work phone. He didn't have a number for the other one, it was too risky for her cover.

'Jezza, it's the boss. Phone me, as soon as you get this message. It's urgent. And watch your backs, both of you. There's a risk your cover has been compromised.'

He tried the same thing with Gina Shaw's phone, with the same result.

Sammy Sampson lifted her head as Ted finished speaking.

'That sounds worrying. Team members out under cover? Sorry for eavesdropping, by the way. Anyway, look, even at first glance I can tell your paperwork is flawless, so I should be able to get my addled brain around it easily enough without you. Why don't you push off and do something more useful? I can always bell you for anything I can't fathom out.

'Just be a love and make me a cuppa before you toddle off to where you need to be. This isn't me pulling rank or anything. It's just that every time I get up and move about, I'm reminded of all the reasons I'm supposed to do it as little as possible at the moment.'

'I drink green tea, but I can find you black tea, or coffee, easily enough.'

She looked up at him as he headed for the kettle.

'Green tea?' she asked with a laugh. 'What kind of a copper are you? Coffee's fine, thanks. Strong, and nothing in it.'

Once she was sorted, Ted headed down to find the team members who were working in the incident room. He particularly wanted to tell Jo the worrying news he'd received about Gina and Jezza's cover being potentially compromised. The sooner he could speak to one or other of them and pull them in, the happier he would feel.

First he had something else to sort out. Something which had been weighing heavily on his conscience the full two weeks he'd been away.

He went first to the front desk in the reception area to find retired Police Sergeant Bill Baxter. Now retired and wearing a different sort of uniform, Bill was a vital point of triage between people who came in to report crime and busy police officers who could do without time wasters. With his years of experience, he could soon sort out which were the genuinely urgent cases in need of immediate action.

'Hello, Ted, how was your leave?' Bill greeted him.

Ted laughed.

'You wouldn't believe me if I told you. I spent the first week sitting in court and the second being involved in a suspicious death case. I did get to the seaside a time or two, though.

'I wanted to ask you how Steve is doing and whether you thought he'd want to talk to me. I'd like to see him. I feel like I let him down in a big way.'

DC Steve Ellis was one of Ted's team who was on extended sick leave after an attempt on his own life. Swift action by Bill and Ted had meant that he'd survived.

'Don't be so soft,' Bill scoffed. 'I bloody live with him and I didn't notice how bad things were getting. And for what it's worth, he thinks he let you down, so he's worried about seeing you again.'

'Would he see me, though? Would it help him? Or would it just bring it all back?'

'You know how quiet he is usually. He's about ten times more so at the moment. He's spending a lot of time with Father Jack on his shoulder screaming swear words down his ear, which he seems to find soothing, for some reason. I'm leaving him be for now.'

Ted had never thought of Bill's foul-mouthed parrot as being therapeutic, but each to their own.

'Anyway, you've got enough on your plate, with a major incident. I'll tell Steve you were asking after him, then maybe we can fix a time when the three of us can sit down over a cuppa and do some straight talking.'

Ted next went to find Jo. The incident room was in full swing so he drew him aside to talk to him. He filled him in on his call from Ian Bradley.

'Shit, Ted, I don't like the sound of that. That puts Jezza and Gina at high risk, even though Gina currently looks nothing like she did before. But it means the gang will be on high alert for any strange female appearing on the patch and that's dangerous for them. We need to pull them.'

'I've left messages for both of them but I've not heard anything back yet. Do you know which safe house they're using?'

'I don't. It was a need to know basis, for extra security. But I can find out.'

'Make it a priority, please. It's dangerous enough for them, an op like this, without having a bent copper somewhere in the mix.'

'Do you know who that is?'

'I don't, yet, but I hope to meet up with Ian when he can find a safe time and a place to do it. No wonder he's been staying hidden. In possession of information like this, he's also in danger. At least we now know why the last big op went so badly wrong, if there's someone bent on the inside. Let's just hope we can get the identity from Ian without putting him or anyone else in danger in the process.

'In the meantime, the longer we leave Jezza and Gina out there on their own, the greater their danger is. I don't think we can afford to wait. We need a pre-emptive strike. Have a word with Kevin Turner and let's get the details to every officer out there, with a full description of what they currently look like.

'Rather than blowing their cover, it can only enhance it if anyone should happen to see the two of them getting arrested and put in the back of an area car, in handcuffs. Although I don't suppose they'll thank us for it.

'If there's anyone else on the team you can spare, even for an hour or so, put them on it. We need to find the pair of them before someone else does.'

* * *

Two officers in an area car were travelling along Wellington Road South towards the town centre. The one in the passenger seat turned to speak to her colleague, who was driving.

'Those two likely lasses, heading towards Merseyway. Are they the two we're supposed to be keeping an eye out for? Descriptions seem to match.'

The driver slowed down, glad of there being enough traffic crawling along to make it seem natural, while he took a good look at them.

'Could well be. What're they wanted for? Are we supposed to pull them?'

'Report in and wait for further instructions, it said.'

She got on the radio while her colleague left the main road and found a place to turn the car round. She gave a detailed description of the two women they'd just seen and asked for further instructions.

'The two women we want brought in are officers from the station working under cover,' she was told. 'It's essential that you do and say nothing to blow their cover. They're unaware that they're to be lifted on sight, so prepare to meet some resistance. One of them is DC Jezza Vine, so the resistance is likely to be strong.'

'Jezza? Blimey, I'd never have known one of them was her from looking at them.'

PC Jenny Wells forgot correct radio procedure for a moment in her surprise. She knew Jezza by sight, but neither of the two people she'd seen walking past had looked anything like the DC Vine she knew from work.

'The two we've just seen do fit the description we were given. I should recognise her from close up, so if it's not those two, what do you want us to do?'

'Again, nothing at all to cause suspicion. If it's not DC Vine, think of something convincing to say. Routine warnings to young women of a man approaching them with indecent suggestions, perhaps?

'If it is them, it's essential their cover is not blown, therefore you are to proceed as for any other arrest. Don't show any sign of recognition. We don't know if they're being watched.

'Whatever it takes, you need to get them in the car and bring them both back here as soon as possible. You're instructed to make it look convincing, so handcuff if necessary. But try to avoid spraying fellow officers unless it becomes essential.'

'Right, Al, you heard what she said, we need to make it look realistic. But watch out for Jezza. I hear she does kick-boxing and I don't imagine she's going to be thrilled at the prospect of being arrested, especially when she knows nothing about it and we can't tell her the reason.'

Thrilled Jezza certainly was not. It was Murphy's law that there were people about so the two officers couldn't say anything to her to risk blowing her cover. Jezza recognised Jenny but it was clear that the Uniform officer wouldn't have known her, disguised as she was, had she not been put in the picture, and Jezza had no ID on her while working under cover. All she could do was to stay in character and verbally resist arrest as strongly as she could.

Jenny wisely left Jezza to her much bigger colleague to deal with. He still had his hands full and finished up cuffing her for his own safety.

As soon as they were in the car and heading the short distance back to the station, Jenny swivelled in her seat to speak to them.

'Sorry about that, ladies, we were under strict instructions to find you urgently and bring you in, by whatever means, and without blowing your cover. Jezza, I honestly wouldn't have known you by sight if we hadn't had the info.

'I better leave the cuffs on while we get you inside and handed over because I don't know the reason for any of this and I don't want to get it wrong.

'You both look amazing, though.'

Jezza looked slightly mollified but was finding the journey uncomfortable.

'This is DC Gina Shaw, by the way. And you've no idea what this is all about?'

'None at all. It just came over as an All Units with instructions to bring you in and to make it look convincing. Which is what we tried to do. And we need to keep it up until we can hand you over to someone.'

Jezza's swearing and struggling as they manhandled her inside and took her to the custody suite were certainly convincing. She had no idea what it was all about, but if it needed to look realistic for any possible onlookers, she was happy to oblige.

The custody sergeant had been put in the picture about who was being brought in and the need for discretion. It was a quiet moment, but he wasn't taking any chances. He wouldn't have recognised Jezza either, apart from her distinctive eyes, close to. He played it exactly as he would have for anyone else being brought into his suite.

He didn't bat an eyelid when he asked PC Wells what they'd been brought in for and she couldn't resist telling him, 'Suspicion of soliciting, sarge.'

Once there was no one about, Jezza had the handcuffs removed, with fulsome apologies from Jenny, and were told they were expected in the incident room, where full explanations would be given.

Ted looked up as soon as the two of them entered the room and strode across to speak to them.

'I'm relieved to see you both, safely back. Sorry about the subterfuge to get you brought in safely. Let's go upstairs and I'll explain all the reasoning behind it,' Ted told them.

He realised he might seem paranoid, not wanting to talk in the incident room which was filled now with officers, including some brought in from other areas to make up numbers. He wasn't about to take any chances. All he knew so far, from Ian Bradley, was that there was a mole somewhere within the system and at the moment he had no idea who, nor where they were from.

Ted headed for Jo's office, which was currently unoccupied, rather than disturbing Superintendent Sampson in his. They stopped to brew up on the way.

'Boss, you're being very mysterious. What's this all about? And was it really necessary to cuff us and bring us in on suspected soliciting?'

Ted had to smile at that, despite the serious situation.

'I judged it necessary, yes, although the soliciting was not my idea. I tried to contact you by phone but could only get the recorded message and I didn't want to wait.

'Gina, I had a call out of the blue from Ian Bradley. Very wary, light on detail. He wants a meet with me. What he told me was sufficiently concerning for me to want you brought in without delay.

'He said he knows some people thought he was the mole but that he isn't though he thinks he knows who it is. He said the person knows you've transferred here, and therefore if the mole knows, there's no guarantee that the people we're after don't know, too.

'You know him a lot better than any of us here. My instinct was to believe him. Was I right to?'

'I would say so, boss,' Gina told him. 'I've known Ian for years. I never believed he'd risk any of the team by giving info about an op. He might have drip-fed some details which were of no real use to anyone for some reason. But nothing like what happened. Perhaps I should meet him?'

'Too risky, Gina, even looking as you do now. I'll go. But for now, you two are strictly back behind a desk, until further instructions. Clear? Jezza?'

'Clear, boss. But first we need to go back to the safe house to get our stuff, including our phones.'

Ted shook his head.

'Not on your own, you don't. Not until I know better what's going on and where the risk is coming from. I'll drive you there myself. I think we can all agree I'm the least copper-like looking person on the team, and I've got my old leather jacket in the car, so I can dress down.'

He was already pulling off his tie and stuffing it in his jacket pocket.

'Well, as we've been pulled in for suspected soliciting, boss, we better make you look like a punter, boss.'

Ted shook his head again, this time in mock despair.

'DC Vine ...' he said.

Chapter Ten

The world of drama had suffered a loss when Jezza Vine abandoned her plans to take up acting and became a police officer instead. She was a natural and never wasted any opportunity to demonstrate her skills. Especially when it involved teasing the boss she worshipped.

She was all over him as they headed for his own car. The trusty little Renault helped his image. Most self-respecting coppers would never be seen driving anything like that.

Ted chucked his suit jacket and tie into the boot and pulled out his old leather jacket. Turning up at the safe house like that, he shouldn't set off any suspicions if by any chance someone was already onto them and watching the place. Hopefully, the breach, if there really was one, had not yet gone that far.

'Boss, at the risk of stating the obvious,' Gina began once Ted had driven out of the car park and was following Jezza's directions to the house, 'if Ian knows I'm working here, then he's clearly been in touch with my old team. And all of them have sworn blind all along that they've had no contact with him for months. So one of them, at least, is hiding something.'

'That was my first thought, too. You've definitely had no contact yourself? You've not been in touch with him, either as colleagues, or as mates? Sorry for asking again, but that would be the most obvious explanation.'

'I really haven't, and that surprises me. Ian and I were always quite close. Friends outside work, when we could manage it, as well as working together. It's not easy, of course, for either of us. Especially as our covers were so different that our paths could never cross by chance.'

'He's in contact with the mole, then,' Jezza said emphatically. 'He's playing them. Drip-feeding them stuff to see how far it goes. That's how he knows who they are.'

'Him,' Gina told her. 'I'm the only female on the team and I'm definitely not the mole. So whoever it is, it's a bloke. Unless they're not on the team itself but somewhere on the fringes. If that's the case, it opens up any number of possibilities and means they could be either gender.'

'Ian's playing a dangerous game, then,' Ted put in. 'If he knows who it is, it's only a question of time before the mole realises they're being played. No wonder he's been keeping well off the radar. The question is, can we bring him in safely?'

'Ian's good. Very good. If he doesn't want to be found, no one will find him, not even us,' Gina told the others. 'If he's contacted you, boss, that's because he trusts you. But it'll still be tricky to meet him without both of you putting your lives in danger.'

They'd reached the house now. The usual scruffily anonymous place with nothing about it to set it apart from all the others in the narrow road. It stood at the end of a row, so it was easy to keep an eye out for anyone getting too close. Fewer walls or other obstacles to conceal someone approaching. More open ground to be covered to reach it.

The garden was nothing but neglected grass, trampled down to be like concrete under the sun, or a sea of mud in the rain. A child's broken tricycle lay in a rusted heap, abandoned where it fell. It all helped with the cover.

'Here were are, then, boss. Home sweet home,' Jezza said with a laugh. 'Are you going to wait in the car? We've not much to collect. The phones are the main thing.'

'I'm not, I'm coming in with you,' Ted replied, in a tone which brooked no argument. 'You two are not leaving my sight until we know for certain who our inside informer is and that they're safely out of harm's way.'

'You don't seriously think anyone knows about this place, do you?' Gina asked him. 'So soon? Very few people knew we were on this op at all, let alone where we were staying. Even you didn't know that, did you?'

Ted was ever the gentleman. His father had brought him up with old-fashioned manners. He would normally have stood aside to let the two of them go first through the low wooden gate which was hanging off its hinges and dragging on the ground as he opened it.

This time he went first, insisting Jezza give him the door keys, and only allowing the two of them to enter once he'd made a quick but careful check of the whole of the premises.

'I don't want us to be here any longer than we need to be, so get your things as quickly as you can. Let me know if anything at all seems out of place to you, though. No matter how insignificant it might seem. And if you do spot something, don't touch anything at all until I say so.'

'Boss, have you been watching too many spy thrillers on TV?' Jezza asked him. 'You don't really think someone's been in here, do you?'

'I don't think anything at the moment, Jezza. I'd just prefer to proceed with extreme caution until I have all the facts at my disposal.'

He'd positioned himself at the side of the main front window now, peering out through the dirty net curtains, checking out lines of sight. All of his previous Firearms training was coming into play automatically. Until he could meet with Ian Bradley he had nothing like as much information as he would have liked. And his only hope was a meeting with someone who, despite his own gut feeling and Gina's assurances, could yet turn out to be a clever double agent in the pay of the dangerous drugs gangs they were tracking.

* * *

Ted waited until he got back to the station to have a full debrief with Jezza and Gina. He pulled Jo from the incident room and the four of them went up to Jo's office.

Ted first put his head round his own office door to check on Superintendent Sampson before they began. Jezza was sorting drinks for them, so he told her to include the Super.

'Ted, once you've finished this major op I'm going to suggest we get you to run a course on how to deal with the admin side of the job. I'm going to be done here much faster than I thought, so I can definitely go and visit some other teams, just for an overview. Ashton, you said, need an eye keeping on them? And I hear I have 'Eck at my disposal to drive me. He and I go back a long way, so that should be fun.'

The driver in question had been christened Hector but was universally known as 'Eck because he was fond of saying 'oh 'eck' whenever anything stronger wasn't suitable.

'Yes, Ashton, for sure. They have been doing a lot better but I do like to drop in unannounced every once in a while, just to make them aware that I'm keeping an eye on them. I've got to debrief now but I've arranged a brew for you. DC Vine, who's bringing it, is one of the undercover team so don't be too alarmed by the look of her.'

Once the four of them were sitting down in Jo's office, Ted asked for Jezza and Gina's feedback on what they'd found out so far.

'Like I said before, the kids we spoke to are really rattled about Noah's death. They were all cagey, not yet ready to trust, but it was clear some of them were buying from Noah. There's one lad, Jay, he calls himself, who seems to know a lot, but he might just be bigging himself up.

'He said there'd been others, older teens, supplying in the town before Noah, but he'd heard most of them had been arrested so things had gone quiet. He also mentioned another youth who can only have been Data from the description he gave. He said the word is he left town when things got a bit hot here and he's not been seen since. Jay didn't know where he is now, or if he does know, he wasn't saying.

'Jay's the one who claims to have seen Noah being picked up by a big four-wheel drive with tinted rear windows a time or two, although no mention of who the driver or passengers might have been.

'It's still the closest thing we have yet to any hint of a connection to Data and the blind dwarf.'

'So now you can see why I wanted you both out of the way as soon as possible. There's a strong chance any of these other youngsters, particularly this Jay, by the sounds of him, might be looking to fill Noah's shoes by getting well in with whichever Big Man is behind it all. If he finds a way of going to them and mentioning two young women appearing on the patch asking questions, and the Big Man has been told about Gina joining the team here, it would be too risky to leave either of you in place a moment longer.'

'But boss, that route is the most likely way to get any info ...' Jezza began to protest.

'No point arguing, Jezza. I can't let you continue when you might be compromised. I'd be hung out to dry, for one thing.'

His expression softened into a fond smile as he added, 'Besides, no one else gives me such a hard time as you do and I might miss that.'

He was straight back into professional mode as he said, 'Go and find out what you can usefully be working on, once you've written up your reports, and I'll just have to hope that Ian makes contact again and has some news for me on the identity of the mole.'

* * *

It was late afternoon when Ted got the phone call he'd been waiting for. Ian Bradley began with the same question and Ted gave the same answer in response. If someone of Bradley's experience was being so ultra-careful, there was a good reason for it.

'Can we meet shortly, Ted? Somewhere on your patch. Mine's too hot at the moment. Somewhere out of town and anonymous, if you have any suggestions?'

'Are you mobile?'

'I can be. Tell me where and when and I'll be there.'

'Take the A6 southbound. There's a pub on the left at the junction with the B6171, with a conveniently placed bus stop close by. I'll pick you up at that bus stop. Can you be there in an hour?'

'I can. I'm sure I've no need to tell you but I will anyway. Watch your back, at all times.'

Ted was still in the incident room, making sure he knew all the details on the case available so far. He went across to Jo's desk to speak to him, keeping his head down and his voice low. He'd done the same with the phone call, even to the point of cupping his hand in front of his mouth as he spoke. He wanted every detail of his meeting with Ian Bradley to be on a strictly need to know basis. He had complete confidence in his DI so had no problem with putting him in the picture.

'I have to ask, boss,' Jo stayed formal in the workplace. 'You're absolutely sure you can trust the DS? After all, you don't know him all that well, and he has been off the radar for a long time. Long enough to have been turned and to be playing both sides against each other.'

'I've considered that possibility, of course. I'd sack myself if I hadn't. But we know there's a leak somewhere. I doubt it's Gina. I saw how gutted she was when that last big op went wrong. I'd hate to think it was any of our own team. So logically speaking, it must be someone on that Manchester Drugs team. Or someone close enough to it to know what they're up to. I need to talk to Ian to find out what he knows or suspects.'

'Back-up?' Jo asked him. It was for form's sake, more than

anything, as he was certain before he suggested it that the boss would have none of it.

Ted shook his head emphatically, almost before his DI had finished speaking.

'Far too risky. I've no reason to believe that Ian himself poses any threat to me and even very skilful followers risk being spotted by someone who knows what they're doing like he does. And even if it's not him, whoever is behind all of these events clearly does.

'I'll go in plenty of time to check the location out and if it's not safe, I'll abort and wait for further contact from Bradley. I can't afford to miss this opportunity, though.'

Jo had one more valiant try.

'You wouldn't let any of us go without back-up.'

Ted gave him a guilty grin.

'One of the advantages of being the boss. Seriously, though, Jo, thanks for your concern, but I'm trained for this sort of stuff and I don't take unnecessary risks. Believe me.

'I'll try to update you as soon as I can but I'll probably turn my phone off while we talk somewhere quiet, so no one can trace me. It'll be fine, don't fuss.'

Ted stopped on the way to buy hot drinks and some food. He hadn't met Bradley many times but he always looked in need of a square meal whenever he had seen him.

He took the chance to make a quick phone call to Trev.

'I'm really sorry but I've no idea what time I'll be back this evening, so go ahead and eat. Don't wait for me. There's been a few changes to my role and I'm back to proper front-line coppering for now, so you know what that means as far as my work hours go.

'I'll tell you all about it when I get back, whenever that is, but don't worry, I've already grabbed something to keep me going until I can get home for a proper meal.'

'Just promise me you aren't doing anything dangerous, Mr Policeman. I know you get bored silly behind a desk, but I'm always much happier when you're safely in the office and the worst you risk is a paper cut or stapling your own finger.'

* * *

Even when he spotted the lanky, scruffy form of the DS waiting at the bus stop, Ted drove on round the block once more for another check before he pulled up briefly to let him get in.

'Hot coffee and bacon rolls,' he told him, nodding towards the passenger foot well, 'so careful where you put your feet. I thought you might be hungry.'

Bradley looked and smelled as if he had been living in his clothes, and probably sleeping in them, for too long. His tobacco-stained fingers were filthy, ingrained dirt around and behind his fingernails. His hair was long, straggly and none too clean, pulled back into a pony tail, and he had much more of a beard than the last time Ted had seen him.

He gave a broad grin, revealing dirty teeth with some gaps, as he said, 'Thanks for the kind thought, but I'm a vegan.'

Then he laughed out loud at Ted's expression and said, 'Am I buggery, I was just taking the piss. I eat whatever I can get hold of. Thanks Ted, I could eat a scabby donkey. Do you mind if I make a start?'

'Go ahead. We're heading out into the countryside because I thought the chances of us being followed way out there would be fairly remote, if we're careful. Plus we aren't going by the most direct route.

'I gather, from your caution in calling me how you did, that we're talking high-risk stuff here?'

Bradley was going at the bacon roll as if it were the first food he'd seen in some time. Just as well Ted had anticipated him being hungry and bought them two each.

'The bad news is that there's definitely a major leak from my team. Someone on the inside is passing info to our drugs-peddling friends, which is why they're staying one step ahead of us at every stage.

'The worse news is that, if they don't yet have someone in their pocket from inside your nick, then they're probably leading up to finding someone.'

Chapter Eleven

Ted drove out towards Mellor but, as he'd told Bradley, not by the most direct route. The roads were quiet. Not much traffic heading out that way on an early Monday evening.

He found the cart track he was looking for and backed the Renault into it, going as far as he could in reverse up the rough, sloping surface, so that the vehicle was barely visible from the road.

He knew there was no vehicular access from the top end, not even for a motorbike or a quad, which was why he'd chosen the place. He and Trev had walked the area frequently enough for him to know it well.

Ian Bradley had already devoured two bacon barms which had barely touched the sides when he passed the bag to Ted, together with his hot drink. Ted took one of the remaining two but handed the other one back to Bradley.

'I'll get a meal when I get home this evening but you look as if you need this more than I do right now.'

'Thanks Ted, you're a lifesaver. I've been ducking and diving for so long I don't always have time to eat. Nor to get cash. I daren't use my bank card in case anyone's trying to trace me. Like I said, I know I was suspected of being the informant and I'd rather stay in the wind until I can prove that I'm not.'

'And you aren't?' Ted's voice went up slightly at the end to make it a query.

'Not me, guv,' Bradley replied in a deliberately bad East Enders accent. 'I'm pretty sure I know who it is, but at the moment, out on a limb like I am, I've no way of proving anything. So you'll have to decide for yourself whether or not you trust me.

'I've stayed in touch on the quiet with each of the team members. I told them all not to breathe a word about the contact. Then I asked each of them who they thought the informer was.'

He paused for a swallow of his coffee, wiping bacon grease from his beard with the back of one dirty hand.

'You know about the fart principle, of course. You fart and you don't want to own it. So you hold your nose and point at someone else. All of them said they had no idea but were trying to find out. All except one. Derek Black.'

Ted remembered the officer called Derek. He'd been the belligerent one who'd been shouting the odds when he and Gina had arrived back to debrief after the planned operation to try to bring in at least one member of the drugs gang, the youth known only as Data, had ended in a death and no arrests.

'Who did Derek say it was?' he asked.

'Gina,' Bradley told him. 'Derek put the blame squarely at Gina's door.'

Ted took a thoughtful swallow of his drink before asking, 'And did you stay in contact with Gina?'

Gina had sworn to him that she'd had no contact with the DS. Ted hoped that was true. He didn't like the idea of having anyone on his team who would lie to his face, even out of some misplaced sense of loyalty.

Bradley shook his head.

'Gina's the one member of the team I trust completely. Nobody on the team knows, except me, but she had a brother. Andy. Bright lad, with a promising future. When he went up to Uni he went off the rails. Big time. Started using. Got in with the wrong crowd and onto the dirty stuff.'

He paused for a bite of the third bacon barm; carried on talking around the mouthful.

'It killed him. Gina was devastated. They were very close. That's why I know, without a doubt, that she would never, ever be passing info to any drugs gang. She hates them with a passion. That's why she works as hard as she does to get as many of them as possible off the streets.'

Ted swallowed his mouthful, helped down by some more of his drink, whilst he formulated his next question.

'Is that the problem? Is she too close? Deliberately passing on disinformation to try to get one over on the gangs and draw them out?'

Bradley was shaking his head before Ted had even finished his questions.

'Not a chance, Ted. I'd stake my reputation, such as it is, on it. It's not me, and I'm certain it's not Gina. But I am pretty sure it's Derek. I drip-fed all of the team a small and insignificant detail to see if it went anywhere. None of them took the bait. No one, except Derek.

'I made up a tale. Nothing important. But I mentioned where I'd be at a certain time of a day I specified. No reason for him to pitch up. But he did, and he wasn't on his own. I was watching from a very safe distance. No one from the team, not anyone else that I know by sight. Let's just say I was very glad whoever it was didn't catch up with me. He didn't look like someone who was about to invite me out for a friendly pint.'

'You need to come in, Ian. You're clearly not safe out there on your own any more. You need to talk to your handler, and soon.'

Bradley drained his coffee cup with an appreciative sigh.

'I'm at the stage where I don't trust anyone, to be honest, Ted. Not even my handler. Well, with the exception of Gina. And you, for some reason, although I don't know you all that well. I like what I've seen of how you work and I'm going off my instincts.

'But for now, I'd rather be out on my own. At least that way I can make my own assessments and decisions all the time, rather than relying on anyone else. As long as I can call you, as and when I need to?'

'Of course you can. Whenever. But I think you're making the wrong choice.'

Ted reached in his pocket for his wallet and took out a twenty pound note, which he handed to the DS.

'Take this. Pay me back whenever. Where do you want dropping off?'

'Anywhere south of the river. I'm not planning on going back to Manchester for the time being. Not until I know more of what's going on with the team. And from the sound of it, I better stay clear of Stockport, too. At least in town, if you've got some of the same people working your patch as mine. And thanks for the loan, that will help a lot.

'Drop me somewhere rural, and don't worry. I'm good at surviving. You might just find your uniformed friends get a few calls from people complaining about strange tramps sleeping in their barns or whatever. If you can pull any strings to stop me getting arrested, I'd be grateful. Although there may come a time when arrest is my best option.'

* * *

DC Maurice Brown was in a car with one of the Police Community Support Officers, Emma Moore. They were prowling round the town, trying to find a young boy who was one of the dead youth Noah Brooks' best friends.

From the information Maurice had been collating, the boy, Ollie Martin, was closest to Noah and may have been one of the last people to see him alive. He was not excluded from school, as Noah had been, but his records showed he was not a frequent attendee and was constantly being chased up because of it.

Emma Moore knew him well and had also known Noah Brooks.

'Smart lads, the pair of them,' she told Maurice as she drove. 'Noah in particular. Such a shame. If he'd had the right help, who knows what he could have achieved.

'Ollie's usually the gobby one, although recently, from what I've heard on the street, Noah had started boasting a lot about what he was getting up to, which is probably what got him killed.'

'I hate seeing kids end up like that,' Maurice told her. 'It's a pity we can't do more preventive policing. Try to straighten them out before they end up like Noah did.'

Emma scoffed. 'I wish. Even if we round them up and refer them, they're often no better off where they finish up.

'Our best bet is probably to park up and walk down to the precinct, see if any of the kids are hanging round down there. We'll soon hear if Ollie is anywhere about. He never shuts up.'

There was a note almost of affection as she spoke about him.

She and Maurice had to trudge halfway round the town centre until they finally spotted a small group of younger youths loitering about. At the sight of her uniform, several of them took off and legged it before they got nearer. Of the two who stayed behind, Ollie Martin was one of them.

'Now then,' Emma greeted them, hooking her thumbs into the armholes of her stab vest. 'Ollie, you know me well enough by now. And this is Detective Constable Maurice Brown. He wants a word with you, about young Noah.'

The young boy, no more than about fourteen, fifteen, Maurice judged as he looked him over, did no more than lift his chin and give an, 'All right?' by way of greeting.

'Are you okay to talk to me, Ollie?' Maurice asked him. 'D'you want a drink of something while we talk? Hot chocolate?'

'I'd rather have a beer,' the boy told him cheekily.

'You know you're under age. Hot chocolate or nothing. Your choice.'

Once he'd agreed, Maurice handed Emma a banknote and asked her to get the drinks from a nearby place which did take-aways. He called a reminder after her to get him a receipt so he could claim it back on expenses.

The other boy who had stayed melted away quietly at the idea of being seen sitting in the open talking to the police. Ollie didn't seem as worried at the prospect. There was a raised flower bed nearby, with a low brick wall. Nothing much remained of the contents except a few tenacious wallflowers which managed to show a splash of defiant colour.

'Are you all right talking to us here, Ollie? It doesn't worry you being seen with the police?'

The boy shrugged one skinny shoulder and perched on the corner of the wall, a good few feet from where Maurice had parked himself.

'Tell me about Noah.'

'Like what?' the boy asked.

'How did he finish up getting in with the wrong crowd, for one thing?'

'He was my mate, right, and I don't like saying anything bad about him. But he liked to big himself up. Even to me. I never knew what was real with him. Y'know what I mean? But some of it must've been true, 'cos of how he died. You don't get killed like that unless you're mixing with the wrong people, do you?'

Emma was back with three hot drinks in a paper holder. She handed them round and gave Maurice his receipt, before sitting on the wall on the other side of the boy, staying a few feet away from him. She didn't want him to feel under any sort of pressure because she knew, from experience, that he would simply run if he started to feel uncomfortable. She wasn't sure she could outpace him over any distance. She was certain Maurice couldn't.

One thing Maurice was good at was talking to young people. Emma had to concede to herself that by the time the three of them had sat there sipping their drinks to the bottom of the cups, they'd heard everything Ollie knew about his friend, not just the edited highlights. She wasn't involved directly in the murder case so she didn't know if Maurice had discovered anything useful. She'd heard enough to know it wasn't for the lack of trying.

Maurice was morose as they walked back to the car.

'How have we come to this?' he mused aloud. 'Kids being used to run drugs for dangerous gangs. We round up one lot and before they've even appeared in court, there's others ready and willing to take their place. We're losing the war, never mind the battle.'

* * *

Adam, the youngest of Ted and Trev's seven cats, was sitting on the windowsill of the front room, patiently waiting for any sign of his favourite human's car reappearing. Some of the other cats had given Ted the cold shoulder treatment when he'd dared to return home with the smell of a dog lingering about him. In Adam's eyes, Ted could do no wrong.

As soon as he saw the lights, the little cat scampered into the hallway and sat by the door, meowing to himself until Ted opened the front door and stepped inside.

'Sorry to be late,' Ted called out, putting his things down and scooping the young cat up as he headed for the kitchen. 'They really have let me out from behind the desk to be a proper policeman once more.'

Trev was cooking, a tea towel flung over one shoulder and a wooden spoon in one hand from where he'd been stirring something which smelled delicious.

Ted leaned in to kiss his partner who asked, 'So you're not Head of Serious Crime any more?'

'I still am, nominally. But we have a major incident on so I'm SIO on that for now.'

Trev sniffed at him suspiciously.

'Your clothes smell strange. Where have you been?'

Ted lifted his arm to his nose to see what he could detect. He hadn't realised how much the odours emanating from DS Ian Bradley had permeated everything in the car with him. Including Ted's own clothes, it seemed.

'I had to do a debrief with an undercover officer. My car was the safest place, out in the wilds up by Mellor. I didn't realise it was that strong. He's been living rough for a while and is a heavy smoker. Sorry, I'll have a shower and get changed before we eat.'

Trev frowned at him.

'That sounds as if it might be dangerous. Ted, I know you like the action stuff, but I worry less about you when you're safely behind a desk.'

'Not dangerous, really. Have you spoken to mam today?'

Ted's attempt at changing the subject was on the clumsy side but the best he could manage off the cuff.

'I phoned her at lunchtime. She sounds fine. Excited about the new house and busily planning where all her furniture is going to go. She said Cariad is missing you. Have you heard any more from DS Morgan?'

'No, not yet. I didn't really expect to so soon. I'll try to call him tomorrow, if I get chance. You know what it can get like, with a big case on.'

Trev put down his spoon and folded his arms around his partner, pulling him close.

'I know this is what you like best and I'm pleased for you. I am. But just please promise me you'll keep a little bit of time for me. For us. And that you won't go putting yourself in any danger.'

Chapter Twelve

Briefing was early, with a major incident running. There were more officers being brought in as needed and that meant there were quite a few faces Ted knew only by sight, if at all. That was standard procedure, with a big enquiry. But after his conversation with Ian Bradley, it was making him feel uneasy.

He needed to know who was on this enlarged team. The wrong word in the wrong ear by someone, even if innocently done, risked not only blowing another operation but potentially putting Gina Shaw in serious danger.

Ted left Jo to run the briefing, only intervening when he felt anything needed clarifying, or if he could usefully add a suggestion.

They all knew how difficult this one would be to solve. CCTV had produced nothing to date and Ted wasn't hopeful that it would. There was none anywhere near the dismal alley where Noah had met his violent death. It was no doubt chosen for precisely that reason. It had all the hallmarks of a carefully planned reprisal killing, from everything he had read so far.

He didn't hold out a lot of hope for any eyewitness accounts, either. It was the sort of case where even if someone had seen something, they might decide they were better off keeping their heads down and saying nothing.

There'd been the usual press and media appeals for information, so far without success. Their best hope, and it was a slim chance, was that ongoing tests might yet pick up even a stray trace of DNA from the killers on the boy's body or the surrounding area which could possibly be a match for something on file somewhere.

Ted didn't want to appear too pessimistic but he was sceptical of the likelihood of success via that route. The only member of the gang they had managed to arrest on their last attempt had been Albanian, ex-Special Forces, with nothing on record about him they could discover anywhere, which was normal in his line of work.

Once the briefing was finished, Ted asked Gina to join him upstairs in his office. It was early yet for Superintendent Sampson to be in and they could always decamp to Jo's room if they needed to.

Ted perched on the front edge of his desk and pushed the spare chair towards Gina with his foot, indicating to her to sit down. He wanted to keep this informal, but he needed to know.

'How long is it since you heard from Ian Bradley?'

She frowned, trying to pinpoint a memory.

'A good while now. Soon after Data got away the first time, on that op on your patch, I think.'

'No contact at all? Not even the odd phone call?'

'None. Like I told you, he said he was going off the radar until he could dig up something useful. Meanwhile we'd picked Data's trail up in Manchester so we were concentrating our efforts to try to bring him in. And you know how that ended, when the gang switched him for a ringer at the last minute after I'd set up that meet with him, and he was shot at the scene. He's still not been identified, unless you know more about that than I do, currently?'

Ted shook his head. 'Still an unknown, as far as I'm aware.

'I have to ask this, Gina, but the last time I spoke to Ian about our plans to round up the youths involved in the trafficking and the porn films, he was making the case for leaving one of them loose so his team, or ours, could keep tabs on them in the hopes of getting nearer to whoever this Big Man is. Is there any chance, then, that Ian had a motive to see that Data got away? On both occasions?

'I'm not suggesting he's gone over to the gang, or even that he's working for both sides. But it was what he wanted, and it might at least explain some of the things which have happened, and why he's been out of contact for so long.'

Gina was shaking her head emphatically.

'No. Never. Not Ian. I wouldn't believe it of him, not unless he was caught red-handed in the act. Can I ask why you're asking these questions? At this particular time, I mean. Have you heard something about Ian?'

Ted hesitated. Ian spoke highly of her, and his own experience of working with her had been positive. But he wasn't someone who trusted easily at the best of times. Eventually, he took a gamble.

'He called me yesterday and we met.'

'Is he all right? What did he say? Has he uncovered the mole?'

There was no mistaking the concern in her voice for her friend and colleague.

'He's as well as he can be. And you must appreciate that whatever we discussed is confidential between us ...'

He was interrupted by the briefest of knocks on the door and Jezza coming striding in without waiting for an invitation.

'DC Vine,' Ted spoke quietly, but it was his warning tone which all of the team, especially Jezza, knew all too well. 'If you go through the motions of knocking, it's customary to wait for an answer before barging in. Leave us, please.'

'But boss, I wanted to talk to you about an idea Gina and I had on how we could best work together next ...'

She could be as stubborn as a mule, Ted thought to himself, looking at her standing her ground, holding his gaze defiantly. Then he smiled inwardly. Something he'd been called often enough in his own career to date. He wondered if this was some sort of show of female solidarity. Had she imagined Gina was in trouble over something so she'd come bounding in to stand beside her? He would be pleased at that. Jezza, not only working well with another female but ready to leap in and defend them.

'And we will talk, Jezza. Hopefully later today, when I can find time. For now, I need to finish speaking to Gina, so please leave us. And can you ask Rob to come up and see me in ten minutes.'

She hesitated a moment longer, looking at Gina to see if she was all right. Then she left the room.

'Right, as I was saying, I spoke to Ian. He's concerned about your welfare in particular because he's convinced the leak in information is coming from within your old team. Which would mean someone there knows you've transferred here, so could potentially have passed that information on to the drugs gang.

'Do you have any theories yourself on who it might be, on your old team?'

Another shake of the head. 'None at all, and I've thought about it enough. I know it's not me and I'd stake my life on it not being Ian either. As for the others, I'd be surprised to hear it was any of them. We all know the suppliers are ruthless and don't care what harm they cause, as long as they get their money, so why would anyone help them?

'It's the collateral damage, too. That young lad who stood in for Data. This boy Noah. How can any police officer let things like that happen? I don't understand.'

They were interrupted once more by the door being opened, this time without a knock. It was Superintendent Sampson who entered.

'Oh, sorry, Ted, I didn't realise you were in here. I can go and get a coffee if you're busy?'

Ted slid off the desk to stand up in a reflex action. Gina also stood, more because she realised her talk with Ted had come to an end than any antiquated notion of springing to her feet for a senior officer.

'We're done here, thanks. Gina, please tell Jezza I will find time to speak to you both later, about whatever her idea is, but I have other things to sort out first.'

He turned back to the Super as Gina left the room to ask, 'Did you want to update me on anything about the Ashton visit before I go back to what I was doing? And do you want coffee? I was just going to make myself a brew.'

'That would be grand, thank you.'

She moved round to Ted's old chair and sat herself down with possibly slightly more caution than the day before. She looked pale, too, dark smudges under her eyes. Ted wondered fleetingly if her reunion with 'Eck, her driver, had ended up in a favourite watering hole, once they'd both knocked off for the day.

'Now, Ashton. It was an interesting spot check. I'm sure it's not politically correct of me to say so, but their DS, Ramsay, isn't it? He certainly needs to grow a pair. He knows his stuff all right, but he's clearly as wet as a washed lettuce. I don't like the idea of them bumbling along without a DI at the helm for much longer, and from what I hear, it's starting to look unlikely that Judy Collier will be fit enough after her accident to go back any time soon.

'I think that's a situation you're going to have to address in the not too distant future, Ted. Unless you want me to sort it for you? I'm happy to do a few more unannounced drop-ins, for now, if that would help in the short term?'

Ted put a mug of coffee in front of her and took a sip at his green tea, which was almost too hot to drink.

'How was 'Eck? Were the two of you reliving old times?' Ted couldn't resist asking, with a grin.

Sammy Sampson groaned theatrically.

'I've been busted, have I? Yes, we did finish up in the pub, and no 'Eck didn't drive back over the limit. He left the car before we went off on the razz. But it was good to catch up. And apart from mentioning Ramsay needing a strong overview, there's nothing much else I need to report from my trip out.'

Ted heard movement outside so went out to find Rob O'Connell, waiting politely a few feet back from the office door.

Ted led the way to Jo's office, while his own was in use. The two of them sat down on either side of the desk.

'Rob, I need you to do something for me. Discreetly and confidentially, please. Report to me only, no mention to anyone else. No written record accessible to anyone.'

'No problem, boss, but it all sounds a bit mysterious.'

'We all know that we've not had the success we should have had tracking this drugs gang. Data's slipped through our fingers far too easily, twice now, and that shouldn't have happened. The obvious explanation for anything like that is always someone on the inside, passing on information.

'I've recently heard from what I consider to be a credible source that there's an informer within the Drugs team we've been working with. I don't yet have a positive ID on who that might be. That means, of course, that now that Gina has joined us, there's a strong possibility that the gang know about that, too. That's why I had Gina and Jezza pulled in from their undercover work. It was simply too big a risk to leave them exposed.

'We've had other officers brought in from various places to make up numbers on the team now. Some we know and have worked with before. Some we don't know. It would be naive and dangerous, in my judgement, at this stage to assume we're dealing with only one inside informer. There may be more, although I hope not.

'What I'd like you to do, Rob, is to go over the details of all the officers who've come in to join us. Look into their details, backgrounds, contacts. Anything you can think of. Plus cross-check them against all the members of the Drugs team, including Gina Shaw.'

Rob frowned as he said, 'Policing the police, boss?'

'Nobody likes doing it, I know. If it helps, think of it more as protecting our own. We know what these people are capable of. You more than most of us, having been at the post-mortem on Noah Brooks. If there's the slightest chance that information from within this nick, or any other, is getting back to them, we need to know about it and put a stop to it as soon as possible.

'It goes without saying that this needs to remain between you and me. I'm not putting anyone else in the picture for the moment. That's not to say I have suspicions about anyone. I'd just feel happier if I had a bit of reassurance that I don't need to have any.

'Are you all right with that?'

'I can see the need for it, so I'll do it.'

'Thanks Rob. Now, I'm planning to go out for a bit so can you please tell Jezza I haven't forgotten her and I'll talk to her and Gina when I get back, some time this afternoon.'

* * *

Now he was back to being a policeman on the ground once more, rather than an administrator with rank, Ted wanted to do something he always tried to do, on any serious crime case he investigated - visit the scene.

He knew the Crime Scene Manager had been Doug, the cat fancier, who had given him Adam the kitten. He knew, too, that no one would have done a more meticulous job than him. Nothing would have been overlooked. Anything and everything which could have provided a crime scene stain or indication, potentially capable of yielding DNA, would have been collected, bagged and sent for analysis.

The in-joke on crime scenes was always that Doug would dig up lumps of tarmac if he thought they could give up anything which would advance the case they were investigating.

Ted had seen the crime scene photographs, including those of the young boy lying dead in his own blood. Nothing could have fully prepared him for the stark reality.

Photos couldn't capture smells and the place was rife with them. It was a narrow service alley, a cul-de-sac, rather than a ginnel passing between buildings to link one road with another. It ended in waste ground and a blank brick wall. High. A good two metres. An impossible height to scale for a terrified young boy, running for his life.

Ted could almost feel the horror the boy would have experienced, diving into what he had probably hoped was a cut-through. Running as fast as his legs could carry him, heart racing, lungs on the point of exploding. Then looking up to see the size of the structure in front of him, with no way over or through it.

The end of the line.

The end of his life.

The whole place stank of urine and excrement, dog and human, with a lingering metallic scent which Ted knew was blood. He'd smelled it often enough. Even with the time-lapse and intervening rainfall, it was still noticeable. Or perhaps he was more finely-tuned to its presence than most.

There were wheelie bins near to the end, with an overflow of black bin bags dumped at the foot of the impenetrably high wall. Ted made a mental note to check with Doug if the tops of the bins had been examined for any signs of the boy trying to scramble on them in a desperate attempt to get a grip on top of the side wall.

If Noah had climbed on the bins, or tried to, there was the slimmest chance that whoever had been pursuing him might also have left their own traces there, although he doubted it. He was certain Doug would have had the same thoughts at the scene but it was always worth checking.

It was just possible that the killers were youths of Noah's age or not much more. Jealous rivalry between street gangs rather than drugs gangs. Although all the intel they had so far suggested that Noah preferred to operate on his own.

One crime scene report had made mention of a partial boot print, simply listed as 'possibly military issue boot'. Ted didn't like that reference. Not at all.

They'd got rid of one foreign mercenary working on the patch. But it was unlikely in the extreme that he was the only one.

And if there were any more of those former Special Forces operatives in the area, it was essential he found and plugged any leaks anywhere before information about Gina reached them. Because if Gina's cover was blown, then Jezza's could be, too.

Chapter Thirteen

It was getting hard to find a quiet corner anywhere, with the enquiry in full swing. Ted was in sore need of tea when he got back from the crime scene. Office space was in short supply. Jo had gone back to his own office to try to get on top of his paperwork before it became totally out of control. Sammy Sampson was still in Ted's old office, working away.

Ted commandeered the rest room as an interim measure, while it was quiet, and messaged Jezza for her and Gina to join him. He had the kettle on and brewed up for the two of them when they came into the room. Head of Serious Crime or not, he didn't, and probably never would, consider himself above doing that for his team members.

He loosened his tie and undid his top shirt button as this was going to be a fairly laid-back meeting. Or at least he hoped it would, knowing how impetuous Jezza could be.

'Right, Jezza, tell me your idea. But bear in mind the chain of hoops it will need to jump through, even if I agree with you, before it gets the go-ahead. So it's not going to happen any time soon.'

'Boss, obviously Gina and I can't carry on doing the same cover here that we started out doing, in case, as you say, they know about Gina's transfer. But what if we do another image change and go back to Manchester ...'

Ted was already shaking his head before she got any further.

'There are so many reasons why that can't happen, Jezza.

You can't simply move onto someone else's patch and start an op without any liaison, not even a courtesy call. And we can't liaise with your old team, Gina, because we have no idea who might be passing on any intel to the gang we're trying to investigate.'

'Boss, the gangs are operating over our borders, not to mention county ones, all the time, that's half the problem. All I'm suggesting is that Gina and I should check out some of the nightlife up in the big city to see if we can get a feel for what's going on. Rather than waiting for gang members to have a sudden attack of conscience and start giving themselves up in droves.'

Jezza could use sarcasm like an offensive weapon, and she was demonstrating that skill now. She wasn't finished yet, it seemed. Her plans were always well thought out, if nothing else.

'What if Gina and I simply have a girls' night out in town, after work? Nothing wrong with that. Nothing suspicious. No need to get official clearance to do it, surely?'

'Except that now you've told me, you've made it official, Jezza. You know how these things work.'

Jezza was visibly getting impatient. She was a good officer, with excellent instincts. Probably her biggest fault was not thinking through the implications of all of her ideas and preferring to avoid too much red tape.

'I could agree to call the idea off then go anyway,' she retorted, a flash of ice blue in her eyes.

'I'm counting on you to be responsible enough not to do that. Jezza, I'm not saying never. I'm simply saying not without a lot of careful planning. Which, of necessity, will focus on your absolute safety at all times.

'If we're going to do this, it needs to be properly thought out, risk assessed, signed off from above and everything else that something like this entails. We'll need people on obs around wherever you happen to be. A full follow team to pick up on you and anyone you identify as suspicious leaving the location. You know how it works. Without all of that in place, not only are the two of you putting yourselves at risk, you're potentially blowing the best way of getting close to the people we need to be keeping an eye on.

'Apart from anything else, I have to consider the budget that would entail and be able to justify all of it.'

'Can we afford the wait though, boss?' Jezza asked insistently. 'Like I said, me and Gina going for a drink after work isn't exactly unusual. Not something we'd normally need to run past you at all. And what if we took a bit of protection with us, in the shape of Virgil?'

Ted should have known she would be several steps ahead of him already. He knew how dynamic and persuasive she could be with the bit between her teeth.

'Virgil's on board with this, then? You talked to him without bringing the idea to me first?'

Jezza beamed at him. The perfect pupil with an answer for everything.

'I did try, boss, but you were busy and you kicked me out. I thought I'd check out the feasibility of it for tonight, then come back to you with a *fait accompli*. We could do it this evening. Just for a quick look at what's going on. No more than that, and then report back to you tomorrow morning.

'Then at least we might have some more info on which to base plans going forward. We may come back with nothing at all, but we won't know until we try.'

'A drink after work, but no more than that. This is not an official op. I'll talk to the three of you together before you sign off today. But the rules are basic. You keep your mobiles on all the time. You stay in contact with one another and you don't try any heroics. This is observation only. Your designated driver has no more than a half, you let me know when you're back safe. And none of that is negotiable.'

Jezza and Gina both nodded meekly. If that was what it

would take for the boss to give them the go-ahead, then so be it.

'Now, I know the two of you are good at changing your appearance. But I'm struggling to see how, looking like you do now, you're going to be able to blend in at the type of clubs you were visiting, Gina, when I first met you. I mean the hair, the bitten nails. Does it really go with the image you need to project?'

Jezza grinned at him. 'Trust me boss, I'm a drama graduate. If we can slope off for an hour or two before we knock off, you can have a look and see what you think. And you know that when Virgil gets his gear on, he looks nothing like a copper. If we look glamorous enough, people will just think we're some sort of celebs, out with their minder.

'It will be fine. It's the nearest chance we have to at least try to find out who's running the high end operation in Manchester since we last lost sight of them.'

* * *

Virgil was driving. His black BMW helped with the image. He and Jezza had used it together before, when she'd needed rescuing from a potentially dangerous situation involving a gang of young girls 'happy slapping' a victim in a park.

Jezza had worked wonders with herself and Gina. She was right in saying they could easily pass for a couple of minor celebs out on the town with their minder, going round the pubs and clubs. They certainly didn't look like most people's idea of police officers.

Virgil had no worries over their cover. His main concern was whether or not Jezza would listen to him if they needed to get out of somewhere sharpish. He knew how hot-headed and impetuous she could be. He didn't know enough about Gina to know how she would react in a tight situation. He thought he'd better set some ground rules as he drove them.

'Right, ladies, can I just say that if you're relying on me to keep you safe, the final decision on when we pull out of anywhere rests with me. If I say we get out, we leave straight away. Then when we're safely back in the car, you can argue, if you must, Jezza.

'It's not just that I don't fancy getting arrested for being in a punch up. I'm more worried about having to explain to the boss if anything happens to either of you. So if I say go, we go.'

Jezza nodded in silence, an angelic expression on her face. Virgil wasn't sure he believed her, but at least he'd tried his best.

Manchester was Gina's home turf. She'd lived and worked in the city for years, so the other two were happy to be guided by her when it came to choosing bars and clubs to visit. She and Jezza were on the exotic cocktails. Virgil stuck to alcohol-free lager. He wanted to keep a clear head.

They were in the third venue when Gina suddenly turned to Virgil, threw her arms round his neck and put her face close to his ear. Jezza wouldn't be able to hear what she was saying from the way they were sitting so she'd have to fill her in later, but she needed to pass her message.

'That's Data who's just come in. The real one. Not a ringer. I'd bet my pension on it. He's headed straight for the gents so I'd guess he's dealing and he's gone there looking for punters.'

She untangled herself from Virgil who waited a moment before standing up.

'Excuse me, ladies, I need the little boys' room.'

As he left, Gina leaned in closer to Jezza to update her.

'Back in the area then, and still dealing, by the look of things,' Jezza said. 'Is this a known place for supply? Or does he just have a weak bladder, if the gents is his first port of call?'

'It's been raided a couple of times, but they just wait for the dust to settle then it all starts up again,' Gina told her.

Jezza was glancing across to where Virgil had disappeared to find the toilets. She wasn't unduly worried about him. The sheer size and bulk of him usually put off most people from challenging him. She'd still feel more at ease when he reappeared.

Gina saw her look and read it correctly.

'Have we got a rescue plan if he doesn't reappear in a reasonable amount of time?'

Jezza shrugged. 'Two drunken birds blundering into the gents' when they're too pissed to find the ladies'? I could kickbox the crap out of anyone I see while you drag Virgil out?'

Gina laughed at the image. 'I'm not sure I could shift someone his size. But I have got pepper spray in my bag, so we should be all right.'

The young man they knew only as Data was openly dealing when Virgil went into the gents. There were three men with him, cash in hand, waiting eagerly for their supply. None of them made any attempt to conceal their transactions. Clearly none of them took Virgil for a police officer, or if they did, they were comfortable enough not to be bothered.

Data eyed up the newcomer appraisingly. Something about the way he looked at him made Virgil feel uncomfortable. It was more than assessing him as a potential drugs punter. Virgil vividly remembered what one of the youths arrested when Data had slipped through their clutches, had said about Data's sexual appetite. She'd talked of him being randy enough to 'knob a dog.'

'There's plenty to go round, my friend, if you're in the market?'

Virgil shook his head. 'You're all right, mate, thanks. That stuff's not a good idea to mix with the gym candy.'

He flexed a powerful arm until his muscles strained at the fabric of his suit jacket, to make his point. It wasn't true, but it was convincing enough. Virgil didn't take anything. Certainly not steroids. His powerful, sculpted body was due entirely to hard, dedicated work, with no chemical intervention.

He decided to use one of the cubicles to give the dealer and buyers some space. It had been an interesting and unexpected discovery, to see Data back in business, and dealing openly, but he wasn't sure how much it advanced them for the moment.

'Well, he's quite blatantly selling in there. He offered me some stuff,' Virgil told the other two when he returned to join them. 'We're going to need to inform the boss and do some sort of a joint op with your old team, Gina. Data is our best hope of getting to the famous Big Man behind all of this.'

The outer door of the bar opened. Gina glanced instinctively in its direction, then suddenly leaned forward again and flung both arms round Virgil's neck.

'Oh, darling, that's fabulous news, thank you,' she said, her voice not like her normal one.

Jezza's eyes were instantly all round the bar to see what Gina had clocked now. She picked up on the casually dressed man who'd just entered and who, after only a cursory glance about, also headed straight for the gents.

Gina waited until he'd disappeared into the toilets before saying to the others, keeping her voice low and her glass in front of her mouth, 'That's one of my old team. Derek. DC Black. Now, there could be any number of valid reasons why he would come in here on a night when Data is selling his stuff in the gents. He might even be a light user. He wouldn't be the first Drugs officer who went down that route.'

'Whatever the reasons for his presence, don't you think we'd better make ourselves scarce?' Virgil asked. 'You two do look a lot different to normal but Gina, do you really want to take the risk of him seeing you and possibly recognising you? Even if he only thinks he does and then later on he puts two and two together and realises who it was.'

'We can't just disappear now, though,' Jezza said, her tone reasonable. 'If there's something going on, we might as well stay long enough to try to find out what it is. Virgil, you bring the car round while Gina and I lurk in a doorway. Don't worry,' she hurried to reassure him, seeing his sceptical look, 'we can do blending in.'

When Virgil still hesitated, Jezza pressed him.

'Go. Get the car. The more we dither about, the more we risk drawing attention to ourselves.'

The car was parked not far away but even so, Virgil must have had his foot down hard to get back with it so quickly. There were yellow lines everywhere but he was quite happy to ignore them. In the unlikely event of anyone coming to move them on, he could always flash his warrant card.

Hopefully the black BMW with two young women slipping into the back seat would look sufficiently like a mini cab making a booked pick-up for it not to seem suspicious.

There was no further sign of Data. He didn't leave the premises while they waited and watched. It was Derek Black who appeared first. He moved a few yards away from the main entrance to stand on a street corner, where he took a packet of cigarettes out of a pocket and lit one up.

Nothing unusual in that. Plenty of people still slipped out of a bar for a crafty smoke. From the way DC Black was looking up and down the road, though, it looked for all the world as if he was waiting for someone to show up.

Gina Shaw spotted the figure heading towards Black first of all and swore to herself. Virgil's and Jezza's heads swivelled in the same direction and locked onto the tall, gangly figure approaching, with a rise and fall to his stride. Once he passed under a street light they could all clearly see the pony tail bouncing against his upper back as he moved.

Jezza spoke first.

'Bloody hell, Gina, isn't that your DS?'

'It is. Ian Bradley. Who's been off the radar for ages. What's he doing here, and why has he come to meet Derek?'

Chapter Fourteen

Endless hours of door-to-door enquiries around where young Noah Brooks had met his violent end had so far produced nothing. It was mainly a commercial area, with no houses, but a lot of the nearby retail properties had flats above them. Flats which appeared to be occupied by the Three Wise Monkeys, judging by the results, or lack of them, reported by frustrated officers who'd been knocking on doors ever since the incident.

DC Graham Winters, one of the officers brought in to make up numbers, who'd worked with the team on previous cases, summed up the general non-existent success at morning briefing the following day.

'Saw nowt, heard nowt and wouldn't tell you even if I had. That's about the sum total of what I was told, and I know I'm not the only one to get that. People are scared. No one wants to be involved, or be seen to be a grass. Not even when a little lad's been killed on their own doorstep.'

Several heads nodded in agreement. Maurice Brown put in, 'That's exactly what I've been finding out trying to talk to the youngsters. It's obvious some of them know more than they're saying, but they're too scared to speak.'

'Having seen Noah at the PM, I don't blame them,' Rob O'Connell said. 'Boss, I think that's something we need to factor in. The more any of us are seen talking to the youngsters, the greater the risk of us putting others of them in danger.'

Jo spoke up. 'You're right, to a degree, Rob. We have to be sensitive to that. On the other hand, we need to ask questions.

Time for another press appeal, boss?' He looked at Ted as he said it. 'With assurances of confidentiality for anyone who comes forward? They may be too afraid to talk on their door-steps, where they risk being seen doing so. We might get a lot of anonymous calls from an appeal which could get us no-where, but we're not exactly drowning in our own success at the moment, so it's surely worth a try, isn't it?'

'I'll speak to the Press Office and get that sorted,' Ted told him. There was not much else of any significance to report so he went on, 'Jo, I'll borrow your office again, if I may. Jezza, you, Virgil and Gina come and join me there, please, for an update.'

There were a few looks of mild curiosity at that, as the three officers left the room at the same time, following Ted. So far none of them had said anything to anyone else about what they were working on behind the scenes. Ted was playing it ultra-cautiously, with outside officers present, not all of whom had yet been checked out to his total satisfaction.

Jezza acted as spokesperson, as the whole foray had been her idea. She set out all the details, fully and factually, while Ted listened in silence. There were only two spare chairs in the room so Virgil stood, arms folded, making the office look even smaller.

'And this definitely looked like a pre-arranged meeting, be-tween DS Bradley and DC Black? Right outside the place where Data was dealing again?' Ted asked for confirmation.

'I would say so, boss. It would surely be too much of a co-incidence for it to have happened by chance, wouldn't it? The DS, who's not been seen by anyone for ages, suddenly decides to take a stroll past a bar the DC has just left to go for a smoke? Or even the other way round. Especially when you add in the factor that Derek headed straight for the men's toilets, where Virgil had seen Data at work.'

'We were able to stay and watch them the whole time they were talking, boss,' Virgil told him. 'They didn't clock us. They didn't even look in our direction, so it didn't look like a covert meet.

'The body language stayed relaxed and amicable, too. Two colleagues, and mates as well, meeting up to chat about something or another.'

'Right, what I'm about to tell the three of you goes no further. I hope that goes without saying. We know there's a leak somewhere, and I'm hoping it's not from any of you.'

The three of them held his gaze effortlessly. He would have put money on none of them being the informer, but he had to cover all eventualities.

'Gina, you know already that I met with Ian Bradley on Monday. He told me he'd been in touch with all of the team members, except for you. He said that was because he didn't think for a moment that you would be working against the team.'

'That's a relief to hear. I thought the opposite might be the case, if he'd been speaking to everyone except me. Did he say who he thought it might be?'

'He did,' Ted told them. 'He named Derek Black.'

The three of them were quiet for a moment. Jezza spoke first.

'So what the heck was he doing meeting with the person he thinks is the mole on the team? Unless he's trying to trap him somehow.'

'If he is, he's playing a very dangerous game, working on his own. He told me he's already tried laying a trap for Black, to see if he reacted. Which he did. So he clearly has grounds to suspect him.

'Gina, do you know who DS Bradley's handler is? Or do you have any way at all to get in touch with him?'

Gina shook her head. 'No one knows, as far as I'm aware. It's done that way to keep the cover as tight as possible. If we don't know, we pose less risk of exposing him, or getting in touch at an inappropriate moment. There are places I could leave a message, but there's no guarantee that Ian would respond.

'But also, boss, I'm surprised at that. Derek's gobby, for sure. Always quick to fly off the handle and point the finger at everyone if things go wrong. But from that to thinking he's the informer ... Well, that surprises me, I have to say. Did Ian say why he thinks that?'

Ted explained about Bradley's famous fart principle and how Black had reacted when he'd been asked outright who he suspected. As well as him having taken the bait about a meeting which Bradley had fed him.

'It isn't me, boss,' Gina told him, her expression earnest. 'I don't even know why Derek would say that. Except he can be a bit of a misogynist sometimes. I've tackled him for it a couple of times. I knew he didn't like that, but I'm stunned if he thinks it's me.'

'We have to keep in mind that he might not. That as Ian Bradley said, he's simply holding his nose and pointing. Gina, if you had to take an educated guess about your former team members, where would your instincts or intuition or whatever be taking you?'

'Honestly, boss? I don't know. I really don't. When you've worked in a tight unit for some time, you find it hard to imagine that any one of them might be on the take or anything.'

'Someone clearly is though,' Ted told her. 'Too many things have gone wrong with these enquiries into the drugs gang for it to be coincidence. If you do have any theories or anything at all you want to discuss with me in private, you can always come and find me.

'Right, for now I'll clearly need to ask at higher level for a way to contact DS Bradley. He told me he's lost confidence in everyone and is even unsure about his handler, so it's clearly not going to be easy. And there's a lot of other factors which will need sorting out. It is possible, I suppose, that DC Black might himself have been working under cover, checking up on

Data. I need to know if he's fed back the information about his visit to your old team, Gina.

'At the moment it seems as if we have potentially two officers working off piste. That's not going to help with our enquiries into Noah's killers. Especially as we think there's a strong link between the cases, which is looking increasingly likely.

'Remember, please, all of this goes no further at this stage. We have no real way of knowing what, if any, information is getting back to the Big Man's gang and from where. Or to anywhere else. Bear in mind, too, that we have officers on our case we don't necessarily know. Certainly not well. I've got someone doing some checking for me on that score. So let's keep a lid on everything.'

Ted went to put his head round his own office door when the three of them left him, to make sure Superintendent Sampson didn't need his input on anything.

'I thought I'd make myself some of my green tea while I'm up here,' he told her. 'Do you want something, while I'm brewing up?'

'Ted, are you a really, really boring person by nature?' she asked him. 'And yes, I'd love a brew, thank you.'

'I probably am. My partner says I'm obsessed with tidying up after him. What makes you ask?'

'I'm trying to find fault with your work. Your high standard rubs off on the way your team members present their reports, too. It's becoming a point of honour to trip you up on something. But I've not succeeded yet. You even make a halfway decent cup of coffee, although you need a better brand,' she added as he put a mug down on the desk in front of her. 'I will do, though. Find something. Even if it's only a missing full stop. I'm a stubborn old bugger.'

Ted laughed to himself as he left the office with his green tea. It had been said before that he was a bit obsessive about reports and figures being kept up to date and accurate.

His mobile phone interrupted his thoughts. DS Morgan,

from Carmarthen once more. He took the call and headed back to Jo's office to talk.

'Hope I'm not interrupting you, Ted? Only I thought you'd want to know, we've got an inquest date and it's come through quicker than we hoped for. It's in just over a week. The coroner hasn't hung about on this one. I wonder if he's as intrigued as the rest of us are. Death by sweetener substitution, if that's what it turns out to be. I wouldn't be surprised if this one makes the national press.

'Of course it's possible that it will just open and adjourn, depending on where we're at with all the documentation by then. We've got your detailed statement, of course, so there's no need to call you as a witness at this stage. But your mother will get a summons to appear, being the last person to see the deceased alive. You know the form. I'm teaching *mamgu* to suck eggs, I know that.'

He slipped the Welsh word for grandmother in naturally enough. It was one Ted remembered from his boyhood.

'I don't for a minute expect you can get away, but is there anyone else who could be with your mam, to support her? We both know these occasions can be a bit of a worry, and she's been through enough already, I would say. We'll help, if we can.'

'I might be able to sort something. I'll keep you posted. Thanks for keeping me in the loop.'

He sat down at Jo's desk, took a swallow of his tea then made a phone call of his own.

'Ted! This is a surprise. Well, of course, if it's that urgent, I could come straight away.'

Jim Baker's voice at the other end of the phone sounded like that of a shipwrecked man who had just seen the lifeboat hurtling down the slipway. Speaking before Ted had said much more than hello.

'I take it you're just about to be dragged out on another visit? I only wanted a quick word, and there's no budget for you to come in and consult, I should warn you, Ted told him.'

'Well, of course, I understand completely. I know you wouldn't call me in if there was another solution.'

Then Ted heard his aside to his wife, deliberately loud enough so he couldn't miss it. He could make out enough of Bella's responses, or at least the tone of them, in the background to tell she was far from amused.

'It's Ted, love. I'm sorry, but he needs me to go in to consult on something urgent.'

... <indistinct response>

'Yes, straight away. I'm really sorry about this, but you know how these things go.'

...

'I know I'm retired, dear, but they're flat out on this one, so what can I say?'

...

'Yes, dear, I know I promised, but Ted's up against it and you know he wouldn't ask if there was any other way. I'll have to go. We can go out tomorrow instead.'

...

'Love, the house has been standing for more than three hundred years. It will still be there tomorrow.'

Bella's final retort was lost in the sound of a door being closed none too gently in the background.

'Ted, you're a lifesaver. I'll be there inside half an hour.'

Ted went to put his head round the Ice Queen's door, as a courtesy, to let her know that Jim Baker was on his way in but as it was not an official request for assistance, it would have no impact on the budget.

She surprised him by smiling and saying, 'I am somehow struggling rather with the image of the former Big Boss being a hen-pecked husband. I'm glad to hear the station still provides a refuge for him.'

* * *

Jim Baker signed himself in and was issued a visitor's pass, but Bill, on the front desk, decided he knew him well enough to risk sending him upstairs by himself. Ted had let him know that he was installed in the Big Boss's old office and that Jim was on his way. He brewed up again, once Bill let him know Jim had arrived. He didn't bother with a spoon, he simply tipped a large pile of coffee granules into a mug and poured water on top of them. No doubt Big Jim would complain it was too weak, as usual. It would be like old times.

'I owe you, Ted, big time. Now, what do you need to know? And I know this is off budget but I honestly don't care.'

Ted set out the details, glad to be back working, even unofficially, with his old boss and good friend.

'Right, well I agree with your assessment, Ted. You can't afford to take the risk of leaving DS Bradley out there. Worst case scenario, he's the dodgy one who's leaking information. Best case, he's a maverick, trying to be clever, and expose who's really behind it all. Playing one side off against the other.

'Neither is very good, and both need to be dealt with. You need him hauling back in, kicking and screaming if necessary, but soon. Then he needs chaining to a desk under close obs at all times so he can't get up to anything, either way he's working it.

'You'll need to talk to the DCS at Central Park. Don Holton. You know him, of course.'

Ted knew the Detective Chief Superintendent, but not well. These days, unless it was in a meeting at the force's HQ, much of the contact he had with anyone outside his immediate team was by phone.

'I'll call him and put in a word for you. We go back a way. You might not get put in touch yourself with Bradley's handler, but I'm sure we can fix it that someone contacts him, and soon, and tells Bradley to get his backside back into the nick and stop playing at cowboys on his own.

'This whole business is messy enough and has been going

on for long enough that it needs stopping, and quickly. It's bloody hard work catching a gang as fly as this one. And it becomes practically impossible when there's a bent copper somewhere in the mix.

'Let's get the bastards found and brought in before another young lad finishes up dead in a stinking alleyway.'

Chapter Fifteen

It was late afternoon, once he'd finished talking to Big Jim, before Ted, with a guilty start, realised he'd better phone Trev to tell him he would be late back and wouldn't make their martial arts session. Trev would probably assume as much, given his change in role, but as a courtesy, Ted would always try to let him know.

'I thought you'd be working late, but thanks for phoning to tell me. Are you making any progress with the case?'

'Circuitous progress. Frustratingly slow. Another thing I was phoning for was to let you know that a date's been fixed for the inquest into Aldwyth's death. In just over a week. It's looking highly unlikely that I'll be able to get down there to be with mam ...'

'I'll go, of course. I said I would and I will. I'll explain the need to Geoff. There should be no problem with some time off work. You'll have to give me the car, though. I can hardly roar up to coroner's court with Annie riding pillion on the back of the bike. Can you manage without?'

'Yes, of course. I can use the bike, or get lifts, or take my official car. It's not as if I'm short of options. Thank you. I'll see you later.

'Oh, before you go, can you give me an honest answer on something, please? Am I a really, really boring person?'

Trev let out a shout of laughter. 'Well, I wouldn't have said really, really. You can be surprisingly spontaneous. Like our wonderful upcoming holiday in Corsica, to which I am so looking forward. So don't even think of backing out. For any reason.

'You're on the obsessive side of meticulous, perhaps. A tidiness freak. But not boring. Who called you that? Do you want me to come round there and bash them up after school?'

It was Ted's turn to laugh. 'It's the new Super who's Acting Head of Serious Crime. Sammy, she's called. She gets to go over all my paperwork, reports and everything while she keeps my seat warm. She's making it a personal mission to find fault with something, she tells me, but so far it seems that I'm winning on points.'

'You have someone else going over your stuff? Does she get to look at anything and everything? I can't imagine you'd like that very much, knowing what a control freak you are. I hope there's nothing indiscreet hidden in your drawers?'

He said it with such latent double meaning that Ted was still laughing as he ended the call.

Then he frowned to himself. Trev had a point. He was paranoid about people going over his things. He had had, of necessity, to turn everything over to Sammy in good faith. But he didn't know her. Didn't know much about her background, except that she came highly recommended.

He made himself a mental note to wait until she'd left for the evening then to go in and do a sweep of his office for any documents or notes he'd filed anywhere which he'd prefer to remain for his own eyes only. He acknowledged to himself just how paranoid that made him seem. But there was definitely an information leak somewhere, there was no denying that, and he still didn't know the source.

It had been useful sitting down with Jim Baker earlier to lay out facts and thoughts. At least he knew Jim would never dismiss any ideas out of hand without weighing them up first. But he was also bluntly spoken and would soon tell Ted if he thought he was straying into the realm of fantasy.

The one thing they were both absolutely in agreement on

was that neither of them had any reason to suspect any member of Ted's team of being behind the leaks. Ted had given it some measured thought. He wouldn't consider he'd done his job properly unless he had. All of his experience and instincts told him that the leak came from the Manchester end of things, from within the Drugs unit. Or from someone closely connected to them.

Jim had kept coming back to the question which was haunting Ted.

'Is it Bradley, though, Ted? After all, he's doing the fart thing himself by pointing his finger squarely at Black. And of course, you only have his word for it that he set up this meeting and Black fell for it. That could be pure fabrication.

'Talk to Don Holton. I'll pave the way, let him know you're not normally prone to flights of fantasy, although he'll know your record, of course. But what's got to happen, as a matter of some urgency, is to bring Bradley in from the cold and then for someone who really knows their stuff to fully debrief him. For as long as that takes.

'You could always suggest that someone should interview Black at some length, too. Put it to him that he was seen on premises where dealing was going on and ask him for an explanation. If he says it was him doing some investigating, let him produce log entries, notes, all the rest of it, not to mention who he cleared it with before proceeding. Although if he's sharp enough, he'll have covered his tracks carefully.

'At the very least, it's possible he's a user, which would make him far too easily compromised to work on any drugs case, and particularly one with violent deaths connected to it. And it could be that Bradley knows that, so would know where to find him. Too many unanswered questions. It needs sorting, as soon as possible.

'Right, I'll phone Don now, see what he says about availability and when he can speak to you. The sooner the better, obviously.'

Jim called the Chief Super's number and was lucky to find him in his office. They chatted for a few moments. It was clear to Ted that the two of them knew each other outside the work environment, probably members of some of the same organisations.

Then Jim laid out the details concisely and asked for a meeting for Ted, adding, 'I've worked with Ted for years. God knows he can be an annoying little bugger, but he's not known for flights of fancy. If I still held any clout, I'd certainly be pressing to get DS Bradley brought in and debriefed as a matter of priority on his say-so.'

He listened for a moment, said, 'Thanks, Don, I'll put him on,' then handed the phone to Ted.

'Ted, I agree with Jim. It sounds as if it's time to bring Bradley in. I can find out who his handler is and phone you back with the details.'

'Sir,' Ted began hesitantly, 'could we do a face to face on this? Only the amount of leaks we've had to date ...'

The DCS chuckled. 'And there I was happy to accept Jim's word that you had your feet on the ground and weren't seeing conspiracy theories around every corner. Are you sure that's necessary?'

'It can't hurt, sir. I'd sooner err on the side of caution with this one. The gang has had the better of us once too often, for my liking.'

'All right, here's what I'll do for you, still going on Jim vouching for you. Get yourself here for eight-thirty tomorrow morning, before my latest fun round of meetings begins. I'll have someone find Bradley's handler and get them here at the same time. We can find an office where you can brief them on anything you need to, on the basis that if secure confidentiality isn't guaranteed within the hallowed walls of Central Park, then we have a much bigger problem than any of us has realised to date.'

'Sorted?' Jim asked as Ted ended the call.

'Looks like it, thanks. I'm going up there tomorrow first thing. I appreciate your help.'

'That sounds like you getting ready to give me my marching orders, Ted,' Jim grumbled. 'And I thought we were friends. If I go back too soon, Bella will extract a terrible revenge for missing the stately home by dragging me off to a garden centre. Can't we at least go and have a look in the incident room and you can show me what progress has been made to date? I might pick up on something you've missed, although I doubt that, in all honesty. I trained you too well.'

* * *

Rob O'Connell was hovering discreetly in the distance once more whilst Ted was showing Big Jim the progress of the enquiry so far. There wasn't a great deal. Tests of DNA from the scene hadn't thrown up any known suspects. Work was being done to try to identify the type of weapons used on Noah Brooks based on photos of the wounds taken post mortem. Such weapons were often illegal but easily available online, so tracing their origins was never easy. But anything was worth a try. They were still waiting on final input on that from Professor Nelson.

The Operation Flood board was at least now fleshing out with what little information was available, including lines linking to previous unsuccessful operations. That included an artist's impression, the only tangible thing they had, of Data, juxtaposed with post-mortem photos of the young man who had been shot when standing in for him. The likeness between them was striking, displayed as they were like that. It was little wonder that even Gina Shaw, who had had direct contact with Data on several occasions before the failed operation, had not spotted the substitution until she saw the unknown young man lying dead on the pavement at her feet.

There were also crime scene photos from another brutal

killing connected to the same gang. The tortured body of a youth, Kane Lomax, had been found hanging from a tree in Heaton Mersey Bowl. A part of his tongue had been sliced off in a clear message to anyone who might have been tempted to break their silence and say anything about the people behind the gang.

Once Jim had dawdled for as long as he dared and made to leave, Rob approached Ted.

'Can we have a word somewhere quiet, boss? Only I have an update.'

Jim waved a large hand at the two of them and growled, 'Go. If I can't find my own way to the main entrance after all these years, there's no bloody hope for me. I can kill a bit more time catching up with Bill when I go to hand my visitor's badge back in.

'Let me know how it goes tomorrow, Ted, at Central Park. Keep me in the loop as much as you can, and don't forget, you only have to call and I'll be here like a shot. With pleasure.'

Both Jo and Mike Hallam were based in the incident room most of the time with the enquiry in full swing, so Ted led the way back up to their shared office with Rob. As he neared his own small room, he had another fleeting thought about Superintendent Sampson. Then he dismissed it. Goodness knows what the DCS would think about his paranoia if he knew he was eyeing up everyone, from senior officers down, as potential moles.

There was one small niggling thought at the back of his mind. Another possible suspect. But for the moment it remained elusive. It was quite likely more evidence of his suspicious mind at work.

Trev was fond of teasing him about his 'trust no one, suspect everyone' methods in the style of Agatha Christie's Hercule Poirot. It was true that Poirot was one of the few fictional detectives for whom Ted had any real respect.

'So, Rob, what have you uncovered?' Ted asked him, as he

opted for his preferred post, perching on the desk while Rob took a seat in response to his nod.

'Something interesting and potentially significant, boss. One of the Manchester officers who's joined us. DC Mari Griffiths. She's Derek Black's live-in girlfriend.'

Ted made to speak but Rob carried on, 'Well, it's apparently a bit of an on-off relationship, currently more off than on by all accounts. She's staying with a friend here in Stockport while she's working with us on the op, rather than going back to the flat she shares with Black.

'It's the only connection of any sort I've found so far, boss, and I don't really know what to make of it.'

'Thanks, Rob, you've done well. And nor do I. There may be nothing to it at all, but like you say, it's a connection and as such, we can't afford to ignore it. Leave it with me for now, thank you. Are you happy carrying on with this for now, see if anything else is thrown up?'

Rob made a face. 'Not exactly happy, boss. It feels like spying on work colleagues, although I can see the necessity for it. I'll carry on for now, if you say so.'

Ted's mobile phone ringing interrupted them both. The screen showed it was Bill Baxter, from the front desk, calling him. Rob looked pleased at the opportunity to escape.

'What time are you knocking off tonight, Ted?'

'I require written notice of that question, Bill,' Ted told him ironically. 'Why, what can I do for you?'

'Steve has agreed to see you, when you have time. And by one of life's moments of synchronicity, today I had to leave the car behind and come in on the bus as the bloody leg wasn't up to driving safely. So I wondered if there was any chance, if you're not planning on a very late night, if you could run me home and come in to have a word with him at the same time? I think it might be a good thing for both of you if you get together quite soon, now he's up for the idea. You know what these reunions can be like - the longer you leave it, the harder it gets. And he's planning his trip to the States quite soon, so you need to talk to him before he goes.'

Bill's leg injury was genuine enough. It was from a serious road accident which had robbed him of some mobility and left recurring pain, but at the same time had seen him awarded a medal for bravery. It did sometimes make it hard for him to drive. Knowing him as well as he did, Ted suspected this was also Bill's way of forcing the issue to get him and Steve together face to face soon, before Ted was too busy to do it and Steve lost his bottle about agreeing to the meet.

'Give me ten, fifteen minutes to hand over to Jo then I'll come and find you.'

Team members were heading back into the incident room to report in and write up notes at the end of the day when Ted went to speak to Jo.

'Any more progress?' he asked him, more in hope than anticipation.

'You know I'm a good Catholic, boss, so I cannot tell a lie. Sadly, no, unless anyone coming back in has anything fresh to report. Are you heading off now?' he asked, noticing that Ted had his things with him.

'I'm running Bill home and he's just finished his shift. Then I'm going to talk to Steve. He's agreed to see me.'

'Give him all our best wishes, if that's appropriate, won't you? I imagine it might feel a bit awkward, for both of you. Hopefully Bill will make a good go-between.'

For all Bill's many outstanding qualities, Ted wouldn't have listed tact and diplomacy near the top, although he had managed to work wonders with Steve.

Bill was limping more than usual as he went with Ted to get into his car. It didn't appear to be put on for effect so perhaps it was genuine and not a device to get Ted back to his house to talk to Steve.

'You will stay in the room, Bill, won't you? It might be easier for both of us if you do.'

'Of course I will, you soft beggar. But he wants to see you, Ted. You know he idolises you.'

As soon as Bill turned his key in the door, Ted following behind him, they both heard the loud squawks of Father Jack, the cockatoo, from the kitchen.

'Drink! Arse! Girls!'

'Go on through, Ted, I'll just hang my coat up, then I'll stick the kettle on.'

Steve was sitting at the kitchen table, his laptop open in front of him, Father Jack sitting on his shoulder and shouting at Ted. Steve looked pale and anxious. He shot to his feet as Ted entered and said, 'Hello, sir.'

Ted had tried many times to get him to be less formal and found it to be a lost cause. He took a seat at the opposite side of the table which encouraged Steve to sit back down. Ted found himself suddenly tongue-tied and feeling inadequate. So much he wanted to say. Words he'd practised to himself in his head so many times. Words which now steadfastly refused to be uttered.

Bill stumped in from the hallway, weighed up the situation and said, his voice laden with heavy sarcasm, 'Well, this is very cosy. I'll put the kettle on. Jack, you come and help me. And for god's sake, the pair of you, just bloody talk to one another.'

Chapter Sixteen

Ted was driving straight to Central Park the next morning, so he phoned Jo on his way. He hadn't yet put his DI fully in the picture about the secondary enquiries trying to identify the informer. It was not for lack of trust. He had every confidence in Jo. But anything as delicate was always best conducted on a minimal disclosure basis.

'Jo, I've got an early meeting at Central Park, and I'm on my way there now. Can you kick off briefing this morning with a very clear and unequivocal reminder to everyone about confidentiality, please? Play the heavy, remind them of the consequences.'

'I will try to look mean and menacing, although as I'm always saying, I'm a lover, not a fighter. Does that mean you think the leak is now from within the heart of things here?'

Ted's hesitation was minimal but would undoubtedly not have escaped Jo's attention.

'Jim says I'm paranoid, but when we don't know, I start seeing possibilities where they probably don't exist. I've even found myself fretting about having the Super in my office, but then I'm a bit territorial.'

'D'you want me to spy on her in your absence? Drop in without knocking on the pretext of offering her a brew and see if I can catch her rifling through your secret files? Not that I know where you keep them, of course.'

There was humour in his tone and Ted had to laugh in return.

'I know, I know, I am starting to sound like a deranged conspiracy theorist. I'd better get a tin foil hat. But there is no getting away from it. Things aren't as tight as they should be, so we need to do whatever we can to identify and plug any leaks.'

'Can I ask if that's what Rob's been working on? Only he's been a bit evasive when I've asked him about his availability and progress.'

Jo was sharp. He didn't miss much. It was what made him a good DI and an excellent second to Ted.

'Something like that,' Ted still sounded evasive. 'Look, I'll update you on everything I know when I get back. I'm trying to find a way to get Ian Bradley brought back in. It feels a bit at the moment as if there are too many of us with a common aim but all pulling in different directions and ploughing our own furrows.

'I'm counting on you to spell out what shouldn't need saying - nothing about Operation Flood leaves the four walls of the incident room without express permission from me, or from you. Thanks, Jo. I'll see you later, but I don't know how long I'll be.'

Ted was shown straight up to the Chief Superintendent's office, where his secretary tapped on the door and showed Ted in.

Holton was in his shirt sleeves, looking workmanlike, sorting through the accumulated daily bumf on his desk. He half rose and held out a welcoming hand. He was not much taller than Ted, which made a pleasant change, medium build, with the beginnings of a spare tyre starting to strain against the fabric of his shirt.

'Take a seat for a moment, Ted. The handler you need to talk to is coming in shortly, and I have to go out before too long, but I thought it might be useful for us to have a brief discussion to begin with.

'The first and most obvious question is should we be

looking at a bigger combined operation? The murder of your wee lad in Stockport together with this whole drugs op and the shooting of that young man here on our patch, plus your earlier unsolved killing. We're no further forward than we were on who was behind that, are we?'

Ted's chin lifted immediately. What Jim Baker always called his stubborn mule face.

'Sir, two things,' he began. 'I'm not saying we should give up on the shooting, of course, but I think the chances of us ever finding who killed the Data lookalike are less than slim at best. That had all the hallmarks of a professional hit job and who-ever was behind it will probably be as skilled in covering their tracks as we are in trying to uncover them.

'Secondly, I'd worry that young Noah would become just another statistic of a bigger enquiry, if we combined the ops. I don't mean that any officer would ever overlook the death of a young person. But for now, he remains the centre of everyone's focus, and I'd really like it to stay that way, if possible.' He left a brief but discernible pause before he added a 'sir.'

'I hear what you say, Ted. But from my side of the desk, it comes down to results. And budgets. Nothing more or less. I know you've had some good arrests and convictions. But the pressure is on from all round with this one. Can you get me the results we need? Because the last thing we want to add into a volatile mix is any in-fighting between different factions within the service. Can you all play nicely in the same sandpit if I leave it as two separate enquiries for now? Serious Crime on the boy's murder, plus the earlier one, on your patch, Drugs and Homicide together on the shooting and the supplying up here?'

'We can, sir, of course. Subject first of all to us finding and plugging the leak. Which is why I'm so keen to get DS Bradley brought back in and debriefed. I'm now concerned that what he told me earlier this week may have been at best economical on truth, at worst, deliberate misinformation.

'Sir, cases like this are hard enough when all officers are

pulling together. But if we have anyone going off piste, let alone working against us, you know the complications that can bring.'

Holton studied him in silence for a moment. Then he sighed and nodded.

'All right, you stay with the Noah Brooks case for now and let's hope for a breakthrough sometime soon. You and I had better have at least a weekly catch-up, by conference call, and keep progress under review.

'Oh, and in case you were wondering, I'm not the mole, so you can safely discuss things with me.'

Ted risked one of the cheeky grins which made him look much younger than his years.

'I did wonder, sir. I wouldn't be much of a detective if I didn't.'

Holton's laugh was interrupted by another knock on the door by his secretary and her putting her head round to announce, 'DI Usher is here. Shall I send him in?'

'Please, Flora. Thank you.'

She stood aside and DI David Usher, DS Ian Bradley's handler, strode into the room. He was comparatively young, new generation. Jeans and a rugby shirt, no sort of old-school etiquette. Ted wore a suit and tie under sufferance as required by the Ice Queen. But for reasons he couldn't entirely rationalise even to himself, he did stick to the formalities which were rapidly disappearing elsewhere.

Holton made the briefest of introductions as he rose and started to get his things together.

'DCI Ted Darling, DI Dave Usher. I'm not sure if you know one another. Flora will show you which room you can use. Take as long as you like to thrash something out, but to save time, Dave, I'm in agreement with Ted on this one. It's time you brought your spy Bradley in from the cold and found out exactly what's been going on.

'Give me a full written update when you've finished. Each

of you. If you have divergent opinions, I want to hear both sides of the argument.'

The secretary showed Ted and DI Usher to an empty room further along the corridor, which was furnished with a water jug, kettle, percolator and the makings of a brew. Ted headed straight for it. He never liked to prejudge any situation but the waves of hostility emanating from Usher were palpable so he was preparing himself for something of an uphill battle.

Usher shook his head to Ted's offer of a hot drink but helped himself to a glass of water then sat down at the small table. His opening aggressive question of, 'So why d'you want Ian brought in, and what's it got to do with you anyway?' wasn't exactly promising. Ted was patient, and he could do tact and diplomatic discourse when necessary. He simply resented the time and effort when dealing with another officer who seemed set on behaving less than professionally, for reasons which so far escaped him.

'Ian contacted me on Monday and we met up,' he began.

He immediately sensed Usher bristle even more at that news. He was clearly unaware that had happened and not happy as a result. Time to set a few ground rules, Ted decided.

'Look, DI Usher,' he hoped his formality might make the point. 'We are both on the same side in this. There's no place for petty, factional in-fighting. We both want to put the same people behind bars and we both have to accept there's a serious security breach somewhere. That's what Ian wanted to talk to me about.'

'He should have come to me. I'm his bloody handler. There's more than one on the team who have serious doubts over you, for a start. We've never had an op go to shit like that before you came on the scene. A few of them raised concerns at the time about you being parked up right by the RV scene like a spare prick at a wedding. You may be a DCI but have you got the training for covert ops?'

Ted was tempted not even to dignify that with a response.

He had fleeting memories of the number of special skills courses he'd done with Mr Green. He understood Usher's suspicion, to a degree. It was a feral response. When any group came under attack, it was nature's reaction to turn on the newest member. He wished he didn't need to waste time in answering the point, but it was time to stamp some authority, if they were to make any progress at all.

'You might be surprised at my level of security clearance. But I'm not answerable to you, and quite frankly, I'm not interested in your opinion of me. All I care about right now is finding the informer who's been making both our jobs more difficult than they need to be.

'You know that Gina Shaw has now joined my team. Ian Bradley contacted me because he seems genuinely concerned about her welfare, because of the leak.'

'We're still looking into who it could be at our end, if anyone.' Usher responded. 'And you should know that we've not yet successfully cleared Gina from suspicion. Bradley was always too soft where she was concerned. If he wanted to talk to anyone about his suspicions, he should have come through me. Did he tell you if he has anyone particular in mind?'

'What he and I discussed remains strictly between the two of us. But he clearly has concerns. Serious concerns. As do I, and mine have increased since some of my officers, out for an off-duty drink together in town, happened to see DS Bradley in circumstances which can only increase my anxiety levels.

'That's why I would suggest that for everyone's safety, including the DS's, you get him back in, and soon. And please have the courtesy to let me know when you do. Meanwhile, my team and I have the savage killing of a young boy to deal with - and not the first one - which is almost certainly connected to the same drugs gang we've both been unsuccessfully trying to track down for too long.'

Ted drained his mug and stood up, pushing his chair back as he did so. He was angry and working hard not to let it show.

Usher's obstructive attitude had annoyed him, especially as there seemed to be no valid reason for his aggression. It was possible that it was simply how he was, which might explain why DCS Holton had asked for separate reports from each of them on their meeting. Perhaps he had known they would be sure to differ considerably.

* * *

There was a slightly more upbeat feel to the atmosphere in the major incident room when Ted arrived back from Central Park. He'd made the briefest stop to pick up a hot bacon barm. His stomach had developed something of an acidic feeling so he'd decided it might be better to give it something more solid to digest rather than his lingering anger over the encounter with DI David Usher.

He went to find Jo to ask for developments.

'We're not putting up the bunting yet, but at least we have another direction to go in. We've had more detailed reports from the PM now. Professor Nelson is disconcertingly knowledgeable about knife injuries, isn't she? She somehow seems too staid and respectable to take an interest in such things, but she seems to be something of an expert.'

Ted had a fleeting memory of Bizzie Nelson at her own hand-fasting, flower buds in her hair, sharing a spliff with her guests under the apple trees in her garden and wondered how 'staid and respectable' Jo would have found that image of her.

'She says some of the injuries Noah suffered, the ones not designed to kill immediately, were inflicted by a *balisong* - a butterfly knife. Illegal to carry in the UK, of course, but not that difficult to get hold of on the street or from some unscrupulous dealers online.'

Ted knew what they were. He'd done extensive weapons training with Mr Green over the years. There weren't many types of blade he hadn't come across.

Butterfly knives, with their concealed blades, were especially deadly, as to the untrained eye it took too long to identify the lethal menace within when folded. The weapons' sides kept a fearsome blade inside concealed from sight until they parted like a butterfly's wings, by which time it could be too late for flight.

'Is it worth making this public? Get some pictures of similar knives out there through the press and media, saying we're trying to trace anyone known to be carrying such a weapon? Perhaps offer a temporary amnesty to anyone handing them in? We could run tests on any we do come by and hope for a match to Noah?'

'I'd need clearance from higher up but I agree it's worth a try. Even if we don't find the murder weapon, or one of them, it might at least pull some weapons in off the street so no one else can be killed or seriously injured by them.'

'The professor has given in her usual detailed description about the precise size and type we're looking for.'

'They come in different colours and patterns, of course,' Ted told him. 'We'd have to be careful not to plant the idea in people's minds that we're looking for one of a particular colour and design. Although if Professor Nelson has the exact blade dimensions, it may be possible to narrow down the permutations of that particular model.'

'It always worries me slightly how much you know about lethal weapons too, boss,' Jo told him.

Ted smiled as he undid his left shirt cuff and pushed the sleeve back slightly, revealing the livid scar, still clearly visible, which ran up the inside of his forearm.

'Don't forget I've been up close and personal with bladed weapons more often than I've been comfortable with.'

Chapter Seventeen

Ted next went back to his own office to find Sammy Sampson. As she was effectively filling his shoes and holding the purse strings which were usually his responsibility, he needed to check with her about the idea of a further press appeal, this time focusing on the butterfly knife.

She looked up at him with a smile as he came in and said, 'You don't have to knock on your own office door, you daft barmpot. I'd heard all the rumours about you being a bolshie little sod yet here you are with manners from the last century.

'Anyway, your kettle's just boiled, if you're looking for a brew, and I haven't been dipping into your foul green stuff. I've been bringing my own coffee in as yours is too weak for me.'

Ted made himself a brew and sat down opposite her. He studied her covertly through the steam rising off his green tea as he took his first careful sip of the scalding liquid. Was he right to stay wary of someone he didn't know well? Or was his imagination working overtime?

'I'm about on top of things here now, as you'd already sorted much of it, and Operation Flood reports coming to me certainly underline that you expect the same high standards from your team members. So I have 'Eck booked for later to pick me up and take me on another tour of your realm, to check all is at it should be out there. Unless there's anything useful I can do to help here in the meantime?'

'As you're now nominally holding the reins, I just wanted to check that you're all right with us putting out another press appeal.'

He set out the details about the weapon and the need to appeal for help from the public to trace its origins. Her face darkened at his words.

'Bastards,' she spat. 'There should be a special place in hell for people who supply things like knives and drugs to children. I've got a little grandson, Benjamin. I know what I'd do to anyone who did anything like that to him. Ever.'

Then she smiled and tried to lift the mood. 'And I know, you're sitting there wondering how someone as youthful as me can possibly have a child old enough to have one of their own, aren't you?'

She made Ted laugh. Try as he might, he couldn't imagine her posing any risk to the integrity of the enquiry. She seemed like a dedicated and hard-working officer who genuinely cared about the people her role was to protect. But then he reminded himself that they'd had an informer inside this very nick before. One no one had ever suspected. Disgraced ex-Police Sergeant Micky Wheeler. Formerly Big Jim's best friend and godfather to his daughter, Rosie. Nobody, even those closest to him, had suspected him, nor known about the helpless gambling addiction which had brought him down to that level.

'You can safely leave it to me to sort things with the Press Office before I go off on my jollies with 'Eck. I'll let the Ice Queen know as well,' she told him, then smiled at his expression. 'Oh, everyone knows what she's called. Even Debs herself. Knowing her as I do, I think she's probably secretly flattered. She's done incredibly well to get as far as she has at her age, and she's not made it by having a thin skin and a warm, cuddly nature, like me, that's for sure.

'Right, I best get on and get it sorted so I'm ready when 'Eck arrives to give me the royal tour. I'm not planning on coming back here at the end of the day so I'll see you tomorrow. Hopefully not too disgracefully hung over, but you know what

'Eck is like.'

Ted suspected it would be a case of six and two threes when the two of them got together, each one egging the other on to greater excess. At least Sammy being out of the building for the rest of the day would give him the opportunity to go through his things to see if there was anything he wanted to store more securely.

The ever-present niggling worry about the informant's identity gave him another thought. It was high time he took Jo into his confidence on that score and put him fully in the picture. Especially to explain to him exactly what Rob had been working on without him knowing. He should have done that already as a courtesy, if nothing else.

He made a quick call to Dave, the landlord of the nearest pub to the nick, The Grapes, to check if the back room was available to him at lunchtime. Then he went to find Jo.

'You and me, the back room of The Grapes for lunch and a full catch-up. There's things I need to tell you which I'd prefer to do on neutral territory.'

'That sounds very mysterious, but I've never been known to turn down a lunch date.'

* * *

The two of them settled for Dave's famous hotpot, with a half of lager for Jo and Ted's trademark non-alcoholic Gunner. They ate in companionable silence for a few minutes, then Ted paused and took a drink.

'I've not been intentionally keeping you in the dark about anything, Jo. But I haven't had the time to keep you up to speed on everything. I thought it was best to do it here, just you and me.

'I have had Rob working on something for me and I should have told you about it much sooner, in detail. Rob's been checking out the new officers we have working with us, looking for any links we didn't know about.'

'And judging by your expression, he's found an unexpected one.'

'I sometimes feel sorry for your children, Jo. It can't ever be easy getting one over on you.'

Jo laughed at that. 'They know better than to even try too often. So, what has he turned up?'

'It may be nothing and I don't want to read too much into it. DC Mari Griffiths is DC Derek Black's girlfriend, although not currently living with him.'

'And that's significant because ...?'

Ted finished his mouthful than started to tell Jo more or less everything which was going on behind the scenes. He realised with a pang of guilt that there was too much Jo didn't know. He should have found the time to tell him all this much earlier. He really did have no reason to mistrust his DI. Far from it. He'd done an excellent job of holding the fort and starting a major enquiry whilst Ted had been tied up in Wales.

Jo kept eating whilst Ted talked, then drank more of his lager once the boss had finished explaining everything DS Bradley had told him.

'As instructed, I read them all the riot act this morning,' Jo then told him. 'I kept an eye on everyone's reactions, especially the newcomers to the team. And I'm used to weighing up six kids who do still sometimes, unwisely, try to get something past their dad.

'I swear there was not a flicker of unease anywhere. Certainly not from Mari. She's a good officer. Meticulous in the work I've seen from her so far. I wouldn't want to lose her from the team. Especially if the only reason is that she might not show the best judgement in her choice of boyfriend. I imagine most of us, at some point in our lives, might have been with the wrong person a time or two.

'Not me, of course,' he added, with the familiar twinkle in his eye. 'I was a child bridegroom to the mother of my children and I haven't strayed since.'

Ted never knew when to take him seriously on such matters. Jo had sworn to him many times that he was a harmless flirt but it was the one thing on which Ted wasn't quite sure whether or not to believe him.

'Well, before we all knock off tonight, perhaps I'd better have a word on the same subject, to hammer the message home. I can have a look myself for reactions, although I doubt I'll spot anything if you didn't.

'I'd like to get away at a halfway decent time if I can, too. A spot of karate might be just what I'm in need of to sharpen myself up a bit. And if the appeal about the butterfly knife does go out tonight, as it hopefully will, we probably need to brace ourselves for the usual avalanche of calls in response, not all of which will be of any remote use to us.'

* * *

Ted's mobile phone was ringing before he'd even taken off his raincoat the following morning, shaken it dry and hung it on the stand in his own office, where he was beginning his day, well before morning briefing. He still needed to make time to have a proper sort through his drawers and shelves to move anything which wasn't relevant to cases in hand. He had almost convinced himself he had no need to, but he knew he'd feel easier in his mind if he at least had a quick flick through everything which was there.

The screen showed him that the call was from DC Steve Ellis.

'Morning, Steve, you're an early bird. What can I do for you?'

'Morning, sir. I saw the appeal on the news last night. About the butterfly knife. I know I'm on sick leave, and not allowed back to the team for the foreseeable future. But I thought I might be able to help a bit, unofficially. So this is me phoning in as a member of the public, not a police officer.'

It was a surprisingly devious start, from young Steve.

'Thank you, Mr Ellis, I appreciate you taking the time and trouble to call us.'

Ted decided to play along with him. This was Steve sounding so much more like his old self. Still nervous, treading warily around his senior officer, but sounding to be bursting with things he wanted to impart. Judging by the time lapse between when the appeals had gone out and the current early hour, and knowing the way Steve worked, he could well have been sitting in front of his computer for much of the night.

'Right, sir. Well, you know I explained to you once before about MMORPGs. You remember, massively multiplayer online role-playing games.'

Ted did vaguely remember. He wasn't sure he'd entirely grasped the whole thing back then, and with the intervening time, he was frantically scratching his head to try to think what it was all about and how it might apply to their current case.

Almost as if he could hear the cogs ticking at the other end of the phone, Steve supplied helpfully and patiently, 'At its simplest, it involves people becoming a character in a fantasy setting. Popular themes often centre around warcraft and science fiction. Like most things on the internet, there's a way for people from all round the world to contact one another and interact away from the game as well.

'Now, it's mostly online and harmless, although to some people it might sound to be on the weird side of eccentric. But there are factions, fortunately few, who tend to get a bit carried away and the war side of it can spill over into their real lives.'

This was the Steve whom Ted missed. Talking about a specialist subject he was passionate about. Explaining things to Ted without a note of patronising. Roles reversed for once. No hesitation. No endless faltering and calling him sir at the end of every sentence. All it did was set off Ted's self-blame again. How could he possibly have failed to notice the small amount of assurance Steve possessed slipping away from him until he'd clearly felt his own life was so worthless it was simply not worth continuing with?

'Some of these people, and I stress again that it's very few, like to collect the sort of weapons they use in the fantasy world. But real ones. Not replicas. And even things which are illegal, like the butterfly knives, are not that difficult to get hold of, if you know your way around the internet.

'I have a couple of anonymous personae which I've set up, and kept, in case I should ever need to do any digging into anything like this. I interact just often enough to be an established presence.

'After what appeared on TV and social media about the butterfly knife, there was quite a buzz about such things on some of those sites. People talk surprisingly openly there.

'Anyway, long story short, I got a couple of leads to people dealing in exactly the type of weapon mentioned, in our area. I'll email you everything I have and please contact me if you need any more help with it.'

'Steve, you are a miracle worker. Thank you so much. This could be just the breakthrough we've been looking for. If we can track down the source of the knife, there's a slim but possible chance we might be able to find who bought it.

'I can't officially ask you to do anything else for us, but I really appreciate this. And remember what I told you. As soon as Occupational Health will even consider you returning to the team, you'll have my backing.'

As soon as he ended the call, Ted asked Jo to come upstairs for an update. He was playing it cautiously again. This was an important lead, a potential breakthrough. Something to be investigated carefully. Certainly nothing which should leave the incident room and possibly get back to the very people they were hoping to trace, giving them enough time to cover their tracks and dispose of any evidence yet again.

True to his word, Steve had emailed all the details he had

to Ted, who printed out a copy to show Jo. It would not leave Ted's possession and would stay, for now, for Jo's eyes only in its entirety.

'Good old Steve, eh? It's great to see that he's clearly doing a lot better than he was. Can we use this, though? Ethically, I mean? Or should we be going after him for attempting to procure an illegal, offensive weapon?'

'He's acting as a member of the public, voluntarily offering information which could be vital to our enquiries. I'll check, but I'm sure it's the sort of occasion where we could arrange some sort of indemnity if necessary. It's our best lead to date. We'd be negligent not to at least look into it.'

* * *

Bill Baxter, on the front desk, phoned through to Maurice Brown, in the incident room.

'Maurice? I've got a lad here at the desk asking to speak to you and no one else. He says his name's Ollie and you know him, but he won't give me his last name, nor his address. He says he's seen about the butterfly knives on the telly and he has some info for you. I wasn't sure if he was on the level but he was very insistent, so I said I'd see if you were free to talk to him.'

'Fair enough, sarge. Me and Emma Moore did tell him to get in touch if he heard anything which might help us. He was mates with young Noah. I'll at least come and have a word with him. If nothing else, I'll ask him why he's not in school when he should be.'

Like almost every other officer in the station old enough to know his history, Maurice still accorded Bill the courtesy of his rank, although he was retired.

Maurice looked round the room. Jo wasn't currently there, to tell him where he was going. He shouldn't be long, hopefully, just to see what young Ollie had to say for himself.

He decided that for form's sake, he should take someone with him when talking to a juvenile. He had another look round, trying to decide who to ask. He thought it might be a good idea for it to be a female officer. Two blokes looming over a little lad could sometimes seem a bit overpowering.

DC Mari Griffiths, from Manchester, was sitting not far from him, looking at something on her computer. She seemed like a nice lass. Friendly enough, if a bit reserved.

'Mari? Have you got a few minutes to help out?' he asked her. 'There's a young lad come in with some info about the knife we're trying to trace. He might be a bit more relaxed with a woman present, if you've got the time.'

Mari smiled up at him. Nice-looking lass too, Maurice thought to himself.

'No problem at all, Maurice. I wouldn't mind a leg-stretch and a bit of time away from the screen. And maybe we can manage a cuppa while we're at it.'

Chapter Eighteen

Ollie Martin looked younger than ever, sitting alone on one of the seats in the reception area, trying not to appear nervous or guilty any time he caught sight of a passing officer. It was clearly not his first time inside a police station.

There was a look almost of relief about him when he saw Maurice's bulky figure heading towards him in the company of a woman in plain clothes.

'Right, young Ollie, first off, why aren't you in school?' Maurice greeted him.

'Inset day,' the boy told him, quick as a flash, with a perfectly straight face.

'My backside, it is. I'll be checking up on you, think on. Right, let's go and find a quiet room somewhere and you can tell us what it is you want to talk to me about. This is Mari, by the way. You can talk in front of her.'

He found them an empty interview room where the two of them sat down opposite the boy. Mari had offered to scribe, taking down anything and everything of relevance, while Maurice posed the questions.

'That knife, like on the telly. The butterfly knife. Noah had one of his own. Just like it. Same model, but a different colour. He showed it me. I wanted a go with it, but he wouldn't let me. He kept showing off with it. He liked to do them tricks, like. Spinning it round in his hand an' stuff. He were crap at it, really, but he'd not had it long.'

'Did someone give it to him?' Maurice asked him.

Ollie shook his head. 'Nah, man, bought it himself, he said. 'For protection, he told me.'

'Can't be cheap, one of those, especially when they're illegal. That must put the price way up. Where'd Noah get that kind of cash?'

Ollie's face took on a sly look as he glanced from one of them to another.

'This is me talking about Noah, right? I never done none of this stuff myself. I'm only telling you so you can get the bastards what killed him. He was me mate.'

'That's all we're interested in at the moment, Ollie. We want to get our hands on Noah's killers as much as you do. I hope you aren't mixed up in anything like he was. If ever you find you're getting dragged into stuff you don't want to do, you get in touch with me.'

Maurice got one of his cards out of his pocket and slid it across the table to the boy.

'Any time. And I mean that.'

Father to twin girls and twin boys, step-father to another boy, Maurice was a big softy where children were concerned. Daddy Hen. He would always go the extra mile to help them.

'What if someone seen me come in here today? Or someone sees me leaving? Will you put me in, like, witness protection, or something? Abroad, somewhere? I never been abroad.'

His eyes looked hopeful. Maurice suspected he watched too much crime drama on television.

'I'll make sure someone drives you back in an unmarked car and drops you off, but not too near your home. Although they'll watch until you get safely back inside.'

'Can I have chips on the way?'

'Give me some information I can use and I might consider it. You can start by telling me how Noah had enough money to buy himself a knife like that. Was he getting paid for what he did?'

'Peanuts, it were, he told me. He did their stuff mostly 'cos he were scared shitless of what they'd do to him if he didn't do what they wanted. Not just to him, he said. He told me what they said they'd do to his mam and his little sister if he didn't cooperate. You're a bloke. You know. But I ain't saying it in front of her.'

He jutted his chin towards Mari Griffiths who was eyes down, writing every detail he uttered which could be of any use to them.

Maurice decided not to press him on that for the moment. He could imagine.

'He told me he were nicking off them sometimes. From the money he collected for them. Not much, 'cos he didn't dare. Just a bit here and there. If he were short when he give 'em the money, they'd knock him about a bit an' threaten him and his family. But he were always good at coming up wi' a story. He could talk his way out of most things, could Noah. Well, I thought he could. But they got him in the end, didn't they?'

'What else did he tell you about what he was doing? You told me before that he liked to big himself up. What did you mean by that? What sort of things did he tell you?'

Ollie made a noise of contempt. 'Crap, it were. Maybe stuff his kid brother and sister would believe but I didn't. Going in a posh car with tinted windows to some big house with, like, bodyguards and everything. All talking in foreign.'

'Did he ever get to see the person in charge? Or say anything about who it was?'

This time there was no mistaking the scorn in the scoffing sound he made.

'The Big Man? Yeah, he told me about him, but he said he never met him. Not close to, like. He saw him through the window in the garden one time, he told me. He said he were a midget. About this big.' He held a hand up to his own chest. 'Wi'dark glasses on, and a white stick. I mean, I'm not a kid. I knew that were just crap. Like I said, all right to tell his little brother, but I wasn't falling for any of it.'

'He didn't say where he went to see this Big Man?'

Ollie shook his head. 'He only went a couple of times and he said that each time they shoved him down on the floor in the back of this Jeep thing they were driving, and put a bag over his head so he couldn't see where they were going. He must have scared the crap out of his little brother and sister, telling them stories like that, but I never believed a word of it. Not really. Although I did believe he were shifting drugs and shit for someone, 'cos that's why he had a bit o'money sometimes. And like I said, if none of it were true, why did they kill him?'

'Yet you say he felt scared enough about something to want to arm himself with a knife, for protection. How did he manage to find where to get one from? They're not exactly easy to come by. Did he have a computer, or a mobile phone of his own?'

Again, a shake of the head. 'He said these blokes he was running stuff for give him one. A phone. To use for doing their stuff. A county line, they call it. But they checked it, all the time. Whenever they met up with him to take the money an' stuff he'd collected, they'd take his phone and check the call history and internet an' stuff, to see what he'd been up to. To make sure he hadn't been doing any dodgy deals on the side. Only doing the stuff they wanted him to do. He said they were very controlling. He pretended it didn't bother him, but I could tell he were scared shitless sometimes.

'So when he wanted to do owt for himself, I let him use my phone. My dad gives me his old ones from work, so they're bloody good. Then there was no risk of them blokes seeing anything he'd been up to. That way he fixed himself up with one of them butterfly knives and was learning how to use it. He said he took it to bed with him every night, in case anyone got in and tried to harm his sister. He really loved her. Not in a weird way, I mean. But they didn't have a dad. Noah tried to protect the others. That's why he got the knife.'

'And d'you know where Noah got the knife from?'

The boy looked cunning now. Ready to play his trump card.

'Oh, yeah. An' I got the proof an' stuff.'

With the air of a conjuror producing a rabbit out of a hat, Ollie took a surprisingly good phone from his coat pocket and put it on the table between him and the two officers. It wasn't new. Not the latest model, but it would have been expensive in its day. Maurice wondered briefly what sort of work the boy's father was in which would give him a phone like that. It could, of course, have been another tall tale. The phone might be knocked off and the father had made up a story about work to tell his son, who'd swallowed the explanation.

'This is my phone. The one I let him use. I've got all the emails and shit between him an' this bloke he got it from. Everything. How he found him, where they arranged to meet. Pictures of it an' what it cost an' all that. I ain't wiped any of it.'

Mari caught up with her scribbling then put her pen down and turned to Maurice.

'Maurice, the fastest way to deal with this would be for me to nip to the MIR and get someone to lift a copy of anything we need from the phone direct. Rather than us messing about reading it all out and me trying to write it down. We've got a couple of good techie types in there who could do that in no time at all. Then you can carry on talking to Ollie and taking notes.

'I shouldn't be long at all and I could bring you both a drink when I come back. Is that all right with you, Ollie? I promise we're not interested in anything else you might have on there. Just the stuff that Noah was doing to make contact about the knife. To trace the person he got it from. That sort of stuff. The rest we'll just ignore, honestly. You can trust us, we're coppers.'

The boys eyes narrowed in suspicion for a moment. He looked to Maurice for guidance. He seemed to have accepted him as trustworthy. Maurice nodded encouragement.

'You'll bring it straight back?' Ollie's look back towards Mari was still on the suspicious side. 'And you won't mess with it or nothing?'

Mari smiled at him. 'Whatever you have on there you don't want me to see, Ollie, don't worry about it. I'm going to hand this straight over to one of our techie experts, and it will be a bloke. They'll copy what we need and I'll bring it straight back.

'Now, what drinks would you like me to bring you back? Tea? Coffee? Something else?'

* * *

Ted had finally found the time to go and have a sort through things in his own office, while Sammy was out on her travels.

From the first flick through the paperwork on his desk, he could see that she was easily as meticulous as he was. Everything was in order; not a thing out of place. He really was getting paranoid, clearly.

Besides, he knew that 'Eck wasn't easily deceived, and he clearly seemed to think highly of her, judging by their off-duty drinking sessions together. That was an endorsement in itself. Sammy had told him the two of them had met years ago when they were both newly posted to the same station in Manchester, had become friends and had stayed in touch, even when their paths had parted and Sammy had started her leapfrog up the promotion ladder.

As much for his own sanity as anything else, Ted needed to find out who the informant was and where they were. And soon. Until then, he was going to spend too much time looking sideways at everyone for the most innocent of things.

He was heading back to the incident room on the ground floor, passing the ladies' toilets, when the door opened and Mari Griffiths came out, almost bumping into him and looking startled as she did so.

They both did the reflex action of stepping back and apologising at the same moment, so they spoke over one another.

'Sorry, sir, I wasn't looking where I was going,' she told him.

'No, my fault, I wasn't either,' Ted told her.

He could see that she had a mobile phone in one hand. Not a model she would have been issued. She saw his eyes on it and held it up.

'Something of possible use to us, boss. A bit of a break-through, hopefully. Ollie Martin, Noah's friend, came in to see Maurice and we've been talking to him. He had plenty to say, too. About Noah having a butterfly knife, for protection, and how he'd bought it himself with money he was siphoning off the drugs he was running.

'This is Ollie's phone. He let Noah use it to arrange to buy the knife so there'd be no trace on his county lines phone of what he'd been doing. Maurice is still talking to Noah in the interview room. I'm just taking the phone to the techie types so they can hopefully quickly lift anything of use to us. We're hoping we might just be able to find the supplier through it and, who knows, get some sort of a lead somewhere, at least.'

Ted frowned. 'But you didn't take it straight to them, then use the ladies afterwards?'

'Sorry,boss, no, I didn't. I wasn't long, but it was a dire necessity, or I would have done it that way.'

She had no difficulty holding his gaze.

Ted hated this feeling. Suspecting everybody, all the time. He needed to be able to trust the officers who were working with him on the team. It was fraught with danger to press her any further. There were all kinds of reasons why her visit could have been urgent, and he instinctively felt he didn't need to know any of them.

By the same token, he wouldn't consider he'd done his job properly if he didn't make at least some basic checks, hopefully without raising any suspicions.

'Yes, of course. Sorry, I didn't mean to be indelicate. That's quite a nice phone, for a young lad to be carrying. May I?' He held his hand out to her and she passed it over with no sign of hesitation.

He made a pretence of looking at it. All he was really inter-ested in was the exact time, which he mentally noted before he handed it back to her.

Even if Maurice was just chatting informally to the boy, he was a trained copper and good in interviews. He'd done all the training, including recent updates. He would have noted by reflex somewhere the precise time that Mari Griffiths had left the room, leaving the two of them alone together. That would give Ted the information he needed to know, about exactly how long she had been alone with full access to those details on the phone.

Chapter Nineteen

Jo Rodriguez was summing up the latest developments at the end of the day, for those who had been out for most of it.

'We shouldn't set too much store by the latest lead about the butterfly knife,' he cautioned. 'If we're not careful it could hinder, rather than help us, at this stage.

'We now know, thanks to witness testimony from Noah's friend, Ollie Martin, and some off-duty work by DC Steve Ellis...'

A small cheer went up from the team regulars at the mention of their absent colleague and friend.

'... we know that Noah had his own butterfly knife, which he'd bought, supposedly for his own protection, with some of the money he was siphoning off the takings he handled for selling the drugs. It seems likely that it was turned against him to inflict at least some of his injuries.

'So even if we manage to recover that weapon, thanks to the public appeal, it may not give us the details to lead us to his killers. If they've handled it, to use it against him, you can be sure it will have been cleaned of the slightest trace. Even assuming we ever find the same one.

'You'll all have had the details of the injuries from the postmortem. The butterfly knife did serious damage but not fatal. The injuries which killed him were done by other knives, at least two, and they were of a military type.'

Maurice Brown was looking glum, sitting with arms folded.

'It's no wonder folks are reluctant to talk to us. Not often we get anything like this right on our doorstep. Not killing a little lad like that, in such a vicious way. Boss, we need to keep an eye on Ollie Martin, somehow. If they think he's been talk-ing to us about anything, he could be next.'

Ted had been perching on a desk at the rear of the room. He slid silently to his feet and moved to the front, to stand by the large whiteboard.

'You're absolutely right, Maurice. I'll talk to Uniform about keeping a discreet eye on him. I also want to stress yet again how important it is that what is discussed in this room stays confidential. At all times.'

He looked round them all as he spoke.

'I know you've heard it all before, more than once.'

His sharp eyes had spotted a couple of eye rolls from offi-cers new to the team who clearly thought the repetition was a bit of overkill.

'You're going to hear it again, too. It's something which can't be stressed often enough.'

He pointed to the crime scene photos on the board. Noah Brooks, lying dead in his own blood in the dirty, stinking alley with no escape route at the end. Kane Lomax, strung up in a tree by the ankles, after being beaten and tortured.

It was to Lomax's graphic photos that Ted pointed as he carried on speaking.

'The only reason we know anything about the so-called Big Man behind all of this is because, after his men did this to a young man, he went in person to throw the part of his tongue they cut out at the teenagers he was using before to shift the drugs. And for those of you who don't know, Kane's tongue was sectioned whilst he was still alive.

'These are the sort of people we're dealing with. Yet some-one, close to this enquiry, has clearly been supplying them with information from within since the beginning. It's the only logi-cal explanation for how they're staying ahead of us at every single turn.'

He was speaking as quietly as he usually did but there was no mistaking the suppressed anger behind his words.

'So I make no apology for the reminder. And get used to it. It won't be the last one you get.

'I'm not asking you to feel you need to start spying on one another. That's no way for any team to work. But if anyone has any concerns at all about anything, you can always come and talk to me in complete confidence.

'But remember, nothing which you see or hear on this enquiry goes any further than this room. To anyone. Even to other serving officers. If they're not on this team, they are not on the circulation list.

'Is that clear enough for everybody?'

There was a collective response of, 'Sir.' Ted seldom read the Riot Act. It had much more impact, therefore, when he did.

'Boss, before we finish, and before I forget to mention it. We shouldn't forget about dogs,' Jezza put in.

'Dogs?' Ted queried.

'You remember from before, on the previous case. I was coordinating the "Just how many breeds of Belgian Shepherd Dog are there?" side of the enquiry. We know that some of the ex-military types on the fringes of that crime were using dog walking as their cover. And you nearly found out at the sharp end that the dogs were trained killing machines, as much as the handlers were.'

'Jezza is absolutely right, and it was an oversight on my part not to flag this up sooner. So whoever is on checking CCTV can you please highlight anyone you see who could possibly look like an ex-military type, particularly if they're walking a dog.

'Jo,' Ted looked across at the DI as he spoke, 'wasn't Noah's body found by a dog walker?'

An officer Ted knew only by sight spoke before Jo could reply.

'It was, boss, and I've interviewed the man who found it, at length. He's a pensioner in his seventies. And unless some armed forces use dogs that look like a woolly greyhound someone put in the machine on a boil wash by mistake so that it shrinks, I think we can probably rule him out on both counts.'

There was a ripple of laughter in the room. A much-needed break in the tension which Ted's pep talk had inevitably produced. Even he had to smile at the description.

'Right, thank you everyone. We'll be working through the weekend, of course, until we can start to make some headway. Jo and I will try to find a way to ensure each of you gets at least some time with your families or friends, on a rota basis.'

* * *

The television was on when Ted let himself into the house. Trev was in front of it, feet up, cats strategically parked on any spare part of his anatomy not already occupied. He was doing a juggling act with a glass of something in one hand, trying to stop them spilling it.

'Oh, look, pussy cats, it's the Corgi-cuddling policeman who occasionally graces us with his presence, when he needs hot food or a clean shirt. He heard me open the sherry so he's come to breathalyse me, no doubt.'

Ted leaned over the back of the sofa to kiss him as he took off his jacket, tie and shoes before sitting down next to him.

'Sorry if you're feeling neglected. It's going to get worse, I'm afraid. We're working flat out all weekend and now I'm not simply a figurehead, I can't nick off as much as before.'

'I understand. I really do. I've just been watching the details on the news about what I presume is the case you're working on. The boy knifed in the alleyway?'

Ted nodded. He didn't talk much about his work at home. Not from any concern about confidentiality where Trev was concerned, but simply because he preferred to keep home as a safe haven when he could.

'Before I forget, unless we get an incredible breakthrough, I won't be able to get to the dojo at all on Wednesday, I don't suppose. So please can you spend some time with the youngsters reminding them why carrying their own knife is never the answer. Hammer home how very easily it can be turned against them, so the best solution is always to run away rather than to try to stand and fight.'

Trev took hold of Ted's hand in his spare one and lifted it up to kiss it.

'Is that what happened with young Noah? He tried to defend himself and someone turned his own weapon on him? They showed some of the footage of the crime scene. I can't believe what his last moments must have been like, knowing there was no escape.'

'I went to have a look in the flesh. It's worse than it probably looks on TV. So please tell them. Make them understand. Never carry a weapon that can be turned against them. Always try to find a way to run. I never want to be visiting a scene like that where any of the ones from our self-defence group have ended their days caught like a rat in a trap.'

* * *

It usually took the equivalent of an earthquake to wake Trev once he was fast asleep. The quiet and pitiful meows of Adam the cat would not normally have been enough to make him so much as stir and turn over in his sleep.

But something reached into the deepest recesses of his brain to drag him back from the warmth and comfort of sleep.

He was, as usual, lying on the diagonal and occupying most of the bed, but his groping hand found no part of Ted next to him. Not even balancing right on the edge of the mattress, as he often had to because of his partner's extravagant sleeping habits.

Trev lifted his head from the pillow and forced his lids open to allow reluctant eyes to register the time from the digital clock on Ted's side of the bed. Just gone five in the morning.

He stretched out a hand to switch on a lamp, blinking at its brightness, then looked across at the closed door where Adam was sitting, complaining bitterly to himself.

Trev rolled out of bed and went to pick him up, then glanced in the wardrobe for a clue as to where Ted might have gone so early. It was his running gear which was conspicuous by its absence.

Trev got back into bed, cuddling the little cat against him.

'We're going to have to get used to it, kid,' he told Adam. 'Daddy's being a proper policeman again. You and I might hate it, but he loves it. It's what he does best. He took the desk job to please me, I know he did. But I'm not sure we're going to get him safely back behind his desk now he's got the taste of it all again. We'd better get used to keeping one another company while he gives it everything he's got, and hope he remembers to keep a little bit of himself for us.'

* * *

Ted was one of the first in to work on Saturday morning. The early run, pounding the pavements, pushing himself to the limits, followed by the sharp needles of a hot shower, had invigorated him. Filled him with an energy he hadn't noticed was missing, until it came flooding back through his veins.

As soon as Jo Rodriguez arrived, not long after him, as other officers were slowly filing into the room and finding their seats, Ted accosted him.

'Jo, I know Noah's brother and sister are really quite young, but might there be something to be gained by talking to them, perhaps? It sounds as if Ollie Martin didn't believe much of what Noah said, but might he possibly have said anything in front of them? A name, or something?

165

'If he was trying to make things better for the family, might he have talked to them, perhaps when they were all trying to get to sleep at night? Him saying things were going to get better because of what he was doing?'

Jo looked dubious. 'I suppose it's possible, boss, but if he was trying to play the father-figure, wouldn't he want to protect them as much as possible? Would he risk saying anything they might repeat somewhere which could be dangerous for them all?

'They are very young, too. It would need someone with relevant training to talk to them.'

Mari Griffiths was just taking her seat not far from where they were talking. She turned to them.

'Sorry, boss, I wasn't meaning to eavesdrop, but if you need someone to talk to young children, I've done recent update training in that. I've worked on cases of drugs-related domestic violence which often means having to talk to children who may have witnessed something.'

Ted's hesitation, although brief, was noticeable. Jo didn't miss it and wondered at its significance.

DC Mari Griffiths clearly spotted it and she bristled with indignation as she looked angrily at Ted and asked, 'Sir, do you have a problem with me being on this op for some reason? Only yesterday you were funny about me going to the loo in work time, which I'm perfectly entitled to do, and now, when I'm offering to do something I'm trained for, you look as if I've made some sort of outrageous suggestion.'

Ted held his hands up in a gesture of appeasement. He'd already checked the timings from yesterday against Maurice's notes. It seemed her visit to the ladies had been nothing more than a brief call of nature. He'd need to have a word with her at length sometime soon, to smooth things over.

He'd no idea what he was going to say to her which didn't sound as bad as it actually was. He'd made a judgement call about her based purely on the company she kept, and that was something he generally deplored.

'Can we talk about this after briefing, Mari, please? And I apologise if I gave you that impression. It wasn't intentional.

'Jo, shall we kick off?'

His DI was still looking at him curiously, as if not recognising him. Ted knew he needed to get a grip. His ever-present suspicion was starting to get in the way of him doing his job properly. Mari Griffiths' suggestion had been a perfectly reasonable one, if she had the relevant training. He would have to get it sorted and smoothed over. The last thing the enquiry needed now was for her to make a formal complaint about the attitude of him as Senior Investigating Officer towards her.

'Maybe something and nothing, boss,' Mike Hallam told him, 'but I've been checking all the witness statements from the evening Noah died for any mention of dog-walkers other than the one who found his body. There are a couple of mentions from earlier on in the evening of a man, or possibly two different men, walking bigger dogs than the one which found him. That was a...' he checked his notes, then said, 'A Bedlington terrier.'

'Do we know why the owner was walking it up that alleyway? It doesn't go anywhere and it's not exactly a nice place, especially not at night, I imagine,' Ted asked him.

'Slipped its lead, boss. The owner says it can be a bit stubborn sometimes. He usually walks it just a few yards down there to do what it needs to but no further. It was pulling to go further than usual and he didn't want to. It ran backwards, wriggled out of its collar, then went off by itself. When he went after it, he found Noah, and luckily phoned for help immediately, then stayed there until they arrived.

'But the earlier reports refer to much bigger dogs. One witness saw a man in dark clothes with a big dog he described as a German Shepherd. He said he gave them a wide birth as they both made him feel uncomfortable and the dog barked at him. This was about half a mile away. Then there was another sighting, roughly halfway between there and where Noah was found. This time the witness had no idea what breed the dog was but said it looked like a police dog, and that the man was talking on his mobile and not speaking English.'

'Boss, it has to be the same lot as last time, surely?' Jezza put in. 'It's far too big a coincidence. That means we need to be following up on Data, and that's one for me and Gina ...'

'Stop right there, Jezza. That's an issue which will need a lot of liaison and discussion before it can go any further. For now, we need to concentrate on what we can do here, around Noah's death. That remains our immediate priority.

'Mike, can you and Mari please follow up on the idea of talking to the younger brother and sister. Contact the Family Liaison Officer and see what could be gained from you going to talk to the mother again, and to the younger children. It's worth a try.'

He inclined his head in Mari's direction as he said it, hoping it would calm things for the moment.

He took himself off to his own office for the rest of the morning to go over every relevant document again. There was something, somewhere in there which they'd overlooked so far, he was sure. There was certainly something niggling away at the back of his brain which, despite his early morning run to clear this thoughts, was steadfastly staying hidden.

He ordered some sandwiches when one of the officers did a food run around lunchtime. Their arrival was his only interruption of the day, but as he began to eat his first one, he was stopped by his phone. An unknown incoming number so he answered non-committally.

Ian Bradley's voice. And he was clearly not happy. Not happy at all.

'What the fuck have you done, Ted, you bloody idiot?'

Chapter Twenty

Ted paused briefly to chew and swallow the mouthful of his lunch which he had just taken. His mind was racing. He'd been expecting to hear from Ian Bradley, if not directly, then to hear that he had been brought in as requested. He hadn't expected such a broadside directed at himself.

'I'm not quite sure what I've done that's so wrong. In light of new information I received, I thought it was time you came in and did some straight talking.'

Bradley's immediate response was more strong language. It was clear he was beyond mere anger.

'Look, I shouldn't really be even talking to you, certainly not by phone. But for some reason my instincts tell me that you're basically a decent bloke who sometimes totally fucks things up but for the best of intentions.

'Your "new information" comes from a black bloke in a black Bimmer, I imagine, who must be thick as shit if he thinks I didn't clock him. And what he saw isn't what he thinks he saw.

'Seriously, Ted, we need to talk. Urgently. But I need to trust you not to tell anyone we're going to do so, and not to get any bloody stupid ideas about trying to lift me when we meet. And believe me, I'm a lot better trained than your Bimmer-bloke, so I will spot a trap a mile away and you won't hear from me again.

'Ted, for Christ's sake, I thought you understood me when I said I don't currently trust anyone. I had hoped I could trust you, but now I'm not so sure.'

'So let's meet. Tell me your version of events. I'll come alone, and I won't be recording anything. You pick a time and place. Last time we met, you said Derek Black was your prime suspect. Next thing my officers, who were actually off duty, not on any official op, see you meeting up with him, so you must realise how that would look. But I'm prepared to listen to your version of events. Tell me when and where.'

Bradley hesitated. Ted could feel his suspicion, coming in waves over the silence. At some point, the DS was going to have to trust someone. He waited for him to say something.

Bradley sighed. 'All right. One more chance. Only one, so don't blow it. Tonight, nine o'clock. Out of town again. Well out of town. I'll phone you an hour before with a venue. But be prepared for it to change, maybe more than once, until I'm sure it's safe to meet.'

It was Ted's turn to sigh as the DS ended the call. Because he'd be working both days over the weekend, he'd at least hoped to have the evening to spend with Trev. That hope had gone out of the window following Bradley's call. He decided there was nothing to be gained by delaying breaking the news.

'How's the shopping going?' he asked when Trev answered his mobile. Ted had given him his card as a sweetener for his absence much of the weekend. He might need to do more than that once he told him he wouldn't be home until some ungodly hour, except for a quick change of clothes.

'I've bought some utterly gorgeous throws for Annie's new house. I thought her old furniture would be a bit dark in such a light setting. My next mission is to find some stunning cushions to go with them. It's just as well I'm taking the car there for the inquest, not the bike.

'Is this you phoning to say you're going to be late tonight?'

'Worse than that, I'm afraid. I have to go out again, so I'll only have time to drop in and change. Not to eat or anything else.'

'What, nothing else?' Trev's voice turned immediately mischievous. 'Will you really not have time to eat?'

'Almost certainly not. I'll have to grab some fish and chips or something when I go out, and I've no idea what time I'll be back. I've got an early start in the morning, too. We want to try to round up the knife-sellers we've got details for. Only two so far, but it's a start.

'So that means we'll have teams out opening up doors with the big red key, nice and early on a Sunday morning, when they'll be least expected. I want to be in on that, but from the warmth and safety of the control room.'

The 'big red key' was the nickname of the heavy enforcer often used by police to gain entry to properties where they might not be greeted with open arms. Ted had briefly liaised with Uniform and Firearms earlier in the day to ensure the ops could go ahead with minimum risk to officers and to the public.

He wasn't expecting the raids to yield anything of direct value to Operation Flood but he would feel better for knowing that they had at least done something in an attempt to keep lethal weapons off the streets.

* * *

Trev had a tuna pasta bake ready in the oven when Ted managed to get home for a quick change. Trev was, as usual, full of enthusiasm for his shopping adventures. Ted did his best to feign an interest in soft furnishings for his mother as he shovelled some food into his mouth after changing out of his work clothes.

He was distracted, and trying not to show it too much. He could understand why Ian Bradley wanted to take full control of their meeting, but it didn't sit well with his own inner control freak. He shouldn't be surprised that someone of Bradley's skills had spotted Virgil watching him. The big question remained why the DS had been meeting with Derek Black in the first place. The officer he'd told Ted was his prime suspect as the inside informer.

He'd managed nearly half a plateful of the food, eaten standing up leaning against a work surface in the kitchen, ready to go at any moment, when his phone rang.

Bradley's voice. Economical on words. He gave Ted a location, well outside town, then rang off before he had time to respond.

Ted put his plate down with an apologetic look.

'Sorry, that's my summons. I have to go. Thanks for making some food for me, it was very nice. I've no idea what time I'll be back.'

He made to lean in to kiss Trev on the cheek but his partner took hold of both of his arms and held him away, looking searchingly at him.

'Is this something dangerous you're doing, Ted? Are you going off somewhere on your own, without any back-up?'

'No, it's nothing like that. I just have to meet an undercover officer so it's all a bit cloak and dagger, that's all. Nothing dangerous.'

Trev's blue gaze was still locked onto Ted's face.

'I believe you, unquestioningly, about whatever you tell me, because I know you're an honest person. Except when it's work. I never know what to believe when it's work.'

'It's honestly true. There's no risk. It's just a bit clandestine. I'll be fine. Trust me. I'm a policeman.'

Ted grinned at him as he said it, kissed him on the cheek, then he was gone, picking up his car keys in the hall and closing the front door quietly behind him.

Trev picked up the nearest cat to cuddle, which was Queen, the most senior of their tribe. She purred her delight, rubbing her head against the underside of his jaw.

'He'd better come home in one piece,' he told the cat quietly.

* * *

Ted stopped to buy fish and chips on his way to the first rendezvous point, which he was convinced would not be the final destination.

He was right. Bradley changed the location twice more before Ted finally parked up on a quiet lay-by out in the sticks. There was no sign of another vehicle anywhere but before Ted had had the chance to do more than take a bite from the batter of his fried fish, he saw a tall figure appear as if from nowhere and walk towards the car.

DS Ian Bradley slid into the front passenger seat next to him, gratefully receiving the bag of fish and chips Ted put in his lap.

'Are we staying here, or moving on again?' Ted asked him.

'Staying. We're safe enough, for now.'

He fell on his fish supper like a starving man once more. Ted let him eat without interruption. He knew he'd talk when he was ready. The fact that he had turned up at all was encouraging. He could wait a while longer for an explanation.

'Anything to drink?' Bradley asked, after he'd been going at the food steadily for a good few minutes.

Ted picked up a bottle from the foot well on his side of the car.

'Mineral water,' he said, half apologetically. 'I didn't know if you were driving here ...'

Bradley threw his head back and started to laugh. It was the sort of uninhibited laughter which soon reached near hysterical point. A release of long pent-up tension.

'Bloody hell, Ted, that's funny,' he said, when he finally recovered his breath long enough to say anything without choking. 'Some of the things we get up to working in deep cover and here you are, worried I'll get booked for drink-driving.'

He took a long pull at the water then gave a loud belch.

'Oops, sorry, I've forgotten my table manners. Right, you

want to know what I was doing meeting Derek Black? Like I want to know why you put your officers onto tailing him, after I told you that's who I suspected.'

'I didn't,' Ted said simply. 'Three of my officers, with my authorisation, cruised some of the clubs in town to see if they could find Data. Not an official op at all. Genuine, if somewhat improbable, coincidence.'

'And they found him. Dealing in the gents' bogs,' Bradley said it as a statement of fact, not a question.

He paused to drink more of the water, then went on, 'Right, when I spoke to you last time I had my doubts, about Derek. But things have moved on from there at a pace and I haven't had time to update you. I was wrong about Derek. I don't now think he's the informer.'

Ted frowned at that. 'But you said you set a trap and he fell for it. Turning up at a place you'd told him about, with a bit of muscle you said you didn't fancy the look of.'

Bradley gave an embarrassed laugh. 'It just goes to show you should never judge by what you see. Turns out that was Derek's cousin, Mick, a nightclub bouncer who does a bit of cage fighting in his spare time. Derek was worried I was up to daft stuff, playing the cowboy on my own, so he wanted to bring me in. Only he didn't expect me to come quietly, hence Mick as back-up.

'Mind, I'm not saying that of itself clears Derek of any suspicion, but the latest instalment probably does. Or at least it's a very clever double bluff, if not.

'After I'd spoken to you about my suspicions, Derek contacted me, out of the blue. Left me a message in the usual place to call him, so I did. We had a long talk. He told me about his cousin. I was inclined to believe him. Then he told me that he knew that the famous Data was back on the scene and dealing openly. He said he'd keep me posted with a when and a where and we should meet up.

'That's exactly what he did. He phoned me about a bar

where he'd had a tip-off that Data was dealing. I wanted to know if he was telling me the truth this time, so I went to check the place out before I met him.

'That's when I clocked your officers coming out. They didn't see me because they weren't looking for someone outside. They were more interested in what was going on inside the bar, and in any more people going in looking to buy.

'I recognised your big black officer from when I came to talk to your team at your nick, of course. I knew one of the women must be Gina, but fair play to both of them, I couldn't really tell which. I saw your man go and get the car and the three of them sit in it. They still didn't clock me, dozy buggers. Not until I decided I better let them, so I doubled back then made a show of appearing to talk to Derek. I'd phoned him to come out at the right moment.'

'All right, so Derek told you about Data. Does that prove anything, though? In terms of clearing him as an informer. We know this gang is ruthless and ready to sacrifice people. Look at the young man who was shot dead after setting him up to look like the real Data to go for a meeting with Gina.

'Perhaps they're doing the same this time. It could well be another lookalike. Or it could even be the real Data and they've decided he's outlived his usefulness to them. They could give him up, in the sure and certain knowledge that with the things he's seen in his time with them, he's not very likely to say anything of any use to anyone. Assuming he even knows much that could lead directly to them.

'If it is the real Data and if we ever manage to arrest and convict him, they're sure to have plenty of their own people inside prisons just waiting to give him a warm welcoming reception, and he would know that.'

'I still think Data is the key to all this, and our best, if not our only, chance of getting anywhere near the famous Big Man who's behind it all. And the best way for us to do that is to do a proper follow of him. Everywhere, all the time, until he leads us to them.'

Ted paused for a swallow from his own water bottle as Bradley replied.

'You know as well as I do what a big op that would be in terms of manpower and everything else. We would need endless follow hours, by people who really know what they're doing, with constant changes of vehicle, of people, and all the rest of it. Plus every single person involved at any level would need the fullest possible vetting to make sure they had no known connections with anyone involved.

'For that reason, I would suggest that you head it up, if you can even get it signed off, and that you personally hand-pick every single person involved. I would suggest too that you should start by avoiding anyone from my old team or close to it, including Derek Black. I don't now think it's him, but I do think he might be close to whoever it is, perhaps without him suspecting a thing.

'You'd need to get clearance at very high level and again, you'd have to be sure of the person you were dealing with. How did you go about finding out who my handler was?'

'I spoke to DCS Holton at HQ. My retired Super, Jim Baker, put me in touch. Are you saying it could be the DCS?'

Bradley shook his head. 'He's someone I would trust. I'm still not coming in, though. Not until you, or someone, collars the informant once and for all. I'd feel much safer on the outside looking after myself until that happens.'

'So if you no longer think it's Derek Black, who do you think it could be?'

Bradley took another pull at his water bottle.

'Okay, if I tell you my thoughts you'll think I've been working in Drugs too long and maybe been sampling too much of the goods. I haven't. I smoke a bit of weed, of course, for the cover, as much as anything. But that's all.

'This is all based on process of elimination, mostly, with not a lot of proof behind it. Yet. Before we part tonight, I'll give you a burner phone number where you can at least leave a message for me, and I will get back to you, when it's safe to do so. Just promise me you won't bring anyone into your team, or into your confidence, without checking with me first.

'And believe me, what I'm about to tell you will seem so far-fetched that there can only be two possible explanations. One is that, as I said, I'm actually using the hard stuff and it's got the better of me.

'The other is much more simple. I'm right in my suspicions.'

Chapter Twenty-one

Ted's mind was racing as he drove back home after his meeting with Ian Bradley. The DS hadn't been exaggerating when he said his latest theory was way off the probability scale. He had also been adamant that there was no way he was coming in for the moment. Short of using his martial arts skills to overcome him, handcuff him and throw him in the back seat, there was nothing Ted could do but accept that.

Ted only agreed to let him leave once Bradley had given him the promised contact phone number and Ted had tried it out to make sure that it worked. He knew it was only temporary. Bradley could ditch it at any moment. But at least it was something.

'I've given you a lot to think about, Ted, I know that. And probably an awful lot to disbelieve. Promise me, though, whatever you do, that you'll exercise extreme caution before you breathe a word of it to anyone. Give me a bit longer to see if I can advance my theory any further. Can you do that for me?'

'I shouldn't,' Ted told him. 'I should take you in, now, myself. Something's stopping me, and I'm not sure what it is. It's certainly not that I believe everything you've told me. I need to talk to someone about this. Someone more senior. For both our sakes.'

'But you can see why I'm not willing to do that, can't you? Who would I talk to, for fuck's sake? Who have you got in mind?'

'Jim Baker,' Ted said promptly. 'I trust him completely.

He's been my boss since I first moved to Stockport. Recently retired but still consulting.'

Bradley nodded his head. 'I know Big Jim. At least by reputation. Can he be trusted?'

'He knows at first hand about betrayal by a bent copper, if that really is what we're dealing with here. And if I can't trust him, then I don't know who I can trust.

'The current acting Head of Serious Crime, while I'm back to being a proper copper, is Superintendent Sampson. Sammy. But I don't know her well enough yet to go to her with something like this. I don't know what connections, if any, she might have to your prime suspect. I know that she started her career in Manchester, but that's as much as I do know, and that's not enough to base any judgement call on.'

'I don't know much about her, either,' Bradley told him. 'I've not heard anything bad about her, but that's a long way from a ringing endorsement from me to take her into your confidence and tell her everything.

'Big Jim I can live with, though. Especially now he's retired. If he ever was passing on info at any time, he's not likely to have access to anything worthwhile now, so he's not much of an asset any more to anyone on the wrong side of the law.

'The same reasoning which makes me rule out Gina, completely. Not only because of her brother, but she was the most likely person to become a suspect when that op to bring Data in went tits up. So now, away from where the main Drugs action is, she's no use to the gang. She won't be privy to the same sort of info she could get at before. Not to mention how gutted I know she was to lose her place on the team. Why would she bring that down on herself? It makes no sense. She lived for her work.

'I know your team and Drugs are ultimately after the same people, but you're further removed from it all than Drugs are, up in the city, so she's too far out of it all now to be an asset.

'So talk to him, Ted. To Big Jim. Tell him what I've told you. All of it. Ask him what he thinks we should do next. But promise me it will go no further until you and I have talked again. And don't get any ideas of trying to trap me. You won't succeed, and it could be the end of a beautiful friendship.'

He grinned as he said it, then he opened the passenger door, slid out and disappeared into the darkness of the night.

* * *

'Planet Earth calling Ted.'

Trev had his head propped up on one bent arm, looking down at his partner as they lay in bed together.

Ted was lying staring up at the ceiling, light from street lamps shining between the curtains, where they'd been pulled in haste and not fully closed. He was clearly miles away, deep in thought.

'I enjoyed myself but I think your mind was somewhere else entirely,' Trev was telling him.

'Sorry, I just have a lot to think about at the moment, with this latest case getting more complicated all the time. I'm glad you enjoyed your shopping, though. Thanks for getting the throws and cushions for mam, she'll like those.'

Trev was still studying him, his expression teasing.

'What colour are they?' he asked.

Ted frowned, trying to concentrate. 'Light coloured. Like early autumn.'

Trev was laughing at him now. 'Ted, you're hopeless. If it was a murder victim you could tell me the site of every stab wound after one glance, no doubt. But not a bad try. Cream, sage and a hint of rust. They'll go perfectly in her new living room.'

'I promise I'll try to get down when she's ready to move in. To help as much as I can. It's just all a bit full on at the moment. You know how it is. And I have to be up and out first thing tomorrow, with the prospect of another long day beckoning.'

'But you're not going to be out doing anything dangerous yourself, are you? You promised.'

'No, I'll be safely indoors, drinking tea with the Duty Inspector, who just happens to be Kevin Turner tomorrow morning, so it will be like old times, me and Kev back in harness together.'

Trev was settling himself down in preparation for sleep. For the moment, at least, Ted had enough room to lie on his back in comfort. He knew it wouldn't last, once Trev fell asleep and started spreading his long legs and his arms to the four corners of the bed.

Ted planted a gentle kiss on his partner's cheek. A small amount of discomfort was a modest price to pay for the amount of support and understanding of the demands of his work which he received in return.

* * *

'Is this going to help with your murder enquiry, Ted?' Inspector Kevin Turner asked him as the two of them sat together to oversee the early morning raid on the knife sellers, at two separate addresses in the still-slumbering town.

'Probably not directly,' Ted told him. 'One of these two sold a knife to Noah. The other's price was too high for him. But now we've identified them, I at least want them put out of business, if not taken off the patch altogether.

'We're likely to be looking at more of the military types we've met before for Noah's death, with their own weapons, and at the moment, we have no direct link to them. They won't have been buying from small-time dealers like these. But this raid will be something constructive, and we all need a bit of a boost to morale with a case like this.'

'Any time we can ever do anything to help, you know you

only have to ask. Anything. None of us likes to see kids get killed at all, let alone like this one was. Especially those of us with kids of our own, and grand-kids.'

'It doesn't help that we've got a leak, from the inside.'

Ted had no qualms about discussing the situation with Kevin, in the broadest terms. They'd worked together for long enough to have a solid mutual trust.

'Do you have a suspect in mind?'

'I don't. But I know a man who does. The trouble is, his theory is so far-fetched I'm not sure who to take it to, to be honest. It needs to be someone senior, but someone who will at least listen and not think I've lost the plot for even entertaining the idea.'

'Big Jim,' Kevin said decidedly. 'You know you can trust Jim with anything, and he will always listen without judging. I'd talk to him, if I were you.'

Then he sat up straighter in his seat and said, 'Here we go, entry to both premises in ten seconds and counting.'

The raids were being meticulously coordinated so they happened at exactly the same time at the two properties, at opposite ends of the town. That way there was virtually zero chance of one of the arms dealers warning off the other for any reason.

Because there was no way of knowing if knives would be the only weapons on the premises at either address, Ted had insisted on a Firearms presence. Those officers would be the first into the properties as soon as the doors ceded to the weight of the heavy enforcers.

Even within the safety of the control room, Ted could feel the adrenaline racing through his body. He'd been in that situation so many times before, first through the door and not knowing exactly what would be lying in wait for him and his team beyond.

It was all over in moments, with no shots fired. The teams had the advantage of complete surprise. Their targets were both fast asleep in bed with clearly no inkling of what lay in store for them. The first they would have known about any of it was the resounding thump of the enforcer hitting the door then the loud shouts of 'Armed police! Stand still!' accompanied by the heavy tread of boots on floors and stairs as the officers streamed in, going from room to room, then calling out as each person was accounted for and secured.

'Job's a good 'un,' Kevin announced with a note of satisfaction in his voice as Ted let out a pent-up sigh of relief. 'If we achieve nothing else today, that should be two less scrotes to make our job a lot harder by giving the youngsters the means to kill one another or get themselves killed.'

* * *

Talking to Big Jim on a Sunday morning was never going to happen. He was a religious man. Always had been. Sung Eucharist mid-morning followed by the Sunday papers, then a long and leisurely lunch. Not always possible when he'd been working, but now he was his own boss - as long as Bella agreed - he could do as he pleased for the weekends.

Ted sent him a text at a time when he hoped the morning service would have finished, or at least Jim would have had his phone on silent, asking him to call when he could. He had plenty to be going on with for the time being. He wanted to oversee the interviews of the knife sellers brought in after the raid, once they had been processed. There was still an outside chance that something might come up in interview which would link in to Operation Flood.

The news that the boy to whom he had sold a knife had ended up stabbed to death by it clearly rattled the man they knew, from the mobile phone exchange, had supplied Noah Brooks with the lethal and illegal butterfly knife. His name was Wilkins and he was a strangely bland and inoffensive type to be involved in the import and sale of prohibited weapons.

DC Mari Griffiths, from Manchester, Derek Black's on/off girlfriend, was interviewing him, while Ted watched over the monitor. She was good, too, he had to concede to himself. Persistent. She kept returning to things he would have picked up on and wanted more detailed answers to.

'I'll ask you again, Mr Wilkins, did the boy, Noah Brooks, say anything to you about why he wanted to arm himself with an illegal weapon?'

The man made a gesture, spreading his hands in feigned innocence.

'You know what these kids are like. They big themselves up. Make themselves out to be more important than they are. He said he was carrying stuff so he needed protection. Stuff for someone he called Mr Big, or the Big Man, or something like that, anyway. I've heard it all before.'

'Yet you knowingly supplied him with a knife which you knew to be illegal to supply and to carry, especially to someone of his age.'

Another evasive gesture. 'If I hadn't, he'd only have gone somewhere else and probably paid over the odds for something rubbish. And at least I only sell knives. A lot of the other dealers, they sell guns, too. I won't have anything to do with supplying guns for kids. It just ends up with killings.'

He seemed immune to the irony of his own words. He had no way of knowing whether or not the knife he had happily sold to a young boy would be used to kill someone, and he seemed not to care. With the details they had from Ollie Martin's phone, they had enough to charge Wilkins with supplying the weapon to a person under the age of eighteen, and for that he could be facing an unlimited fine plus up to six months in prison. One less such type to worry about on the patch.

Ted made himself a note to have a word with Mari Griffiths when she'd finished all the formalities, to acknowledge the good job she'd done. It might hopefully go some way to smoothing things over with her, and he believed in praise where it was due.

He got a phone call from Jim Baker at roughly the time he imagined he would have got home from church. Jim was only too happy to agree to come in for a chat, off the budget, after lunch. Ted imagined it would once again give him a valid excuse to avoid garden centres or stately homes and gardens. Jim was a keen gardener himself, but his interest didn't extend to looking at other people's historical ones, or doing anything other then going into a garden centre with a fixed idea in his mind of what he wanted to buy.

Ted had the kettle on ready for his mid-afternoon arrival. He decided to take the risk of pinching some of Sammy's stronger coffee. He hoped she wouldn't object, in the circumstances. It might be more to Jim's taste.

'I don't mind if you've brought me in for nothing at all, Ted. I honestly don't. I never thought I'd be nostalgic about the sudden call in with a big case. But just occasionally, I'm pathetically grateful for the excuse. So, what can I help with?'

If Jim noticed an improvement in the coffee he didn't comment. But he didn't pull his usual face or complain about it being like dishwater, as he often did, which was something.

'I honestly didn't know where to go with this one, Jim. It's a real hot potato. A word to the wrong person could be catastrophic. But at least I know I can trust you, one hundred per cent.'

'I should bloody well hope so. After all we've been through together, over the years. Very few people have ever seen me drunk, let alone crying like a baby, and you've seen both. And I know you've never breathed a word, which means a lot.'

'I've spoken to Ian Bradley again, at length. To say he was furious would be an understatement. He didn't like me speaking to the DCS.'

Big Jim snorted into his coffee. 'He's getting paranoid if he doesn't trust Don Holton. Is he claiming there's some sort of conspiracy going right to the top? Because if he is, he's been smoking the wrong stuff.'

Ted shook his head. 'It's not the DCS he's worried about. It's his handler. It's DI Dave Usher he says he doesn't trust.'

Chapter Twenty-two

Big Jim was quiet for a moment, taking another thoughtful swallow of his coffee, still with no adverse comment. Then he looked at Ted and said, 'That's the biggest load of old bollocks I've heard in a long time. Are you sure you're not being played for a fool, Ted?'

'I'm not sure of anything on this one,' Ted admitted, 'except that we know there's a leak and has been for some time, and we don't know where it's coming from.'

'But a DI, and an undercover officer handler at that? What would be his motive? If it's purely financial, he'd need a bloody secure account somewhere like the Cayman Islands because he'd know how easily an internal investigation could get access to all his financial affairs. He can't be that stupid - he made DI relatively young.

'I grant you he probably easily has both means and opportunity. But it's the motive which has me struggling at the moment. What does Bradley say about him, about his background?'

'He's not a joiner. He seldom goes for a drink with the team, even after a good result. Obsessively private about his personal life, so no one knows all that much about him.'

Jim grunted at that. 'Nowt wrong with keeping your home life private. That could equally apply to you, Ted. Does that mean we should start suspecting you?'

Ted spread his hands in mock offence. 'I throw a party for the team every Christmas,' he smiled. Then he was serious again. 'But from what Bradley said, Usher is very closed on that front. Unusually so. All Bradley knows is that he's married, seemingly happily, and they have a teenage daughter. Bradley said he did hear on the grapevine that the daughter was very ill a couple of years ago. Hospitalised, touch and go, that sort of thing, but seems to be all right now. But that was from station gossip, nothing concrete, and we all know that's not always reliable. Although if he's had hefty medical bills for any private treatment, that might well have given him a financial motive.'

'But it's only five minutes since Bradley was telling you the mole was definitely this DC Black and he'd tricked him into revealing himself. You're sure that Bradley isn't just becoming paranoid because he's been under cover for too long? Is he using and is that clouding his judgement?'

'He smokes a bit of weed and admits to it. That rather goes with the territory, I imagine. But setting motive aside for now, Usher certainly has the knowledge to be an informer. We kept Drugs in the loop on our attempts to bring in Data, that time when he slipped neatly through our fingers. He'd have had access to such information all along. In fact he'd have access to pretty much everything to do with recent enquiries.'

'But so would anyone else on the team or close to it, including Bradley. Is he spinning you a line to stop you looking into him too closely?'

Ted shook his head. 'He really had no reason to contact me at all. He seemed to be genuinely concerned for Gina Shaw's safety, which is why I pulled her back in, thanks to his tip-off. Why would he do that, if he's the informer?'

'Buggered if I know,' Big Jim admitted. 'Smokescreen, perhaps?

'Presumably you've asked me here for some words of wisdom on how to proceed with this. I have to confess, I haven't a clue. This is one occasion when I'm quite glad I'm not involved. It's a bloody minefield, whichever way you tread. But you definitely need to get clearance from higher up before you can do anything. You could do worse than start by talking to Sammy Sampson. No doubt she'd have some sound advice to give. And you know by now she doesn't mince her words, so prepare for an earful, if she thinks it's as far-fetched an idea as I do.'

Big Jim looked up to the ceiling at Ted's barely perceptible hesitation and said, 'Bloody hell, Ted, don't tell me you've turned so paranoid you suspect Sammy? You must realise what an uphill struggle she's had to make superintendent in CID, being a mere woman. And let's not kid ourselves that there's no leftover vestiges of sexism in the police, because we both know that's just bollocks. Things are improving slowly, but there are still too many -isms where there shouldn't be any, and there's no point denying it.'

'I don't suspect her, no, although you know me, I'm never keen on anyone going over my things. But I don't really know her well enough to talk to about something like this. You've known me for years and you think I've lost the plot over this, don't you? So what might she say?'

'I wouldn't go that far. I've known you long enough to know your judgement is usually sound. Although you've had your moments. But don't lose sight of correct procedure, which you know perfectly well would be to take what you've been told to your immediate senior officer. And that is, of course, currently Sammy, especially as she is now Acting Head of Serious Crime.

'She'd probably need to go a lot higher up, too, with a hot potato like this. If we are looking at serious police corruption, you know as well as I do that it will need to be investigated independently, from officers outside this force - outside the area, too, preferably - and with no connections to anyone serving in it.

'You called me in to ask my advice and that's it. Follow correct procedure. Discuss it with Sammy. I've said my piece, now it's up to you whether or not you take any notice of what I've suggested or if you decide to go off somewhere doing your own thing. But be bloody careful if you opt for that route. No one likes a whistle-blower. Especially if they get it wrong.'

* * *

After Jim had left, reluctantly, as he'd received a summons from Bella that she was waiting to be taken out on a promised trip, Ted decided to settle down to something he was good at - report writing.

Big Jim had originally asked Ted to join his team, his first experience of CID, on the strength of a detailed report which Ted had done for him at short notice. He was good at detail. It would help him to put his own thoughts in order and would also give him a written document he could present to Sammy Sampson, and anyone else who would need to be involved. It could set out in simple terms what information he had and what he felt was needed to make a balanced decision on who should be the target of any enquiry going forward into the identity of their inside informer.

It should have been a simple task. It was turning out to be increasingly depressing the more he wrote, as it became clear that everything was based on suspicion and conjecture. Ted knew that if any of his team had handed him a report so thin on facts he would have thrown it straight back and told them to make a proper job of it.

The best he could hope for was that if he presented it to Sammy, and she in turn agreed it should go further, it would at least show a need for an in-depth enquiry into what had been going wrong. It was urgent, too, because clearly, with the increasingly strong links between Operation Flood and the drugs gang, they couldn't make any progress as long as there was a risk that the people they were hunting were in the know at every step.

Once he'd polished it as much as he could, he went to find Jo for a sit-rep on any developments.

'I had an email from Professor Nelson this morning, surprisingly,' Jo told him. 'I thought she'd be having a weekend off like most normal mortals do, I believe. I thought it was only silly sods like us who worked through weekends and pretended it was worth it for the overtime.

'Anyway she says she's been working on comparing the knife wounds from Kane Lomax, our Body in the Bowl, to those found on young Noah's body. From the military knives, not the butterfly knife, because we've now been told that he bought that one himself. She says she hopes to have some further information on that tomorrow morning. She's apparently planning on using the comparison work as an exercise for her pathology students.'

'Even if she can prove a link, it doesn't fill me with optimism, I have to say. They haven't left us a single usable link to them anywhere so far. Any DNA or fingerprints they may have left are unlikely to lead to anyone on record in this country or any other database we might get access to,' Ted told him. 'They'll be anonymous, and specially chosen because of that.'

'You're unusually pessimistic, boss. We have to keep going on the basis that somewhere there'll be the key, no matter how small, to take us a step forward at least.

'Meanwhile we've a couple of fresh leads to follow up. We're still looking at CCTV footage and we've found a man in black getting a big brute of a dog out of a van on the evening Noah was killed, and within easy walking distance of the murder scene.'

Seeing Ted about to ask a question, he replied to it before it was posed. 'Usual story, boss. A lot of hours to trawl through and we've only just got to it. We started with all the closer stuff first, of course. Hard to pick out the reg number of the van but we're working on getting it enhanced. If it is to do with our case, no doubt the plates will be false or cloned, but we can't overlook anything.

'And speaking of leads with a time lag, you aren't going to like this, but again there does appear to be a valid reason for the delay in it getting to us.

'We've had a call from a duty sergeant in Altrincham, about a Misper. Apparently a young woman has been going into their nick roughly once a week for some time now, to report her boyfriend as missing. They've gone through the motions but she hasn't been taken all that seriously because she doesn't know her boyfriend's name, she told them. Only his nickname.'

Ted was frowning, already ahead of him.

'I'm getting a bad feeling about what you're going to tell me.'

Jo nodded. 'Sorry to say, boss, that your bad feeling is probably right. The sergeant told me the young woman has learning difficulties - Down's syndrome - and because she couldn't supply many details, no real name, no age, no idea where he's from, where he works, or anything else, they've initially treated it as a bit of a fantasy on her part. An imaginary boyfriend, if you like.

'It wasn't, in fact, until her third visit that anyone started to take it seriously and do some proper investigating. It looks as if the reports had been cuffed up until then, but the sergeant promised me a witch-hunt is under way and backsides will be kicked.

'Checks were then made. The young woman, Robyn Pascoe, she's called, has her own flat but the parents live nearby and appear to be supportive. They weren't aware of a significant boyfriend. They did say she tends not to understand the nature of relationships at a normal adult level, so anyone who says a kind word to her becomes her boyfriend, in her imagination.

'Officers have now also asked at her workplace. Robyn has a part-time job waiting on at the cafe in a garden centre. They said the same thing. She forms the wrong impression of what people say to her, and they hadn't heard of any budding romance.

'Luckily, finally, a PC with a bit of gumption went round to the flat and sure enough, there's plenty of evidence of a male presence having been staying there. Said PC went as far as bagging a few items which could hopefully give up some DNA on the elusive, presumed missing, boyfriend, which might be very good news for us, because it might well link in with our earlier cuckooing case.'

Jo was smiling now at the expression on Ted's face.

'I can see that you're way ahead of me. The only thing Robyn does know about her boyfriend is that he calls himself Data.'

'Right, let's get Jezza and Gina round to talk to Robyn as soon as possible. Jezza was really good with Abigail Buller in our similar case, and Gina has the advantage of having seen Data up close on more than one occasion. She might be able to check that this really is the same person, if she talks to Robyn.

'We need to turn the place inside out to see if Data has left any trace of anything useful at all, but that means we need to be very sure Robyn is capable of giving informed consent for a search. Otherwise we need to liaise with the parents. We don't want the slightest slip-up in procedure which could come back to bite us in the future.

'What's the name of the PC who did all the right things?'

'PC Kate Prescott.'

'Make sure someone thanks her, from me, for being on the ball. And let's see if she's free to go with Jezza and Gina to talk some more to Robyn.'

Jo was still smiling. 'Not so pessimistic now, then?'

'I'm staying realistic. I don't for a moment think Data will obligingly have left anything incriminating in the form of names and addresses, or anything like that. It's possible, even probable, that he has several "girlfriends" on the go so he has somewhere to crash whenever he needs to. Altrincham suggests money, perhaps ...'

Jo nodded at that. 'From the address, I'd say yes, very much so.'

'In which case he's not likely to abandon Robyn unless he has a very good reason to leave there. Let's get the two of them over there as soon as possible, preferably with PC Prescott.

'Oh, and Jo, when you brief Jezza and Gina for this, tell them they need to raise with the parents the fact that Abigail ended up pregnant from her time with Data. Obviously they can't give away any confidential information, but they need to find a way to float the idea, at least.

'If the parents weren't even aware that Robyn was seeing someone, let alone living with them, there's a chance, as with Abigail, that there's been no thought of any such thing.'

* * *

'It's nice to have you home at a decent time, for once. You look a bit more positive, too, than you have done lately. Have you had a breakthrough with the case?' Trev asked Ted when he got home and found him in the kitchen, laying the table, a glass of wine to hand.

Ted greeted him with a kiss then bent to stroke each of the cats in turn. Adam was, as ever, first in the queue.

'Not exactly, but we've at least got a positive direction to go off in in search of one, and we were really in need of something because it's been a frustrating case so far.'

'How are you getting on with your new lady boss? Sammy?'

'All right, so far. She's relaxed and informal, for one thing. The trouble is, tomorrow I need to talk to her about something which might make her think I'm completely deranged. Or very gullible, at the least. Even Jim had his doubts when I ran it past him.'

'I can't think of anyone less gullible off hand. But then, she doesn't know you like I do.

'Is there anything you want to do this evening while you're back at a decent time, for once? Go out on the bike for a bit of a blow, or something? Supper won't be ready for at least an hour. Longer, if I turn the heat down.'

'I'm not sure about going out, unless you want to? I just feel like relaxing and forgetting all about work for once.'

'In which case,' Trev told him, putting the glass down away from the cats and taking Ted's hand, 'I might have the perfect suggestion.'

Chapter Twenty-three

Jezza took her own car to drive herself and Gina Shaw over to Altrincham. Now the team was expanding in numbers, service vehicles were in high demand, so mileage had been authorised on private cars for specified use.

They were going to pick up PC Kate Prescott first from her own station. She had arranged for them to meet Robyn Pascoe and her parents at the flat where Robyn lived. Robyn wasn't at work on Mondays because she did a shift at the garden centre cafe on Saturdays.

Kate was young, keen, and, thankfully for the enquiry, on the ball. She started by apologising as she got into the back of the car.

'I'm sorry this wasn't picked up on sooner at our end. It should have been treated seriously from the start but I think someone put the boyfriend idea down to wishful thinking from Robyn, when they really should have taken it further.'

'What put you onto the link with our cases? Jezza asked her.

'They wanted a female officer to talk to Robyn. Just going through the motions really, as it was the third or fourth time she'd been in and it hadn't been taken seriously up to then. She seemed to me to be genuine in what she was saying, and the name Data rang a bell with me. When I'd taken Robyn's statement and she'd gone, I ran the details through the system, which I don't think anyone had done before, and I got a match on the alias Data from your cases.

'I took it to my sergeant and he got in touch with your team. I think that rather hit the panic button at our nick because it hadn't been picked up on before.'

'My turn to be sexist now,' Jezza told her, grinning at her briefly in the rear view mirror, 'but let me guess. You were the first female officer to talk to Robyn and to look into what she said?'

Kate laughed at that. 'To be fair to my mere male colleagues who were more dismissive, because Robyn's speech is a little indistinct, there could be a tendency to assume her cognitive skills are less than they are. Especially when she's trying to report a Misper and doesn't even know their name. I found her easy to understand.'

'That's good to know,' Jezza told her. 'We needed a Makaton interpreter to talk to our victim of the delightful Data, Abigail.'

'I also found that she has quite good basic literacy and numeracy skills, and when I went to the flat, she keeps it beautifully. Very house proud. She went to a specialist further education college, residential, where she was taught to be as independent as possible. I was lucky to find a comb and a toothbrush which she said were Data's, still in the bathroom, which I've not yet sent for testing as I didn't know what you wanted me to do.'

'Fantastic, thank you,' Jezza told her. 'We have his DNA from our cuckooing case but he's not on the system anywhere, no previous. But if we can match him to your samples, we'll at least know where he's spent some time recently, which is a real breakthrough for us. And we really need to get a positive lead to Data. He's our only real connection to the drugs gang we've been tracking without success for too long.

'I imagine this is all going to come as a big shock to the parents, if it's the first they've heard about a boyfriend, but our Data has form for such things, and most of it is pretty nasty.'

She filled Kate in on more of the detail as she drove. Her

description of some of Data's antics, particularly the porn films, drew a few expletives from her back-seat passenger.

'Does Robyn have any way to contact Data and has she been trying to?' Gina asked.

'I asked her about that,' Kate told him. 'She said she has a mobile phone number for him and she's been trying it, but at the moment he's not replying to any of her calls or texts.'

'With the phone number, at least, we might be able to get somewhere,' Gina replied. 'What we really need is to try to get Data to go back and visit her, then follow him to see where he might lead us. But to do that, we'd need to get him to show himself. If there's money about where Robyn is concerned, judging by his record so far, he's not just going to drop her until he has to. Unless he's found another easy target who's worth even more to him.'

'I think we need to be quite sparing with what we tell Robyn and her parents at this stage,' Jezza cautioned. 'It's presumably going to come as enough of a shock to her family that she's been seeing a boyfriend at all, never mind hearing that it's quite possible that he's been filming their most intimate moments together and plastering them all over the internet.'

They agreed that to begin with, Jezza would take the lead in both the questioning and deciding what details were divulged, and that those would stay on a strictly as and when necessary basis.

Robyn Pascoe's home turned out to be a spacious ground floor flat in a large semi-detached house on a pleasant tree-lined road. The whole area reeked of money. There was a sleek Audi parked in the driveway, which Kate told them belonged to Robyn's parents, who lived not far away and had agreed to be present.

Robyn herself opened the door to them before they needed to ring the bell. She had clearly been looking out for their arrival. She smiled at Kate as at an old friend.

'Hello, Kate, please come in,' then to the others, 'Hello, I'm

Robyn, please come in.'

The perfect hostess. Welcoming important guests. Jezza felt a sudden pang of guilt that this was another young woman whose heart she was likely to break with the news that the handsome boyfriend she thought she'd acquired was not all he had appeared to be. Just as she had had to do with Abigail Buller.

Kate saved the introductions until Robyn had shown them into a bright, expensively furnished sitting room. Jezza was herself from a moneyed background. She recognised the signs. Nothing flashy or ostentatious. Absolutely nothing which might have been delivered in a flat pack from some Scandinavian chain store.

The couple who rose from the sofa as they entered the room were both older than Jezza had anticipated. Perhaps in their sixties. Robyn herself looked no more than early twenties.

'I'm Ralph Pascoe, Robyn's father, and this is my wife Miriam.'

The man introduced himself and his wife and shook hands all round. Quietly self-assured, a handshake confidently firm without the need to grip hard to assert himself. A man no doubt used to being in charge of any situation.

'Please sit down,' Robyn instructed them. 'Would you like some tea, or some coffee?'

'No, thank you, Robyn,' Jezza told her. 'I think Kate told you, Gina and I would very much like to talk to you about your boyfriend, Data.'

'I'm sorry to interrupt, officer,' Ralph Pascoe put in, his tone still polite, 'but the news that Robyn had a boyfriend at all came as a total surprise to my wife and me. We had no idea. He was certainly never here when we visited, which we do often.'

I can well believe that, Jezza thought to herself. Data was far too fly to show himself to his target's parents too early on, if at all.

Robyn gave a little girl's giggle and blushed as she said,

'Data wanted it to be a surprise. We were going to tell you when we got engaged. Data was going to buy me a ring.'

Ralph Pascoe smiled fondly enough towards his daughter but then he became the consummate businessman as he turned back to Jezza.

'Fortunately, officer, I keep a very close eye on my daughter's finances. I'm all too aware that, although she is very good with simple figures, it would be so very easy for someone unscrupulous to separate her from rather a lot of money.

'Would it be indiscreet of me to ask if one of the reasons this Data is clearly known to the police is that this is not the first time he's done something like this?'

'Please call me Jessica,' Jezza told him, surprising herself with the rare use of her full name. Something about this setting, these people, had somehow transported her back to her own youth, before she started using the abbreviated form of her name. 'And I'm afraid I can't discuss all the details of our enquiry.'

Pascoe was looking at her shrewdly. He understood the message. His wife appeared equally as sharp. She told Jezza, 'I imagine there could be other implications to consider about this liaison but thankfully, that is all taken care of, so that of itself presents no worries.'

They were both certainly on the ball. It made Jezza's job easier, not having to spell everything out. At least it meant there was not an unplanned pregnancy to be dealt with this time. She turned again to Robyn.

'Robyn, how long is it since you last saw Data?'

'About a week,' Robyn told her promptly.

Her mother smiled at her and told Jezza, 'Robyn's good at some numbers, but not dates, for some reason. Her week might be someone else's month.'

Kate spoke at that point. 'Have you seen Data since you first reported him missing at the police station?'

The young woman shook her head at that and said, 'No,

that's why I went back again in two days.'

'Just over three weeks since the first report, then,' Kate confirmed for Jezza's benefit.

Pascoe was frowning now and asked his daughter, 'Darling, did you give this Data a key to the flat?'

'Yes, daddy, I did. So he wouldn't have to wait outside in the rain if he got here before I finished work.'

He stood up and took out a mobile phone. 'Excuse me, please, Jessica, I'll just phone my secretary to arrange a locksmith to come to the house as soon as possible. Obviously my wife and I will stay here with Robyn until the locks have been changed. In case this charming Data person should decide to come back.'

'Have you heard anything from Data at all since you saw him last?' Jezza asked.

Robyn shook her head. 'No. I keep trying to phone him, but even when I leave a message, he doesn't phone me back. That's why I went to the police because I was worried about him. Do you think he's all right? Perhaps he's had an accident, do you think?'

The look of hope on her face was almost too much for Jezza. She found herself struggling to stay professional. It was going to get harder, too, with the rest of the questions she was going to have to ask Robyn.

'I hope we'll be able to help to find him, now my colleagues and I are on the case. Robyn, did Data ever take any photos of the two of you? At any time? When you were perhaps alone together in the flat? And did he ever bring any of his friends round here?'

She saw the mother's hand go to her face, which had suddenly paled visibly. She was quick on the uptake; had seen the direction in which Jezza's questions could be heading.

'He wanted to. He said we'd have a party, for our engagement, and he'd bring some of his friends. He asked me if I had any friends to invite, from where I went to college. But then I haven't seen him for a week so I don't know when the party is going to be.'

'Well, the first thing we need to do is to find Data,' Jezza told Robyn. 'May I please have the telephone number you have for him, and your own number too, Robyn?'

Gina Shaw posed her questions next. She needed to know if the person Robyn referred to as Data was, in fact, the one they were looking for. Robyn's description was vague - black hair, brown skin, dark eyes, handsome - so Gina produced the artist's impression she herself had helped to create. The only likeness they had of the person known as Data.

Robyn beamed and nodded enthusiastically. 'Yes, that's Data. Look, mummy, isn't he nice looking? That's my boy-friend. We're going to get engaged.'

When they'd finished, Ralph Pascoe showed them to the door, but not before Robyn had hugged each of them in turn and thanked them for coming.

'You'll all be Robyn's new best friends now. Her trusting nature and genuine love for everyone are her biggest dangers. But don't worry, my wife and I will be keeping a much closer watch over her from now on. We want her to enjoy her inde-pendence, but not at the expense of her safety.'

* * *

This time Ted's quiet tap on his own office door was a mere formality as he did it at the same time as opening the door and walking in.

'Before we start, I have to confess to pinching some of your coffee for Big Jim, who paid me a visit yesterday.'

Superintendent Sammy Sampson's face was perfectly straight as she told him, 'I know. I count the grains whenever I leave the office. There were a hundred and sixty-three missing this morning.'

Then she laughed out loud at her own joke. 'No problem at

all. Feel free to help yourself any time, especially if it will save poor Jim from that cheap, weak stuff you have.'

She switched in an instant to more serious mode as she said, 'More importantly, was this a meeting of old friends, or something to do with work? And if the latter, can I ask why you were discussing it with him and not with me first?'

Ted took a seat in response to her nod. Then he answered her frankly, 'Because it all sounds so improbable I wanted to run it past someone who knows me well before bringing it to you.'

He'd brought a copy of his report, scant on fact though it was, which he put on the desk in front of Sammy, then gave her a detailed summary of everything he knew so far. She listened in neutral silence, her face not giving anything away.

When he'd finished, she said, 'So because you don't know me well, discovered that I started out in Manchester, and I now have free run of your office and files, you needed reassurance that you could take me into your confidence. Is that a fair summary?'

Her expression was still impossible to read. Ted risked a grin as he said, 'I wouldn't be much of a copper if I didn't suspect everyone, would I?'

She laughed at that. 'That's what I like to hear. Never trust anyone.'

As the laughter stopped she was once more serious and professional. 'Right, this is definitely something which needs clearance at higher level. I'll get on to the DCS. Luckily he and I go back a long way. I know him well enough to know what Don is really short for, and it's not Donald, as people assume. Then you and I need to go and see him and get clearance to run a proper op to find this mole once and for all and deal with them.

'I can't abide a bent copper, whatever their reasons. The job is bloody hard enough, especially these days with all the politically correct crap that gets thrown at us, and every bugger filming everything we do to stick on social media. Usually doctored and out of context, of course.

'So let's get this sorted, once and for all. I'll try and get an appointment for us at the end of the day, and I'll get 'Eck to drive us there. Then once we've sorted out the business side of things, the four of us can go for a bevy together. Just like old times.'

Chapter Twenty-four

Sammy Sampson was in luck with her call to Detective Chief Superintendent, Don Holton. He had a scheduled desk day, he was groaning under a mountain of paperwork, so the prospect of a night out on the tiles with old friends at the end of it all certainly appealed.

He suggested that she and Ted should be at his office for five so they could discuss whatever it was they needed to talk to him about without interruption. Then 'Eck could leave the official car parked at HQ and the four of them could take a taxi somewhere to spend a convivial evening.

'Are we eating as well as sinking a few, and is it likely to be a long session? Just so I can warn the wife,' he asked her.

'Oh, I think we should, don't you? It's been too long since you and I went out on the lash together - Donovan.'

'You breathe one word about my full name anywhere ...'

Sammy's only reply was to start signing *Mellow Yellow* as she ended the call.

She tried Ted's phone to put him in the picture. She was still supposed to limit the amount of walking around that she did. His number was engaged so she left him a message then, with a sigh, she turned to her own admin tasks for the day.

Ted had had a call from DS Rhys Morgan at Carmarthen.

'I wanted to check that your partner was still going to be able to come down to be with your mam for the inquest on Friday, Ted. It would be nice if she has family with her, but if not you can trust us to look after her properly.'

'Thanks for checking but yes, it's all sorted. He'll drive down on Thursday evening and probably spend a day or so there after the inquest. They get on well together, and I'm likely to be flat out again this weekend.'

'Good to hear someone gets on with their mother-in-law. Mine probably thinks public boiling in oil is too good for me.

'Anyway, we're really hoping for an unlawful killing conclusion at the inquest, which would green-light a full scale murder enquiry for us, and that would be the best possible outcome. We're pretty confident, with what we've got so far. We can usually rely on the coroner to do the right thing, but we both know it's never a foregone conclusion, eh? So keep your fingers crossed for us.'

Ted gave Sammy a quick call back in response to her message. He groaned inwardly when she told him the plans for the evening, after the formal meeting with the DCS. Since he'd given up drinking when his dad had died, Ted was never keen on the kind of boozy evenings which were still quite a feature in the job. It didn't seem as if he was being given much choice with this one. It was presented to him as a done deal, by two senior officers.

He gave Trev a quick call to warn him he'd be late, and to confirm arrangements for the inquest. Trev was full of excitement and bursting with news of his own.

'I'm a godfather! Willow's had the baby. A little girl. They're calling her Aspen Jade. She sent me the photos and she is too adorable. I can't wait to meet her. But of course I'll make sure Annie is all right before I even think about that.

'Are you sure we shouldn't think about adopting, Ted?'

'Very sure,' Ted told him dryly. 'And so would you be, with a teething baby whose cries probably even you wouldn't sleep through.'

'Another kitten, then? You know seeing baby things makes me broody.'

'No more kittens.' Ted tried to make his tone firm, but he

was never sure if Trev would get the message. 'Anyway, I was calling to say sorry but I've no idea what time I'll be back to-night.'

He explained the plans for the evening then went on, 'I'll try not to make it too late. I might not have a lot of choice, though. I think Sammy likes to party, and she outranks me. Plus we're going with the DCS who outranks me even more.'

He ended the call, wondering how many cats he might be going home to, then went to find Jo.

'Jo, we keep hearing about a black 4x4, but we're not having much luck tracking it down. Is it worth putting someone onto that as a dedicated action?'

'We've consistently drawn a blank on that front, boss.' Jo was staying formal as they were in the incident room, with other officers about. 'The one Steve went after when it picked up Data from near the park was on false plates, when we ran it through the system, so we got nowhere, and it disappeared into thin air.

'If it's still around I think we both know it will be on differ-ent plates now. My gut feeling is that one has been sold on out of the country long since. You're talking serious money for one of those things. Well into six figures, some of the top of the range ones.'

'Which is why there can't be all that many around here. Maybe we can try tracking down anything like it registered in the area. I imagine there are a few in Wilmslow or Alderley Edge. Proper WAG-Wagons, I would think. But yes, there's nothing to be lost by putting someone onto going through the system and tracking anything like that on our patch or beyond.'

The wealthy towns in Cheshire had long been a magnet for football stars and their other halves, the famous Wives and Girlfriends or WAGs, who could afford the elevated property prices there.

'Put Maurice onto finding them all,' Ted told him. 'You know he's good at anything like that.'

Jo made a face. 'Good, methodical, but not quick, boss. Can we really afford the time?'

'Can we afford not to at least explore that avenue?' Ted countered. 'We've heard that Noah spoke about a black 4x4, and that's not the first time we've heard of such a vehicle being mentioned. Put Maurice on it, but chivvy him a bit if he's making a meal of it. And can you liaise with Road Patrol. Ask them for a campaign of stopping and document checking any big 4x4s on our patch. Start with the top of the range ones, don't bother yet with cheap foreign imports. And tell them especially black ones, although if they've changed it, they might have changed colour, too. Use the excuse of increasing thefts; checking and offering advice. And of course we need to know about it immediately if any of them have a dwarf as a passenger.'

Jo laughed at that. 'Of course, if this was crime fiction, that's exactly what would happen. It would be great if real life was like that.'

'On the subject of the other matter I mentioned,' Ted was being cagey again, with people within earshot. 'I'm going up to HQ late afternoon with Sammy to meet with the DCS. The two things are totally intertwined. I don't see how we can tackle either without dealing with the other. So let me know when Jezza and Gina get back. I want to hear what the latest is on Data as that might also affect how the discussion goes with the DCS.'

* * *

Jezza and Gina arrived back with sandwiches and hot drinks for Ted and Jo, as well as their own, Gina having phoned ahead to take their orders. It would be a working lunch, up in Jo's office, by way of a debrief on their morning visit to meet Robyn.

They ate in companionable silence until the first of the sandwiches had been consumed. Ted could see Jezza was bursting to put forward ideas. It always worried him slightly when she was like that. She'd always been impulsive. Whatever her ideas were, they'd always been good, but he might have to apply the brakes quite sharply, at least until he'd had clearance from higher authority.

'Right, we now know where Data was staying. Robyn ID'd him from the artist's impression ...'

Ted stopped her already. 'We don't know that, Jezza. For so many reasons. Not until the DNA check. Robyn may well have identified the picture as the person she knows as Data. But Gina, you know as well as I do that you didn't recognise the stand-in Data until you saw him up close, so I'm assuming he bore more than a strong likeness to the Data you've met. And therefore that he looked like the picture. This one could be another stand-in, for reasons we don't yet know.'

'It's got to be him though, boss,' Jezza said stubbornly. 'The behaviour fits. He's doing exactly what he did with Abigail Buller. Worming his way into the home of a rich and vulnerable young woman ...'

'But then disappearing without, seemingly, having done any of his usual charming tricks, like the porn films with her, or taking any of her money,' Ted cut in again.

'It's only been three weeks, though, boss, since he was there. It's the closest we've got to him in a long time. It's got to be worth a shot, surely? Anyway,' she gave him an exaggerated eye roll and folded her arms in stroppy teenager mode, 'I hate it when you're right.'

Ted took a sip of the cappuccino he'd asked for, by way of a change. He'd declined a double shot and it was about right for him as it was.

'Tell me your ideas anyway, Jezza, yours and Gina's. I'm always willing to listen, and I'm going to talk to the DCS, with Superintendent Sampson, later today. So if any of your proposals have legs, I can at least put them forward.

'But first of all I need to stress yet again that everything we discuss in here remains confidential. It goes no further, unless I say so. I know I keep repeating myself on this, but we have an informer inside the system and we don't yet know who or where.'

'No shit, Sherlock,' Jezza couldn't help muttering to herself then, seeing the look Ted gave her, she went on, 'Sorry, boss, but we all know that. And you should know by now that it's none of us on our own team.'

'We can't assume anything, Jezza. So, let me hear your ideas.'

'Well, we might not know for sure yet if this is the real Data,' she inclined her head towards Ted as she said that. 'But we do know that Data likes money, and easy targets. And Robyn represents both. So with the right support in place, we could try to draw Data out, to get him to get back in contact with her and perhaps even to go and visit her.

'My idea is that we get Robyn to try phoning Data again.'

She saw Ted open his mouth to point out the flaw and hurried on, 'Yes, I know he's been ignoring her. What if she phones him, says she knows he's struggling for the money to buy her a ring, which she understands is why he's been ignoring her, but her father has given them some money to buy one, and to throw an engagement party.

'I had a long talk with the parents while Gina was talking to Robyn about Data. They're very supportive. They said they're happy to do anything they can to help to bring him in, as long as Robyn's safety can be assured at all times. Even if it costs them a bit of money. They clearly have plenty to spare.'

'And can it?' Ted asked her. 'Can Robyn's safety be assured?'

'Clearly Gina can't be visible if and when Data comes to the house, because he's seen her before. Even with the new look, he'd be bound to know who it was up close. But he's never seen me. I could be there, posing as one of Robyn's friends, as he's been asking her if she has friends who could come to their so-called engagement party. Although I think we know what he actually has in mind for them.'

Ted's expression changed immediately to one of scepticism, but before he could speak, Jezza smiled as she pointed to herself and said, 'Boss, you've seen me fool the team once, but you ain't seen nothing yet. BA (Hons) in Acting, and if I say so myself, I wasn't half bad at it.

'I can be anything I need to be to pull this off. All we need to do is to get Data to come to the house, which he's very likely to do at the mere mention of money. Gina can be in another room, with Robyn's parents, who are supportive and want to help.

'I can be in the room with Data and Robyn. The idea is simply to bring him to the house and give him some money for the ring, supposedly. Like I said, the parents are quite happy to put some up, knowing they might not get it back. They're not short of a bob or two and they've both said they'd consider it a worthwhile investment to get Data out of their daughter's life once and for all, and to stop him harming anyone else.

'We're not looking to apprehend him at this point because we want him to lead us somewhere. Preferably to at least wherever he meets with the Big Man, if he doesn't go straight to where he's currently living. So we set up a follow and track him wherever he does go.

'If for any reason at all he turns nasty, I'm sure my kickboxing would help, and we could maybe have a bit of extra muscle in the house somewhere. What d'you think, boss?'

'And what if Data is armed, Jezza?' Ted asked her, cutting across Jo who had also opened his mouth to speak, probably to voice the same thought.

'We have no reason to believe that he would be,' she told him.

It was Ted's turn to roll his eyes to the ceiling.

'Jezza, I can't put "we had no reason to believe" on a risk assessment and you know that, perfectly well. The clue is in the title. What assessment have you done of the risks involved in such an option?'

'Jezza, you seem to be assuming that Data will just turn up alone and on foot. But what if he doesn't?' Jo asked her. 'We can be fairly sure that the gang regard him as a valuable asset, which is why they sacrificed the unknown young man rather than risk anyone getting their hands on the real Data. Not to mention them lifting him almost from under our noses at Alexandra Park that time.

'What if they drive him there, wait for him, then whisk him away as soon as he gets his hands on the money? As the boss keeps reminding us, the men who drive for and protect the famous Big Man are trained ex-military. Even if we put the most experienced follow team at our disposal onto tracking him, there's no guarantee we wouldn't lose them.'

'I agree, Jo, and more than that, I wouldn't be at all surprised if they sacrificed Data if that became necessary. He's a valuable asset, yes, but not more valuable than the whole of the operation. If they had to, they'd kill him without a second thought to protect the identity and location of the Big Man. I'm certain of that.'

'Could we not put a tracker in with the money Robyn gives him?' Jezza suggested.

Ted was already shaking his head before she'd even finished the sentence.

'Jezza, these are highly trained, professional and utterly ruthless people. It is their job to protect the operation, and whoever this Big Man is, at the cost of their own lives, if necessary. They'd be onto anything like that in an instant. It would stand no chance.

'But I agree with you that this is probably our best hope to date of getting to Data and perhaps getting him to lead us to the Big Man. There are so many elephant traps to avoid in something like this, it's probably as well I'm seeing the DCS later today. Apart from the logistics of it all, there are a lot of ethical issues which we'd need to be very sure of so that, if we manage to get a result and put a case together, it doesn't get kicked out at the eleventh hour.'

What he wasn't about to mention to any of them, not until he'd discussed it with the DCS and with Sammy, was that Jezza's idea also gave them their best chance to date of finding out who was really passing on information from inside the force to the drugs gang. Information which had led to several deaths. And that would be the biggest prize of all.

Chapter Twenty-five

Ted sent his report up to HQ before going there, in case the DCS had a moment to glance at it before he and Sammy arrived. It was scant enough, so it wouldn't take him long. Ted wasn't happy with it. He wished it had more substance, but it did at least highlight the need to throw resources behind outing the informer, before they could hope to make any significant progress with the investigation into the drugs gang and their associated crimes.

Sammy and DCS Holton greeted each other like the old friends they clearly were. He invited her and Ted to take a seat, picked up the flimsy report and looked at Ted as he said, 'To say it's light on detail, Ted, is an overstatement, wouldn't you agree?'

'I'm not proud of it, sir,' Ted told him frankly. 'The lack of detail highlights, though, why I think it's essential we deal with this matter as soon as possible. Every move we've made all along has got back to the very people we're trying to investigate. I don't see how we can expect to make significant progress until we identify and deal with the informer.'

'And where is DS Bradley now? I'd be happier if I could hear his rationale for such a seemingly far-fetched theory from his own mouth. We could do worse than start by bringing him in.'

'If he's right in his fears, I can understand why he wants to keep a low profile, though,' Sammy put in, her tone reasonable. 'Do you know DI Usher, Don? I can't say I've come across him myself.'

'I know of him, but not enough to make any sort of judgement call. I know his DCI, Ken Birchall, quite well, though. Why don't I give him a ring now, on speaker, then we can all hear what he has to say on the subject. And don't look like that, Ted, I will, of course, stress that this needs to be kept schtum.'

Birchall answered on the third ring. He and Holton exchanged pleasantries, then the DCS got down to business.

'Ken, tell me what you know about DI Usher from Drugs. And this exchange is on a strictly need to know basis, which means that Usher himself doesn't need to.'

'Sounds interesting, boss. Okay, potted biography. Good officer, kicks arses to get things done. A tendency to be a bit prickly sometimes, and definitely not the sociable type. Can I ask why the interest?'

'You can ask,' the DCS told him, 'though that doesn't mean you'll get answers, at this stage. On the take would you say?'

'Dave?' Birchall's single word suggested shock at the mere suggestion. 'I wouldn't have thought so. Who from and what for?'

'Can I ask a question?' Ted asked.

'Ken, I'm with Superintendent Sampson and DCI Ted Darling, from Stockport. Over to you, Ted.'

'Do you know about DI Usher's daughter? Her illness, and her time in hospital?'

There was a noticeable hesitation, then Birchall said, 'Boss, I'm really not comfortable with this. Random questions about Dave's private life, without me knowing the reasons. Is he under investigation for something? Because like I said, as far as I'm concerned, he's a good copper, doing a good job.'

The DCS responded, keeping his tone neutral.

'It would help us to know about his daughter, if you have any information, Ken. It need go no further at this stage, you have my word on that.'

There was another short pause before Birchall said, 'Fair enough, then, boss. If this is all in confidence. Dave's daughter did something very silly when she was just a kid. About fifteen, I think. Got offered some sort of shit at a party and foolishly accepted. I'm not sure if it was an overdose or some sort of a reaction. I do know she was blue-lighted to A&E and it was touch and go for quite some time.

'Dave was in bits, of course, so he took some compassionate leave until he at least knew she was out of danger and going to live. So if you're even thinking he might be taking a bung from drugs gangs to look the other way, then I'd say you're barking up completely the wrong tree. A lot of officers in Drugs have valid reasons to hate the whole culture with a passion. Like Gina Shaw, for another one. If we really are talking in confidence, then I don't know if you know that drugs killed her kid brother.

'If you really want to find out who might have turned and be working for the other side, why not go after DS Ian Bradley? He's so far off the radar not even Dave Usher can get hold of him these days, so who knows what he's up to. He needs hauling in and putting through the ringer to find out why he's off the radar and avoiding all contact.

'That's for you to decide, boss, of course, but until I'd satisfied myself Bradley hasn't gone rogue, I wouldn't be looking elsewhere, and certainly not at Dave Usher.'

'He has a point, Ted,' the DCS told him as he ended the call. 'I must say I'd be happier if we had Bradley somewhere we can keep a very close eye on him, and could hear what he has to say for himself. Can you contact him? Get him to come in?'

'He'd want assurances,' Ted told him. 'I would, too, in case he's right in what he's told me. A safe house. Preferably one only I know the location of. And Firearms protection for him while he's there.'

'You can have a safe house, but I want to know the location myself. Unless you don't trust me? And he can have an AFO on babysitting duty round the clock.'

'Two AFOs,' Ted told him firmly. 'The people we're dealing with are highly trained and dangerous. And I'm basing that risk assessment on my former training and service as both an Authorized Firearms Officer and a Specialist Firearms Officer.' He left one of his trademark pauses before he added the 'sir.'

Holton sighed theatrically as he said, 'All right, two. But let's for goodness sake get him in and spoken to, soon as.

'Now, what about the other idea? Using this young lady Robyn to bring your suspect Data out into the open. I can't say I'm entirely comfortable with that, either, and I can visualise CPS throwing up all sorts of objections from an ethical point of view. Can this Robyn give informed consent for anything, for instance?

'Run me through exactly what you have in mind and how you intend to make it work with minimum risk and best chance of success. And without blowing the budget. What's your primary objective?'

'Twofold,' Ted told him. 'We're hoping that the mere mention of money will bring Data running. We don't at all want to try to arrest him at this stage. He's too valuable for that, because he's our best way of trying to get closer to the so-called Big Man.

'It's a gamble, I grant you, but what I'm hoping is that the hint of cash up for grabs will be too much for him to resist. So we'll keep the house under surveillance until either he shows up or it's fairly obvious he's got bigger fish to fry and isn't going to appear.

'If he appears, we simply watch, wait, then follow him when he leaves. We need a very experienced follow team on this one. The best we have. There are two possible positive outcomes. He might hopefully lead them to the Big Man, so at least we'd get some idea of where he's operating from.'

'You can have three cars and a motorbike. The best units we have.'

'Four cars and two motorbikes,' Ted countered. 'And I want

someone in a nearby house, which we need to choose carefully. One with line of sight to the Pascoe house. We're dealing with professionals here and we need to be equipped and on the ball. We know they've already used a motorbike, for the shooting, and they got clean away from us that time. We're only likely to get one chance at doing it this way. It would be wrong to blow the opportunity because of budgetary considerations.'

'All right, but it can't be for a limitless time. We can't have teams sitting about on the off-chance of getting a result.

'You said two-fold. What's the second part of the op?'

'We use it to draw out the enemy within, the informant, once and for all. We let slip the details to anyone we suspect, to include DI Usher, despite what his DCI says about him. I'll bring DS Bradley in but he's not going to be able to overpower two AFOs and go anywhere. I'll also make sure he has no telephone contact with the outside world. So if someone turns up, to stop Data from being arrested or followed, the leak can't have come from Bradley.'

Sammy Sampson spoke next, having been listening attentively in silence as Ted set out his plans.

'It's not foolproof though, Ted. Don and I will know the details. One of us could be the mole. Not to mention people on your own team who will need to be in on this. DCs Vine and Shaw, for a start.

'If someone from the gang turns up to pull Data out of harm's way, you still won't have any certain way of knowing where the leak came from, surely.'

'I'm taking a gamble on this, and I don't usually,' Ted told them. 'I'm hoping it's a calculated one. If Dave Usher is the mole, and I concede it's a long way from being certain yet, there's a good chance that it's not just for money. That the gang has some sort of a hold over him. Something so powerful it has him dancing at the end of their strings. So I think he'll turn up in person, to whisk Data out of the way.

'Think about it. If he needs to keep on the right side of

them, so that whatever they're threatening him with doesn't happen, what better way to get in their good books than by rescuing their golden boy for them. That's what I think is likely to happen.'

'That's a hell of a big gamble, Ted, and I wouldn't share your confidence based on a report with detail as thin as this.'

Holton jabbed a finger at the print-out on his desk as he spoke.

'There is another way,' Ted told him, holding his gaze. 'We keep the details of the op to a very few officers, not including DI Usher. Instead, you authorise a full investigation into everything about him. His finances, the whole of what happened with his daughter, including who paid for what medical care, and so on. And we put a tracker on his car, before he gets wind of anything of that sort going on.'

DCS Holton picked up the report now and waved it at Ted, his voice rising.

'If there's not enough here for the first option, there certainly isn't enough for anything like that. Not remotely. The only way I'd agree to that is if we did the same thing for every officer involved at any stage on any of the enquiries linked to this drugs gang. And you know that would be a physical and a financial impossibility, within any useful sort of a time frame.

'So you leave me no choice. We'll try it your way. As long as CPS don't raise any serious impediments, we'll go with the idea of trying to draw Data in and letting a few selected people in on what's happening. Then we'll wait to see who, if anyone, turns up to lift Data. But I want Bradley brought in and safely babysat long before any of that happens. Clear?'

'Clear, sir,' Ted replied, then risked, 'I could go now and make a start on finding DS Bradley and getting him to a safe house, with armed babysitters.'

'No you bloody won't,' Holton told him, but smiling now. 'You've just blown a massive hole in my budget for about the next quarter, so the very least you can do in return is to get the first round of drinks in.'

He looked at Sammy as he asked, 'Pub?'

She smiled at him.

'I thought you'd never ask. Pub it is.'

* * *

It was certainly a lively evening. 'Eck was waiting for them downstairs, where he'd been chatting to people he knew. A taxi was summoned and swiftly whisked them to a pub not far away which looked presentable and had a good menu.

As instructed, Ted got the first round in. Clearly the first of many, he imagined, the way the three of them were going at it. He sat quietly with his Gunner, feeling slightly out of it, not just as the only non-drinker, but because the three of them had all served together before and knew each other well. He rather wished the DCS had agreed to him going off to find Bradley. He would have preferred to be doing something constructive.

He finally managed to slip away when the other three decided to go on to a club they knew. Ted called himself a taxi to the station, took the train to Stockport and walked to the nick to pick up his car.

It was gone midnight by the time he got home. He could hear the television, turned down low, coming from the front room, where some lights were still on.

He found Trev half-asleep on the sofa, clearly the right side of almost a bottle of wine. He opened one sleepy blue eye when Ted rearranged cats so he could sit down next to him. Adam had already started climbing up his trouser leg as soon as he appeared. Ted carefully counted them all as he did so. Trev saw the gesture and laughed.

'No, no new kittens, officer. Not yet, anyway. But I did open a bottle of good wine to welcome Aspen Jade to the world. What about you? How was your night on the town?'

'You know I don't much like that sort of thing. We had a

good meal, though.'

'And what about your meeting with the DCS? Did you get what you wanted out of it? Are you going to be able to catch the baddies?'

Ted leaned his head back against the sofa cushions and sighed.

'I'm not sure. The problem is that I suspect the biggest baddy of them all is a bent copper. And you know how hard they are to catch.'

Chapter Twenty-six

After morning briefing, Ted once again sat down with Jo, Jezza and Gina in Jo's office, to report on on his meeting with the DCS.

Jo had further news from Professor Nelson on the knife wounds, which he'd presented at the briefing. The Professor was now able to say categorically that one of the knives used to kill Noah Brooks was an exact match for the type which had also been used on Kane Lomax, their earlier victim, the body in the Bowl.

The bad news was that it was a bog standard military knife commonly issued to armed forces, particularly those in the Balkans region and most of Eastern Europe.

'The Professor warned me there was no magical fiction formula to tell one such weapon from another purely from the wounds they inflict. Not unless there was some sort of notch or damage to the blade, and in that case no self-respecting killer would be likely to use it because it would simply be leaving a signature each time it was used,' Jo summed up.

'The only glimmer of hope on the knife or the wounds it inflicted is that, in both cases, it was wielded by someone using their left hand. It's not much but it's something.'

'What's bothering me at the moment is even if we do successfully track down Data and get a lead to the Big Man, I doubt his henchmen will be under the same roof at the same time. Not all of them, for sure. He'll have his close protection guards by him constantly, no doubt, but if we do succeed in collaring them - and that would take a major Firearms op - they'll probably be illegals, no doubt wanted in other countries too, so we may not get to keep them here long enough to bring them to justice.'

'If we manage to get the Big Man though, would that not shut the operation down, boss? At least for now? Isn't it likely that he keeps a lot of info to himself? Supply line, that sort of thing?'

'Possibly. But what I really want is his hired private army as well. As many of them as possible. We owe that to Noah, and to Kane Lomax. I'd really like to get at least one of them who was involved in killing either or both of them.

'So with that as the objective, what the four of us need to do now is to formulate how we're going to use Data to get us as close to the Big Man as possible, with the minimum risk. Once we've finished discussing a plan, Jezza and Gina, you're going to write me up a fully risk-assessed proposal suitable for me to send to the DCS to sign off on. And it needs to be watertight. Not so much as a missing comma. Got it?'

Jezza nodded meekly, which always worried Ted.

'Got it, boss, it shall be flawless.'

'I've had agreement for four cars and two motorbikes for a follow, plus someone in a nearby house to keep obs and run the follow operation. The two of you need to go back to see the Pascoes - the parents and Robyn together - once more to iron out the details before you finish your proposal. I would strongly suggest a different look this time. More like possible friends of Robyn. Jezza, you in particular, if you want to play that part if and when Data turns up.

'I'd really like a Firearms presence, given who we could potentially be dealing with, but if any of the trained military types are about, they'd smell them a mile off. The next best thing would be some muscle inside the house. Virgil would be ideal but he might not exactly blend into the surroundings, to get him inside. I'm sure he'd be the first to agree with that assessment.'

There was a hint of self-satisfaction to Jezza's smile at that.

'Ahead of you there, boss. We discussed some logistics with Mr Pascoe in case we could get the go-ahead. I knew Virgil would be a good choice and we have the perfect cover, as long as he doesn't mind the possible stereotyping. Mr Pascoe's company sponsors several charities, including some schools and orphanages in Africa. Virgil could be visiting him in connection with those, for the benefit of anyone taking an interest.'

Ted wasn't surprised that Jezza seemed to have all the answers. He would expect nothing less from her.

'So you already have an OP sorted, I take it?'

This time she gave him a smug grin.

'Probably, boss, but we need to confirm. Mr Pascoe told me the lady who lives diagonally opposite, Mrs Forsyth, keeps a bit of an eye on Robyn for them from time to time. Her front upstairs bedroom has a big bay window, with an excellent view of Robyn's flat. It would be perfect. It has net curtains and the window has big mature trees in front of it in the garden. You can still see out through the branches, but it does tend to mask anyone who might be watching up there from anyone on the outside glancing that way.

'We haven't talked to her yet, of course, pending approval, but the Pascoes think she'd jump at the idea of being useful. A big advantage is that she hardly ever goes out anywhere these days so she's no one to gossip to about it.'

'I'd need to clear it with whoever is running the follow team, of course, but it sounds like a strong probable.'

'Boss, Robyn says that Data always comes and goes on foot, so do we need walkers as well as vehicle followers?' Gina asked him. 'Only I've done the course recently, if it helps. He might well recognise me close up, but from a distance I'm pretty sure he wouldn't, looking like I do now. He might, of course, only be walking as far as the nearest bus stop. But then he might be walking somewhere to get picked up.'

'The team will need full details of the location, so we'll need to highlight things like bus stops. Harder to do a follow if he jumps on a bus, with all the stops and starts, so they need to be ready for any eventuality. The most productive outcome for us in all of this is if our inside informer turns up to whisk him away. So it goes without saying that no word of him being followed gets out anywhere. The mole must think that we're simply going to grab him the minute he gets inside the Pascoes' home. If he even turns up. So they'd want to lift him before he gets anywhere near to the house.'

'In respect of when he might show up, assuming Gina and I go back to see the Pascoes this afternoon when Robyn is back from work, they've already said he's never been there after six in the evening, because he knows they visit her then, every day, although he has sometimes turned up very late and stayed the night. He knows she works mornings and doesn't get home until half two, three o'clock, most days, and that she's off on Mondays. So that theoretically gives us a narrow window of about three hours on each of four days, or possibly at some time on a Monday, but that's unlikely,' Jezza told him. 'He doesn't visit at the weekend and never usually on Mondays as he knows she often spends time with her mother then, or with both her parents when Mr Pascoe isn't at work. If we get Robyn to phone and leave him a message when we go back there after lunch, there's a good chance he'll want to come soon, if there's cash on offer.'

'It can't be too soon, though,' Ted warned her. 'We need time to set this up properly. Can you get Robyn to say something convincing about coming on a specific day? I don't like taking advantage of her, and that could really present some ethical issues. But could her father perhaps say he needs to go to the bank to draw the cash? Would Robyn accept that?'

Jezza stood up, looking purposeful.

'Only one way to find out, boss. Don't worry, we'll try to be as ethical as anything. We can record the whole discussion for

CPS so they can decide if we crossed a line or not. But first we better go and make a start on that report, Gina. We'll no doubt have a lot to add when we get back from Altrincham.'

Ted next went upstairs to see Sammy. She was looking decidedly fragile after the night before.

She held up a warning hand.

'Whatever you've come to say, Ted, please make it very quiet. I'm definitely getting too old for that sort of a carry on.'

Ted smiled his sympathy.

'What time did the party end?'

'I think I got back home about three o'clock this morning, but I was honestly beyond reading the time on the clock. So what can I do for you?'

'I just need your signature on a few forms, sorting out the safe house and the Firearms presence to babysit DS Bradley. I'm intending to try bringing him in later today.'

'It's a good job I trust you implicitly, Ted. I'm not up to reading anything just now so I could be signing my life away to you. So who are you taking with you to lift the DS?'

'No one.'

She looked up sharply at that, suddenly fully wide awake and functioning again.

'No one? How are you going to manage on your own, without putting yourself at risk? Have you done a risk assessment? Is there a copy on file? And have I got a copy somewhere amongst all this bumf?'

Ted gave her an enigmatic smile as he said, 'Oh, I think I'll probably manage without too much trouble. People tend to underestimate me. They only see the short, skinny little runt. They don't know about the inner ninja.'

She was still looking at him searchingly.

'Hmm, I can't imagine for a moment you'd let one of your team go alone to lift someone who probably has not the slightest intention of allowing himself to be brought in. I'm not officially sanctioning this. In fact, I half wish you hadn't mentioned it, because if it all blows up in your face the fallout will land on me as well. But you seem confident enough so I'll have to trust you. Just keep me posted and let me know when the DS is somewhere safe and under constant obs.'

He had the safe house sorted and Firearms officers on standby before he put in a call to DS Ian Bradley. As he'd suspected, he had to leave a message on the burner phone number Bradley had given him, then wait for him to call back. When he did, it was with the usual coded checks before he would agree to talk.

'I need a meet, Ian. ASAP. I have news following on from our last conversation. Developments, you could say. But as usual, not by phone. And it needs to be today. My turn to pick the place, but you should know by now that you can trust me.'

He told him when and where, then asked if he needed food again. Almost as an afterthought, he added, 'Oh, and I'll be in my service vehicle. Here's the make, model and number, so you know it's me. Mine's in the garage at the moment.'

It wasn't, at all. It was parked outside on the station car park, as functional as it ever was. But Ted wanted the much faster and more efficient central locking of his service vehicle. He needed the element of surprise very much on his side.

He stopped off on the way to buy the promised bacon barms and coffee, still arriving at the RV point well ahead of time, so he could keep an eye out for any sign of anything untoward. Bradley had, understandably, been wary of the daylight meeting, but Ted had managed to convince him of its necessity.

He sat waiting patiently, munching his way through a roll, looking relaxed and not particularly alert. Nevertheless his eyes were everywhere, missing nothing, and he clocked Bradley approaching long before he reached the vehicle.

Ted allowed the soft clunk of the passenger door closing to cover the sound of him hitting the central locking. It was natural enough, even if Bradley had heard it. It would stop them being suddenly interrupted by anyone opening, or attempting to open, one of the doors.

'Dinner is served,' he said with a note of irony, as he put a bag of barms and a hot coffee into Bradley's eager hands.

The instant he was temporarily occupied, Ted's handcuffs appeared in a flash and were around Bradley's skinny and none too clean wrists before he could even understand what was happening.

'What the fuck?'

He was clearly none too happy.

'Sorry about that, Ian,' Ted told him pleasantly enough, 'but we need you in now and I was under strict orders from the DCS not to take no for an answer. We're running the op you wanted to try to draw Usher out, if he is the mole, but there was no way Holton was going to sign off on it as long as you were in the wind and unaccounted for. I can't say I blame him. It could all be a set-up on your part to get Usher out of the way. So you're going to a nice safe house for the time being. You won't be leaving it until he or I say so, and don't even think about trying to, because you'll have AFOs babysitting you round the clock.

'Fuck you, Ted!' Bradley spat at him.

'You're angry, I get it,' Ted told him, his tone still mild. 'When you've calmed down a bit and thought about it, you'll see it from my point of view and realise I didn't have a choice. Eat your scran and drink your coffee while we're parked, so you don't spill it and scald yourself. Oh, and I got you a few things to tide you over. A change of clothes, some trainers, a wash kit, that sort of stuff. I had to guess at your size, so I hope it's all okay.'

He risked a grin towards Bradley as he said, 'The clothes and shoes should be okay. When you do martial arts, like I do, you get quite good at guesstimating the size and weight of a potential opponent. They're only cheap supermarket finest, but they'll do for now. I also got you a razor and some scissors. I think it might perhaps be time for you to change your look for a bit, for your own safety. Don't you?

'I know you're pissed off with me and you feel betrayed. But I'd rather we were allies in this. I'm sure you'd have done exactly the same in my shoes.'

Bradley had put the sandwich bag down in his lap and lifted the coffee cup to his mouth with his still-cuffed hands.

'You're an annoying little bastard, Ted. D'you know that?' he asked, although his tone was at least starting to mellow.

'So I've been told, on many occasions,' Ted laughed. 'I'm just a copper, doing what any good copper would do in the circumstances. What you'd almost certainly have done faced with the same scenario.

'Anyway, I'll leave you to eat and drink before I drive off. I'll just let your babysitters know what time to expect us. Oh, and I'll need your mobile phone. At least until the op is over and we've had a sight of who our mole is, if not got them safely under lock and key.'

Chapter Twenty-seven

The two Firearms officers were waiting in their vehicle outside the safe house, following Ted's instructions. He hadn't wanted them standing outside on display, drawing attention to the fact that something out of the ordinary was going on.

He flashed them his ID then told them to wait where they were while he went to open the front door, carrying with him the supermarket bags with the things he'd bought for Bradley, including some food. Only then did he return to the vehicles and nod to them to get out of theirs. They were instantly on the alert, scanning all around for any signs of anything suspicious.

He left Bradley's handcuffs in place while he helped him out of the car and hustled him into the house, the two AFOs following them, walking backwards, eyes everywhere, ready to cover them at the first hint of danger. Ted was praying that neither of the two of them had seen Bradley before, or if they had at some stage, not looking like he did now. He didn't know either of them by sight but then thought with a jolt that they would probably both have still been at school when he was at Longsight in his Firearms days.

Once they were safely inside and Ted had checked for himself that both entry doors were securely locked and bolted from the inside, and no signs of anything untoward upstairs, he removed Bradley's handcuffs and held out his hand for his mobile phone. The DS hesitated but he could see that Ted was determined so he fished it out of his pocket and handed it over.

Ted then turned to the two officers, one male, one female.

'I know it's a pain in the backside when some senior officer from CID starts telling you how to do your job, but I've done it. I started out in Firearms. This is Ian, and that's all you need to know about him. Your job is to keep him safe. He does not leave this house at all, for any reason, and he has no contact with the outside world. No phone calls in or out. No matter what he tells you.

'The same for the two of you. I want both of you inside, on full alert, for the whole of your shift. I've no reason at this stage to think the safe house location is compromised, but none of us should underestimate that possibility. This case involves some highly trained mercenaries, so you take no risks at all at any stage. Is that clear?'

'Sir,' the two officers said in unison, although Ted could feel the scepticism directed towards him. He was used to it. He'd known it throughout his career.

'I've had basic provisions provided so you won't starve, Ian. But nobody comes to the house without my say-so. So don't even think of ordering in a sneaky pizza or anything like that.'

'What about fags, Ted? Did you think of those? Only I'm running low on roll-ups and I'd hate these poor young officers to have to witness me going through tobacco withdrawal.'

'I didn't think, sorry. Tell me what you want and I'll go and get it now.'

'I've got ciggies in the vehicle, sir, I could go and fetch those,' the younger of the two officers told Ted. Then she could happily have bitten off the end of her tongue at the long, appraising look he gave her.

She stumbled on, stammering, 'Sorry, sir, I mean I could give you the keys to go and get them, to save you having to come back again.'

Bradley stepped in, feeling sorry for the young officer. He sensed it was merely the wrong turn of phrase and didn't feel any less secure with her as his babysitter because of it.

'It's fine, Ted, I have enough for tonight, if you can arrange something for me from tomorrow.'

'Sorry, sir,' the AFO muttered again.

Ted didn't quite thaw, but his expression was less severe as he spoke again.

'I need the two of you to stay on the ball, please. Position yourself so you have clear line of sight to both doors and as many other approach and entry points as you can. There's a half landing up the stairs with a good view to the front door, and there's also a window so you can see the road junction at the corner. It has net curtains, too. It's up to you two, of course, but if I was doing this, that's a place I would favour.

'Right, if you're sure you'll survive until tomorrow, Ian, I'll be on my way,' Ted told him.

He looked at the younger officer as he said, 'Perhaps you'd see me to the door and make sure it's securely locked and bolted behind me, please.'

The please went down well, together with the genuine smile he gave her.

'Don't worry about it,' he told her, once they were out of earshot of the other two. 'We all make mistakes. If I had longer, I'd tell you about the time I made a total pillock of myself by waving a Heckler at a Senior Crown Prosecutor because I didn't know him.'

She smiled at that. 'You were really an AFO then?'

'SFO, actually, before I left Firearms,' he told her, waiting while she opened the door and checked carefully all around before she stepped aside to let him out. It reassured him. She clearly did know what she was doing; she'd just made an unfortunate slip of the tongue, which he wouldn't hold against her.

'Have a good shift and please, whatever Ian says, don't let him phone anyone. And be careful. I've no reason to believe he's dangerous, but he is a wily fox, and he doesn't like having been pulled in to be babysat. So don't trust him, at all, and make sure you know where he is in the house at any moment. Even to the point of one of you standing outside the lav when he uses it, no matter what he says to that.'

He drove the car a good mile away from the safe house, by an indirect route, before he stopped to report to the DCS. He wasn't taking any chances. He'd done enough of Mr Green's special training courses, including Escape and Evasion, often shoulder to shoulder with military operatives from the most specialist of units, never to forget the basic precautions. Even when they might seem like overkill.

'Mission accomplished, boss,' Ted told him. 'The DS isn't exactly thrilled, but he's installed in the safe house with his armed babysitters. Are you happy with me debriefing him and recording it? I'd be happier if it could be done without moving him anywhere at the moment, just in case.'

'In view of the seriousness of his allegations, I think you should take Sammy with you. Hopefully, after a night out with her letting her hair down, you accept by now that she's one of us and that you can trust her implicitly. I think her presence might show Bradley we're taking him seriously but not to the point of believing everything he says without proof.

'As you gathered, she and I have known each other for a very long time, and worked together a lot. She's very good in interviews. Nobody gets anything past her, and she has the ad-vantage of not yet having spoken to Bradley. I think she'd be a usefully impartial and incisive person to be part of the debrief.'

Ted had no real choice but to accept. The fewer people who heard what Bradley had to say, the better he'd like it but he was outranked on the decision. He fully intended to send the two AFOs to wait outside in the vehicle during the debrief.

They were getting close to attaining their target in this case - the closest they'd yet been. Ted could feel it. He didn't want to risk a leak at the eleventh hour. Only the controlled one they were planning to feed to DI Dave Usher.

'One more thing I need you to do for me, please, boss. We're going to try to lure Data in on Friday afternoon, if we can. You'll have the full written report and risk assessment of everything. But we will need, please, the description and registration number of any vehicle DI Usher might turn up in, if he does come looking for Data. Service vehicle as well as his own personal car.'

'And if it's not him that turns up? What then? Are you pre-judging this one, Ted?'

'I don't think so, sir. The follow team will be ready whoever turns up - if anyone does. It would just give us a bit of a heads-up if we knew in good time that it was the DI.'

'Are you planning to be there yourself?'

'I don't think I should, no. Not at close quarters, anyway. I think I'd be better off watching from the monitors somewhere out of sight. I had to show myself as a police officer when the Data stand-in was shot dead on the last attempt to get him. The situation escalated rapidly and someone needed to step in and take control. Gina, DC Shaw, kept her cover intact though. We both made sure of that. Plus her appearance has changed dra-matically since then.

'I think it would be too much of a risk for me to be any-where near the place when Data turns up, if he does, and we try to follow him. He might have been at the site of the shooting, even though he wasn't spotted there, so he could conceivably have seen me. And if it is the DI who turns up, he's seen me, of course.'

The DCS sighed hard.

'Let's just get someone for it, Ted. It's about bloody time we did. Take Sammy with you to talk to Bradley and let me have a full report on the debrief as soon as possible, if not sooner.

* * *

Ted had barely reached his desk the following morning when his mobile phone rang and the screen showed him it was Steve calling him once more.

'Sir, is this a good time to talk to you?' he began. His tone was not his usual hesitant one. It was the one he'd used when phoning with news about the knife suppliers. Confident, eager. Ted felt a small surge of optimism. Perhaps he had something equally as useful for him.

'It is, Steve, but first tell me how you're doing. In yourself, I mean. How are you?'

'Oh, I'm fine, thank you,' Steve's tone was so dismissive he might simply have been recovering from a mild bout of flu rather than from a seemingly determined attempt on his own life.

'While I'm on leave I thought I'd do a bit of rummaging around on the dark web. The sort of thing which would require all sorts of forms and permissions if I was doing it from work. Similar to how I found the knife sellers, but this time looking for drug suppliers in our area.

'I didn't want to go too far without checking with you that you were happy with what I'm doing and if you think it might be useful to you. Only I'm working towards setting up a meeting with someone who might just possibly be connected to our Big Man. But nothing beyond that as yet. No firm plans to meet.'

'Steve, I'm getting on a bit, I think, and my hearing doesn't seem to be what it was. I didn't quite catch where you did this research but never mind, no need to repeat it,' Ted told him.

To his surprise, Steve laughed out loud at that. He couldn't remember Steve doing much laughing. He always seemed so serious, even in a social setting. It was good to hear.

'Seriously, though, Steve, this is really useful, thank you, but clearly you can't take it any further. I'm going to talk to Jo about it now and we'll see if we can't set up a meet, carefully stage managed, in liaison with you. So thank you.'

'You're welcome, sir. Oh, and just to mention, I finish my sick leave this weekend, then I'm taking some annual leave and going to the States for a fortnight, to see Océane. And when I get back, I'm hoping to take over her post as a CFI, until I can think about coming back to a job somewhere.'

'As I've said, Steve, you'll have a glowing reference from me for whatever you decide to do. And thanks again for this. I'll get Jo to contact you.'

* * *

'Robyn, Gina and I need to talk to you again about Data,' Jezza began when the two of them sat down with Robyn in the living room of her flat, with both her parents present. 'And I'm afraid you might not like what we have to tell you.'

Robyn was smiling at them. 'We're going to get engaged,' she told them proudly.

'I'm sorry to tell you this, Robyn,' Jezza instinctively moved nearer and took hold of both the young woman's hands as she spoke. 'But no, you aren't. I'm afraid this is something Data does, quite often. He meets a young woman like yourself, pretends it's a big love affair, but in reality he uses her to get his hands on money.'

Robyn's face turned solemn as she first studied Jezza then turned to look at her parents, who were smiling their encouragement at her.

Then she smiled again and said in a flat monotone, 'Oh dear, how sad, never mind,' which made her mother laugh out loud.

'That's the spirit, darling,' then, turning to the officers, she laughed again as she said, 'That's one of Robyn's favourite lines from television. She loves watching the reruns of "*It Ain't Half Hot Mum*", for some reason. But that's a good philosophy to live by, don't you think?

'So now we're hopefully past the worst, why don't I put the kettle on. I'm sure we'd all like a cup of tea.'

Robyn seemed genuinely to be over the initial news already, so Jezza decided to press on.

'Robyn, I can see you're very mature about all of this. Some of Data's targeted young women have been a lot more hurt by him, though. So we'd very much like to speak to him, and to do that, we need to find him. We wondered if you could help us with that? It would mean you phoning him again, with a special message. It wouldn't be entirely true, though, so would you be happy to do that to help us?'

'Like drama, you mean?' Robyn asked her.

'Robyn loves drama,' her father told them. 'She did it at college and she was very good at it.'

'That's excellent. I love it, too. I studied acting at University before I joined the police. Shall we have a practice of what we need you to say?'

Robyn was good. She had her little speech word perfect after just one run through. She phoned Data's number, recited her message, then ended the call and looked eagerly at Jezza for approval.

'That was fantastic, Robyn. Well done, and thank you so much. Now, remember, if Data tries to contact you, or perhaps turns up except at the time you've told him, please phone me or Gina immediately and we'll get someone round here. If not, we'll see you again on Friday early afternoon, with our colleague. He looks a bit big and scary but he's a lovely man, very kind, and he's here to help to look after you and make sure you won't be in any danger.'

'Don't worry, Jessica,' Ralph Pascoe assured her as he showed the two of them to the door after they'd had their cup of tea. 'Either my wife or I will be with Robyn all the time until the appointed hour, and we'll both be here on Friday. We're more than happy to do anything we can to help you catch the delightful Data, especially after everything you've told us about him.'

Chapter Twenty-eight

'It's a good lead from Steve, as usual,' Ted told Jo when they finally found a quiet moment to catch up. 'I think it might possibly take us somewhere. I also think it's something that needs to wait until after Friday's op, for a couple of reasons.

'The first is that the most likely person to use would be Virgil, but we also need him in the house for if and when Data turns up, and I think that needs to take priority. Until we at least have some clue about who the mole may be, anything else seems pointless.

'I take it no one else knows about the op, except those directly involved in it? Let's try to keep it that way. The two of us should have a get-together at close of play today with Virgil, Gina and Jezza, to go over once more how things are going to pan out tomorrow. If all goes according to plan.'

'I've kept a tight lid on it, don't worry about that, Ted. I've taken Rob off looking at new members of the team for this case and put him on to other things. I would never suspect him, but this way he's hopefully distracted from the mere idea of an inside informer.

'Do you really think it is Dave Usher? And do you think he'll risk showing himself tomorrow?'

'I honestly don't know, Jo, but my instincts tell me he's the most likely. If it is him, it depends on his motive. If it's purely for money, he might not take the risk of turning up. But if, for instance, they are blackmailing him, because they have some sort of a hold over him, he may be desperate enough to try anything.'

'But how are you going to make sure he's the only one who

gets the heads-up on the plan for Data? And more importantly, gets him to believe the idea is to arrest him in the house, and not to follow him anywhere, which is what's really going to happen. Hopefully. We ideally need him to show himself and try to lift Data before he gets suspicious or spots one of the followers.'

Ted gave him a sly grin.

'You know what it's like, Jo. Sometimes documents go out with the wrong circulation address list. Someone's not cleared it from the time before and hits send without checking.'

'You are worryingly devious sometimes, Ted,' Jo told him, smiling in his turn.

'Desperate times, desperate measures, Jo. For the record, I'd be happy if it turns out not to be DI Usher. I just want whoever it is off the scene and out of our way so we can finally start to make some progress. Hopefully.

'Meanwhile can you give Steve a ring, find out all the details he has for us, but stress we can't do anything until we know how things pan out on Friday. So he's going to be in the States if and when we follow up his lead. But promise him we'll let him know what happens.

'If you know a prayer to produce miracles, we could do with some help. Favourite outcome would be for tomorrow's op not only to show us our mole, but to lead us straight to wherever our Mr Big has his lair.'

'Saint Anthony of Padua is the one, boss. I'll endeavour to light a candle to him before we begin.

'Will we pull the informant in afterwards, assuming they do lead us somewhere, or leave them for now?'

'That'll be a damage limitation decision, taken by those much higher up than a mere mortal like me. Let's just concentrate on drawing them out then take it from there.'

'But if Dave Usher doesn't turn up, that won't automatically clear him, though, will it?' Jo asked. 'He could have got wind of the op, or been too wary to show himself in broad daylight. Or even simply not had time to open his incoming mail.'

'Unusually for me, I'm setting great store on a hunch which says he'll show. And if he does, it's essential we don't lose him. I can't risk being anywhere near the scene, having been at the place where the shooting happened. I've asked to be in a comms vehicle some distance away. Which is why I want you in the OP, Jo, to personally update me on every move the followers make. I especially want a heads up if you get an ID on anyone who turns up, and I need to know as soon as possible which direction they're heading in.

'We're getting so close, finally. I don't want anything at all to go wrong at this stage. Which is why I'm going to slope off at a decent time this evening to get to the dojo. A hard physical workout usually sharpens up the thought processes somewhat, but I also want another chance to impress on our young members of the self-defence club all the associated risks of getting involved with drugs. I wouldn't want the team to have to investigate any of them meeting an end like young Noah did.'

* * *

It was a totally transformed DS Bradley who was waiting for Ted and Sammy the following morning. Ted drove them in his service vehicle to where he was being babysat. He'd had a message sent through to the armed detail guarding Bradley that they would be arriving, and gave a rough time. He knew better than to pitch up unannounced.

He couldn't help but notice the difficulty Sammy Sampson had getting in and out of the car, and he didn't miss the slight wince of pain as she sat down.

He was stiff enough himself. He'd had a good judo session which had served to highlight that he didn't do it often enough to stay at peak fitness. It wasn't always easy, with the constraints of his job, but it had left him resolved to make the effort more often.

The AFOs had clearly been looking out for them. One came to the door to let them in, insisting on seeing both their photo ID cards before he did so. Ted was impressed at their vigilance. He could see the second officer on the half landing, where he could cover his oppo and deal with whoever came through the door, should he need to.

Bradley was sitting waiting for them in the living room, looking completely different to when Ted had delivered him there. He had cut off his pony tail and given the rest of his hair a buzz cut. He'd also shaved off his beard. Dressed now in the clothes Ted had got for him, he looked totally different, although his tall, gaunt frame and distinctive rise and fall gait would strike a chord easily enough in anyone observant as soon as he walked anywhere.

Ted handed him the cigarettes he'd got for him on the way, then set up the equipment to record the interview. Sammy chose the small dining table and chairs. Ted suspected it was easier for her to sit on a higher chair than the low and squashy sofa or armchair which were the alternatives.

Ted had sent the two firearms officers, different ones on this shift, to go and sit in their vehicle to maintain confidentiality. He didn't want them standing about in full view outside, raising suspicions from nosy neighbours.

Bradley fell on the cigarettes like a drowning man on a lifebuoy. His 'Is it all right if I smoke?' was clearly only for show. He was pulled up short by the coldly formal tone of Sammy Sampson.

'No, sergeant, it is not all right if you smoke during a formal interview. Sit down.'

Bradley's eyebrows climbed up almost to where his fringe would have been, if he had any hair left to speak of, but he said nothing. He sat down at the table opposite the superintendent, while Ted started the recording then took his seat and went through the formalities, leaving Sammy to begin the questioning.

'You've made what are effectively serious allegations against a senior officer, your own undercover handler, Detective Inspector David Usher, DS Bradley. So far I'm not aware of any kind of proof you have provided in support of them. Would you care to enlighten me?'

Bradley made a wry face.

'In case you hadn't noticed, superintendent,' he told her, with heavy irony, 'I'm not exactly best placed to use all the wondrous resources of officers in the nick. Working out in the field, the best I can generally manage is an internet cafe for a bit of browsing, which is neither use nor ornament to me in my circumstances.

'For anything official by way of research, I would have to go through my handler. And that would be ...' he left a pause for dramatic effect ...'DI Dave Usher. You can perhaps see my dilemma.'

Ted could see what the DCS had meant about Sammy's interview technique. Her face gave nothing away but she picked up on the slightest nuance.

'So now is your chance to tell DCI Darling and myself everything behind your suspicions so that we can carry out our own investigations into whether or not they have any basis.

'But while this interview is being recorded, can I just say, for the record, that DI Usher's name is not the first which you have put forward as being the source of leaked information. I believe you previously claimed, quite recently, that it was DC Derek Black. Is that correct?'

'I was mistaken,' he inclined his head as he said it. 'I set up a way to test the theory and discovered I was wrong.'

'And what steps have you taken to test your theory about the DI?'

There was a noticeable tremor now to the DS's hands. Bradley saw Ted looking and he lifted and spread them.

'Tobacco withdrawal, Ted,' he told him. 'Not nerves because I'm lying to you. I told you it would happen.'

The superintendent remained unmoved.

'Then I suggest we crack on and make some progress, so you can have a break, sergeant. Tell me about how you've tested your latest theory.'

'With the greatest respect, ma'am,' he began in a voice which dripped with sarcasm, 'there's bugger all I can do, in my circumstances. I'm trying to avoid my handler in the belief, mistaken or otherwise, that anything I do say to him will go straight to the very drugs gang I'm trying to investigate.

'I also felt that any personal meeting between him and me could potentially pose a serious threat to my safety. So it was at that point that I made further contact with DCI Darling, to tell him of my suspicions about Usher. And here I am. Being interrogated.'

'Interviewed, DS Bradley,' the superintendent told him, 'as per standard procedure.

'So tell me anything at all that you have been able to find out on which you base your suspicions. Preferably something concrete.'

'Let's start with his daughter. Poppy. She did finish up in hospital with a drugs reaction and/or overdose when she was just fifteen. That's a couple of years ago. You can check that easily enough with hospital records. He told some of us, though not many, about it himself, so it's not that much of a secret, although he only hinted at the cause. He didn't mention drugs outright.

'What's less well known is that his daughter then went into a private clinic, up the coast, to be thoroughly sorted out and set back on the right path. Now that place I have been able to research online and the fees are eye-watering. Unless Usher has private means, they'd be beyond the pocket of a mere DI.'

'You're saying the DI turned to the very drug dealers he's supposed to be trying to bring to justice for financial help for his daughter after a drugs overdose? Is that not a little far-fetched?'

'We all know the dangers posed by a police officer in serious financial difficulties. It makes them open to any kind of pressure from criminals. Especially for someone working in areas such as Drugs.

'And if you want to see that your daughter is never given access to buying any future supplies, who better to approach for that reassurance than the Big Man himself, who seems to control the city and beyond, on the drugs front.

'Imagine what a trade he could offer. *"See that no one ever again sells anything to my daughter and I'll keep you supplied with everything you need to know to keep operating and avoid being pulled in and the supply chain being broken".*'

'Have you put any of this to DI Usher himself? Or did you go direct to DCI Darling?'

Bradley's look towards her suggested he clearly thought she didn't know the ins and outs of his job, and the inherent dangers which went with it.

'No, I didn't. For two very good reasons. If I'm wrong, it could ruin our relationship. Believe me, if you've never done this kind of work yourself, you can't imagine how important total trust is between a field officer and their handler. Once that goes, the working relationship is dead in the water, for evermore.

'If I'm right, then by telling him my suspicions I would be putting my life at risk. As simple as that. You don't imagine for a moment he could afford to let me walk away to pass on my theory to higher authorities, do you? I certainly wasn't going to take the chance of that happening.'

* * *

As Ted and Sammy got back into the service vehicle, once they'd concluded the interview, Sammy turned to look at Ted as she asked, 'What did you think of his story, Ted? Did you believe him?'

'Did you?' Ted countered, putting the car in gear and pulling away smoothly.

'I asked first, I outrank you, and it's ladies first,' she told him, but with a smile.

Ted chuckled at her sense of humour. She was definitely growing on him. And the DCS had been absolutely right. He wouldn't fancy being interviewed by her himself. She was relentless. Ian Bradley had been gagging for his cigarette and a cup of strong coffee by the time she'd finished with him. It had been fair and legitimate questioning, without undue pressure, but she'd left no question unasked. And most of them had been asked several times in a different format.

'For what it's worth, yes, I believed him. His theory is a very plausible one which at least merits being carefully looked into. Certainly Usher's financial situation, and the bills from the clinic. Because we both know all too well, as Bradley reminded us, a police officer in financial difficulties presents a very soft target, especially if they have family members who could be targeted in turn, and are therefore a danger to any case they're associated with.'

'And there's no way, as far as you know, that Bradley could have heard about the planned op tomorrow? I'm just speculating that there could simply be bad blood between the two of them, so Bradley is setting Usher up to take the fall for something he's not involved with.'

'Not as far as I know. He's been kept out of the loop completely. Unless there's another mole somewhere who's supplying him with information, although I don't see how they could currently contact him. But if that is the case, we have a bigger problem than we've realised so far.'

'Right, well, so that none of us ends up looking like total pillocks tomorrow because we haven't crossed all the t's and dotted the i's, first thing I'm going to do when we get back to the nick is to authorise in-depth investigations into the private lives and finances of both DI Usher, and DS Bradley.

'But before that, be a love and stop somewhere we can get a cuppa and a decent butty, will you? Breakfast is but a distant memory and my belly thinks my throat's cut.'

Chapter Twenty-nine

Ted began his end of the day meeting with Jezza, Gina, Virgil and Jo by giving them the broad outline of the interview with Ian Bradley and the possible motives he'd put forward for DI Dave Usher to be the mole. The four of them would have key roles to play the following day and Ted was leaving nothing to chance.

Jezza gave one of her characteristic tuts of impatience as she asked, with a note of irony, 'Permission to speak freely, boss?'

'Don't you always, Jezza? Please, go ahead.'

'With all due respect, boss,' she began. Ted was convinced she only ever said that to needle him as she knew he didn't like it. 'Aren't you overlooking the blindingly bloody obvious? Yes, the DI's daughter and the whole drugs thing are powerful motivators. But then if the DI was in a position to go directly to the Big Man or any of his team to beg for their help, then surely he was in a position to bring the lot of them down instead? And wouldn't that be better all round? Clean up the town, get a big tick on his record for results, job done, with his honour and his career prospects intact.'

'She has a point, boss,' Jo put in.

'So what's your theory, Jezza?' Ted asked her, although he had an idea which way her thinking was taking her.

'They approached him in the first place, not the other way round. Either they heard somehow about his daughter getting into drugs. Or, and here's the cynical thing, they picked him because they knew he had a daughter. They deliberately started her on drugs. Enough to scare, not enough to kill, because they know what they're doing. Then they contacted the DI. Full of apology. So sorry, should never have happened, we can see that it never happens again. We'll pay to get her straightened out, and we'll ensure no one in the city or anywhere close to ever supplies her with anything again.'

Ted was nodding before she'd ever finished speaking.

'You make a very good point, Jezza. I should have considered that myself. And of course, if you're right, there will be even less of a trail. If the DI isn't being paid for his information, it's going to be that much harder to find the evidence.'

'There's something else we need to consider and set up before tomorrow, boss,' Jo began but Ted was ahead of him.

'If it is the DI who turns up tomorrow to whisk Data away, and not someone else we haven't even thought about yet, we're going to need a plan in place to take his daughter, and probably his wife too, into immediate protective custody before we can remotely think about arresting and questioning him. If his daughter is anywhere the Big Man's lot can get their hands on her, he would never tell us anything at all.

'Jo, we won't know until tomorrow who it is we're really dealing with, but if it's Usher, we'll need to make that a priority. Meanwhile, the objective for tomorrow is to watch and wait, to see who turns up to intercept Data.

'If no one does, then it's up to your acting skills, Jezza, to convince Data that he's wasting his time with Robyn and to send him on his way. And Virgil, you're our secret weapon. If young Data won't take no for an answer it will be your job to show him the error of his ways - and show him the door. He'll still be followed, of course, to see where he takes us. But the safety and welfare of Robyn and of her parents, not to mention the three of you, is paramount, so please remember that.'

As the others were leaving the office Ted asked Jo, 'D'you fancy a swift one in The Grapes?'

Jo didn't. Not remotely. What he wanted to do was to get home to his family. To relieve his wife who would have been looking after Mateo all day as well as trying to do her own work. Helping him with the physiotherapy exercises he had now been given and was meant to do every day, which he didn't unless chased and only then did them with much protest.

He wanted to cook dinner for the whole family. For all eight of them to sit down at the table together for some proper family time, then to check and help with homework.

The boss so seldom suggested social drinking, except after a good result, that he sensed he was in need of it, so instead he said, 'Love to, Ted. Just let me phone my real boss, the mother of my children, and then I'm all yours.'

Ted went to get his things from his own office while Jo made the call. The simple fact was that Ted had so much on his mind, with such an important operation the next day and so much riding on the outcome, that he didn't feel quite ready to go back to the house when Trev would have left already for his trip to Wales for the inquest. He'd get a warm welcome from the cats, but he felt in real need of some human company, if only for an hour or so.

Ted got the drinks in and they found a quiet corner of the bar. It was not yet busy.

'How are things going with the Welsh case, Ted? Your mother's friend, did you say?'

Ted had only told him the bare outline of the case. There hadn't been time for more than that when he'd arrived back to the midst of a major incident.

'The inquest is tomorrow,' Ted told him. 'Trev's gone down to be with my mother because she'll be called as a witness and she's a bit nervous about it. The local CID are hoping for an unlawful killing conclusion, of course. Then they can go after their prime suspect.'

Jo took a sip of his pint then wiped his top lip. Now he understood the reason for the after work drink. The boss probably didn't fancy an empty house, with so much on his mind.

'It's going to be a very interesting case, I imagine. I hope they get the right result.'

They made inconsequential small talk for a few minutes then Ted smiled as he said, 'It's fine, Jo. You get off home. I was being selfish, avoiding an empty house - well, apart from the cats - and wanting a bit of company. You've got a family to go home to. I'll see you in the morning, bright and early, and let's hope for a successful outcome. And thanks for your company.'

* * *

Mrs Forsyth, the elderly woman who lived diagonally opposite Robyn Pascoe's flat was up bright and early, long before the appointed hour when she'd been told that police officers would arrive to set up an observation post in her front bedroom.

She was washed, smartly dressed, hair neatly styled, the kettle on and the best biscuits selected from the tin, tastefully arranged on a tray with the good china teacups. She couldn't remember when she'd last had so much excitement to look forward to. It was certainly different to her usual mundane days, sitting in her window, watching the few people who passed in the quiet and reserved slice of suburbia where she lived.

The large van which turned into her driveway bore a convincing-looking but totally false logo for a company offering installation of fitted kitchens, bathrooms and bedrooms. Any equipment which went into the house would be in anonymous cardboard cartons which should raise neither suspicion nor much interest from anyone who might see them. Officers going in and out all wore overalls with the same logo on them.

Jo was there before the van arrived and had parked outside the house. He was dressed in what he hoped looked like suitable clothes for someone from the company there to oversee the fictitious installation and to make sure the supposed client was happy every step of the way.

Mrs Forsyth was hovering just inside the door, offering tea and biscuits to anyone who appeared. These days there was nothing unusual about tradesmen showing ID before entering a property, so Jo made sure to show his. Then he skilfully manoeuvred her to the kitchen and kept her there chatting, out of the way. The less attention that was drawn to the property until everything was done, the better he would like it.

Data wasn't due to arrive until three in the afternoon, if he turned up at all. They'd been told that Robyn had at least had a reply to her text from him, saying he would be there. No doubt the prospect of some cash was enough to entice him. But all of them knew the risks of not setting up early enough for a delicate operation. Data was a valuable asset to the gang. There was always a chance he was being watched by them at all times.

A large part of police work always involved a good measure of waiting around. Today's op was going to be no different. Robyn wouldn't be home from her work until about two-thirty and Data was not due for at least half an hour after that. Jezza would meet Robyn at her workplace and come back with her. She'd hopefully look like one of her friends. As Data had been keen for Robyn to bring some of them to their supposed engagement party, he shouldn't be worried by her presence if he himself arrived early to check out the location.

In case Data or anyone else was keeping an eye out, Robyn's parents also arrived early at the flat, with Gina and Virgil in the back of the car. Once they and Mrs Pascoe had got out of the vehicle, Mr Pascoe parked the car outside in the road, a short distance away, rather than on the driveway, where it might possibly scare Data off. Mrs Pascoe had offered to feed them all while they waited.

In the meantime, Ted had positioned himself in another van, some distance away from the main action. Another bland vehicle with another false logo. The phone number on both vehicles would go straight to an answering service which would sound genuine enough. This second van contained equipment for a direct audio link with the followers, plus a video link to footage being shot from the front upstairs bedroom of Mrs Forsyth's house, opposite the target property.

Most of the followers would also be in place in good time, but not so early as to draw undue attention as they waited for action. They would stick out like the proverbial sore thumb if they were parked and hanging about for too long in one place, or simply cruising about aimlessly.

Robyn's flat had the big advantage of being situated roughly halfway down a relatively quiet road, so not only would Data be seen approaching from some distance away, if he came on foot as Robyn had told them he usually did, but so too could any vehicles.

They had the registration numbers of any car which DI Dave Usher might possibly use if it was him and if he did come to grab Data. They at least stood a good chance of finding out who their target was. Now all that any of them could do was to wait and to watch.

* * *

It was always the way, on an operation like this. Flat calm, for minutes, sometimes hours, at a time. Then suddenly ...

'We have a young IC4 male on foot heading in the direction of the target property road. Age estimate late teens/early twenties. He's got off a bus coming from town lower down the road. Alone, walking briskly, doesn't appear to be suspicious of observation.'

The tension levels of all those watching and waiting went up palpably. Particularly for Ted and Gina who had both been present on the previous occasion when they thought they had Data walking neatly into a trap, only to find that the gang had sent in a decoy to test out the meeting. They had then calmly sacrificed him when he was no longer useful to them.

'Now turning into the road for the target property. Anyone else have eyes on?'

'We have him in sight now, walking down towards us.'

The officer in Mrs Forsyth's bedroom with Jo joined in. Jo was getting his first look at the person believed to be Data.

Robyn was back from work now and in the house with her parents and Jezza. Watching the two of them, Robyn and Jezza, walking down the road together, arm in arm, chatting away like the best of friends, Jo was sure that seeing Jezza in that role wouldn't raise any suspicions from anyone who might be watching. He knew Jezza well, knew it would be her with Robyn, yet watching her like that, in character, he found it hard to reconcile her with the feisty DC Vine he knew through work.

'We have a black Ford coming up now, from the same direction as the IC4 male. Just running a check on the reg number now.'

A different voice this time, who repeated the number aloud. Ted, in the second van, had committed to memory the car numbers the DCS had given him for vehicles to which DI Dave Usher would normally have access.

The number was a match. It was Usher's own personal vehicle. But who was driving it?

'Turning into the same road as the IC4 male now. Driver only. IC1 male. No further details.'

'We need a visual on that driver. I need a firm ID. Jo, can you get anything on camera from the OP?' Ted asked him.

He was feeling detached and helpless. He would be able to tell if it was Usher if he got a decent shot from the camera filming the scene. Being blind-sided in the van was increasing his frustration.

He'd made sure that Jo, Jezza and Virgil had all seen a photo of DI Usher, so they would be able to identify him. Gina already knew him by sight but she was keeping out of sight in the flat as she could be recognised either by Data or by DI Usher, if it was him.

What Ted was desperate for now was some sight of the driver and a definite ID on who it was.

'We have eyes on the vehicle now and the camera running. Impossible to tell at this distance who's at the wheel.

'It's coming up behind the IC4 male now. He's still on our side of the road. He's not yet crossed over to go towards the flat. Car is slowing down to crawling pace. Passenger side window is being lowered. Pedestrian has slowed right down and turned to speak to the driver. He's leaning in through the window.'

It was Jo's voice still, giving Ted the vital running commentary he needed on what was going on and hopefully, soon, a positive ID on the driver.

'There's a bit of a debate going on between them. It looks as if it's getting heated. Data is making to walk away. Driver is leaning towards him, trying to grab his arm. I have a good visual on the driver now.'

Then Jo's voice turned more serious and formal.

'This is DI Rodriguez for DCI Darling. It's a positive ID on our prime suspect. He is the driver.'

Ted didn't know whether to be relieved or disappointed that it was Usher. He tried to focus on the task in hand. Time later to think of the ramifications.

'DCI Darling to all follow units. Please don't lose sight of this target. We need to know their end destination and if it's at all possible, we need some footage of it. But proceed with extreme caution. If they're going where we think they might be, it will be well protected and you'll be under scrutiny as soon as you get anywhere near.

'So observation only please. Stay in contact and stay alert. Give us a heads-up as soon as you can on where they're headed and try to get us a final destination.

'Good luck.'

Chapter Thirty

Ted could feel his heart start to thud in his chest as adrenaline levels rocketed. A new voice now, the first of the follow cars beginning the pursuit. Vehicles would be switched regularly, one turning off to give way to another, so that the driver being pursued didn't see the same vehicle behind them for too long at a time.

Ted was busy trying to second guess where Usher would be taking Data. Would he head straight to the Big Man? Did he even know where to find him? He suspected that the DI probably did. If the man had the sort of hold over him that Jezza had suggested, and Ted was beginning to find that more and more plausible, he could risk his informer having such information, safe in the knowledge that he would be too afraid of the consequences to his family if he tried to do anything with it.

'In pursuit of target vehicle which is currently heading north west. Driver appears unaware at this stage that he has a tail.'

The driver added road names and numbers for exact location, shadowing the black Ford for several turns before announcing, 'Traffic lights on red ahead. I'm taking the left filter lane before he notices I've been behind him for some time.'

Another voice picked up the commentary.

'I'm three cars behind target vehicle and have eyeball on him now. Lights are changing to green.'

Everyone listening to the running commentary was clearly going to be feeling the same as Ted. Heart rate increasing, mouth going dry, palms getting damp.

The slightest error now could lose them the chance to get anywhere near the Big Man.

'He's turning again. Now heading west out of town. I'm continuing straight on.'

A succession of different voices as the followers relieved and replaced one another as needed. The team so far had no trouble at all keeping the target vehicle in their sights. Whatever was running through Usher's mind as he drove, always keeping carefully within the speed limit, it certainly wasn't keeping an eye out for pursuit. He seemed to have swallowed the line he was fed in the circulated false report that the attempt to arrest Data was going to take place inside the flat. He would no doubt be imagining the reception committee waiting patiently there.

It was a measure of how panicked he was that he appeared not to have thought of the alternative. He must be totally spooked and running scared.

The less good news in terms of the pursuit was that Usher's route was now taking him out into the countryside. An expensive area. Big, detached properties, well secured. Widely spaced, often with their own impressive security systems. Not at all the ideal place for a covert follow.

All Ted needed from the operation was sight of the end destination. Wherever Usher might be taking Data, he needed to know the location so it could be carefully checked out with a view to any further action. Luckily plenty of vehicles had dash cams these days, and motor cyclists were often equipped with a helmet cam. Insurers liked it. It helped with disputes after a collision. There was nothing unusual in seeing them. Footage from those cameras might at least help them pinpoint the Big Man's lair for a future raid.

It was one of the bike riders, now out into quiet rural roads, who signalled something happening.

'Target vehicle is now pulling into a lay-by and stopping. I can't risk doing the same. Can someone pick up?'

'I can shortly, but I won't have eyes on for a couple of minutes yet.'

It was a voice from one of the car drivers who'd dropped back some time ago.

Ted seldom swore. It took a lot of provocation to make him do so. He almost forgot all radio protocol and did so, but managed to grit his teeth and said instead, 'That leaves us without visual for longer than I'd like. Sit rep ASAP, please.'

'I have eyes on him now. He's just pulled out of the lay-by in front of me. Accelerating away in front of me. I can see the vehicle clearly enough and I cannot see a front seat passenger. Repeat vehicle appears now to have one occupant only.'

This time Ted did swear on air. He simply couldn't help himself. The frustration was too much.

'Stick to the target vehicle. Do not lose him. We need to know where he's going. All other available units, we need to check that lay-by for any sign of Data in case he's been dumped for some reason, alive or dead.'

Ted's mind was racing. Had Usher suddenly realised he was being followed, lost control of himself and disposed of Data? That didn't make sense, though. If he turned up empty-handed, he would hardly be well received.

Something was niggling away at the back of Ted's mind. Something he couldn't quite put his finger on. Something he'd read in a report somewhere. About Noah Brooks boasting of having been taken to visit the Big Man.

'Wait!' he suddenly bellowed. 'He's still in the vehicle. Data. He's either in the back under the parcel shelf, alive, or he's in the rear foot well, with something over his eyes at least, so he has no idea where he's going. A witness told us the dead boy, Noah, had boasted about being taken to visit the Big Man like that.

'One vehicle only to check the lay-by. The rest of you concentrate on the target vehicle. I want to know where it goes.'

It seemed an agonisingly slow time to all the listeners before another of the followers announced, 'He's using his mobile while he drives. Let's hope that's to signal ahead that he's nearly at his destination. Very quiet and rural here so it won't be easy getting close.'

A long pause. A collective holding of breath. Then the same voice again. One of the bikers.

'He's turning right off the road into a driveway with electronic gates which are being opened for him, seemingly remotely. Got my helmet cam pointing straight at him but I can't slow down much or it will look too suspicious.'

A different voice. 'I'm close enough behind you to drive past in less than two minutes. I'll at least be able to see if the target vehicle leaves the property my way, and if you have anywhere to stop without raising suspicion you can see if he comes in your direction.'

As soon as the followers relayed an exact location for Usher's destination, everyone with internet access was pulling up apps and entering the coordinates. In short order, Ted found himself looking at an impressive detached property with a conservatory on one side which took up the footprint of an average pair of semi-detached houses. Tall trees and immaculate green lawns surrounded the house and the whole extensive acreage was surrounded by high sight-screened fencing, affording complete privacy.

Ted stared in silence for a long moment at the image on his phone screen, mentally trying to put a price tag on the property and hardly daring to.

Then he spoke very quietly to himself under his breath.

'Got you, Big Man. Got you.'

* * *

The donkey work was done, for now. There were no reports of Data having been found under a hedge by the lay-by so Ted was as confident as he could be that his hunch had been correct. Usher had put him in the back of the car, or down in the foot well, so he couldn't see which property he was being taken to.

Next began the mammoth task of collating all the intelligence collected during the operation. Ted wanted a better recce of the property and surrounding area before they even thought about the raid which would be necessary. He'd ideally like a helicopter overfly of the site, or at least a drone. Before they could begin to risk assess a raid, they needed to know exactly what they would be up against when they went in.

He was remembering, with a chill, what he'd found out about some of the Big Man's henchmen on that earlier case. Some, at least, were from *Batalioni i Operacioneve Speciale,* an Albian Special Forces outfit, known as BOS or The Unit. Their motto, 'We better die for something than live for nothing', told him all he needed to know about the possible outcome of a siege at that property.

He needed to get back to the nick to report in to the DCS, and to Sammy, and think about what their next move could safely be. He thanked everyone still in radio contact for a successful op so far, and told them all to stand down. No point anyone hanging about to tail Usher any further. They knew where he lived, and worked.

As he walked back to his own car, he took out his mobile phone, which had been switched to silent mode throughout. There was a voicemail from DS Morgan in Carmarthen.

'Ted, we got it. Unlawful killing conclusion from the coroner. I'm off to sort out a warrant right now so we can go and haul in the lovely Gemma and ask her what she knows about medication substitution. Oh, and it's early days yet but we have found another of her aromatherapy clients who died suddenly, so we'll be looking into that one, too. I'll call you back again as soon as I have some further news for you.'

There was a brief text from Trev. 'Unlawful killing,' with a long line of exclamation marks after it and a row of kisses. Ted phoned him back.

'Ted! Isn't it fantastic? Unlawful killing. DS Morgan said he was rushing off to sort out bringing Gemma in. What a result! Annie was fantastic as a witness, she really was. I was so proud of her. D'you want to speak to her? She's right here.'

'I honestly haven't time at the moment, sorry. I have to go. Give her my love, tell her I'm pleased for her, and I'll try to catch up with you this evening, perhaps. We've just finished the first part of a big op and now the real work starts. I've got reports to write and grovelling to do to get the officers I need for the next part, and that's not going to be easy. Go and celebrate somewhere with a cup of tea and a cake, at least, then you can tell me all about it when I do manage to phone.'

There was a wistful note of disappointment in Trev's voice as he said his goodbyes. He should know by now that although Ted did his best, and he had at least called, his family could never be his main focus when he was working.

* * *

Ted wasn't at all surprised to find Sammy still in his old office when he got back to the Stockport nick and went to find her. She'd been kept in the picture all through the operation, but she would no doubt want to hear everything from the horse's mouth.

The DCS, too, was still in his office, waiting for news. Sammy made it a conference call so Ted could update both of them at the same time.

'There was no way we could safely leave anyone around to keep an eye on further developments. It's quiet and rural. Loiterers would stick out a mile off. Not just the suspect's house but others in the same area have security cameras everywhere possible. So we won't know if Data stays there or if Usher takes him somewhere. I'm not too worried about Data for the moment, I think he's the least of our concerns. It's the Big Man I want, and his bodyguards.

'We can't risk a raid until we've carried out full surveillance. If the place is crawling with his Albanian mercenaries, there's no telling what security measures they may have put in place. Which is why I want an aerial survey, as well as anything we can do on the ground without raising suspicions.'

He saw and heard the DCS's exaggerated sigh at the mere thought of the budget. Then Holton said, 'At least tell me this is all in our own area and I don't have to go grovelling to Cheshire for permission to play in their sandpit? I know we're talking county lines here, but that could really complicate things for us.'

'All safely within the Trafford boundary, boss. At least that's one thing made simpler. But I can't stress enough how important it is to do our homework before we go blundering in.

'I want to try and have a walk out that way myself over the weekend, if I can borrow a little dog from someone. A nice one, that won't bite me. I'm not very good with dogs, but I managed to walk a Corgi okay.'

Sammy looked at him as she said, 'You need a dog? My daughter has an Iggy. He'd be perfect. Gentle as anything.'

Ted shot her a suspicious look, not sure if he was being teased.

'I don't even know what an Iggy is,' he told her candidly.

'An Italian greyhound. Good quiet little dog, very dignified. Luca, she calls him. I'm sure she'd let you borrow him if you promise to take good care of him.'

Reading the next question formulating in Ted's brain she laughed and said, 'No, he doesn't bite. She has a young kiddy, remember, so she wouldn't have anything snappy in the house.

'I take it your masterplan consists of walking past the place with a dog as an alibi, so you can have a close look at it? Is that not risky? Have some of them not seen you before?'

'I've got a baseball cap I've used before, in Spain, to look different. I can do dressing down. DC Vine can always help me. It's her speciality and she's very good at it.'

'Just think of the bloody paperwork if the SIO on the case gets himself shot on the doorstep of the drugs baron we've been trying to bring in, without success, for far too long,' Holton grumbled.

Ted gave them both his most disarming smile. He wanted to do this. The control freak in him wanted to see for himself exactly what they would be up against.

'I'm also very good at running away from danger when necessary, if the dog can keep up.'

'It's a greyhound, Ted,' Sammy told him. 'A little'un, admittedly, but still a greyhound.'

'When are you planning to do all of this?' the DCS asked him.

'Over the weekend, whenever I can borrow the dog, and you can give the go-ahead for the rest of it. With a view to a raid, if it's safe to proceed, early next week.

'There's a layby some way down the road from the house. It should look natural enough to park my car there - and believe me, it looks nothing like a copper's car - to take the dog for a leg stretch and a pee, as if I was off on a journey somewhere. I'll also get some drive-by surveillance done to see if that brings us anything new.

'But I really do need a view from the air, in case there are any nasty surprises lying in wait for us. Then and only then can we plan exactly when to go in. And I want Firearms for that. Plenty of them. Have we got enough for a warrant to search?'

'Suspicion of Class A drugs on the premises? I would think so,' Holton told him. 'What are you going to do about Usher? I have to say I'm shocked and disappointed to hear it was him who turned up. And what about DS Bradley? Does this put him in the clear, as far as you're concerned?'

'Not yet,' Ted told him. 'I'm going to leave him where he is until after the raid. Then we can be sure he's not going to be doing or saying anything to anyone. Not that he knows much. I'll go and see him this evening with some food and cigarettes, but I won't be telling him anything.

'Boss, one more thing. If we manage to get inside the property, and that's a big if, and if we can get to the CCTV tapes before anyone wipes them, there's a good chance that they, too, will show Usher arriving at the property. Hopefully also letting Data out of the back of his car and delivering him to the Big Man or one of his men.

'Meanwhile the helmet cam footage should be plenty for us to bring him in for questioning, at least. But the minute we do that, we need at the same time to put his wife and especially his daughter straight into protective custody somewhere. With them still out there, Usher will tell us nothing, in case any of the Big Man's men go for them.

'Because that will be the hold they've had over Usher all along. They know where his family are.'

Chapter Thirty-one

For once, Ted was glad that Trev was away for the weekend and not planning to arrive home until late on Sunday evening. Trev was looking forward to visiting Willow on his way back, at her invitation, to meet his new baby god-daughter. That would keep him happy and occupied, which eased Ted's conscience as he was planning on working through both days and would probably be late home on Sunday.

Sammy had taken him to meet the Italian greyhound, Luca, owned by her daughter, when they'd both finished work on Friday. She warned him of the Iggy reputation of being somewhat aloof, and she hadn't been exaggerating.

Even Ted didn't feel threatened as the dainty little creature trotted up to him to sniff his trousers, which inevitably smelled of cats. Its smooth coat was a greyish shade which reminded Ted of a mouse. The inspection finished, it turned and went back to its basket without a backward glance.

Ted looked anxiously at the dog's owner, his new boss's daughter, as he asked, 'He doesn't think much of me, does he?'

Laura Sampson laughed. She looked so like her mother and had the same ready, infectious laugh.

'Oh, that was an effusive welcome and a seal of approval from Luca. He's not very demonstrative. You'll be fine with him, and I know you'll look after him. Mum speaks very highly of you, and she doesn't do that often.'

Sammy Sampson shot her a mock glare.

'Don't tell him that, he'll get ideas above his station. Right, then, Ted, I'm not planning on coming in over the weekend, but I'm on the end of the phone if you need to run anything past me, and I might well see you when you come to pick up Luca and drop him off. I like to spend as much of my time off as possible with my grandson. And my daughter, of course.'

She smiled with open affection at Laura as she said that. Ted was always interested to see the softer family side of the officers he served with.

Ted decided to stop for a takeaway on his way back to the house. There was plenty of food in. Trev had stocked up enough to last him for a week, at least, as he was obsessed with seeing he ate properly. But Ted didn't really want to spend time cooking while he had so much on his mind, and so many notes to make for himself.

First, of course, he would have to fend off and see to seven cats claiming to be on the point of starvation, as well as clearing up after them.

Adam was the first to pounce, the minute Ted opened the front door. Ted scooped him up and put him on his shoulder while he gently shooed the others away from the door, so that he could close it as he attempted to herd them all back into the kitchen.

'I don't believe a word of it,' he told them sternly. 'You forget it was me who fed you this morning. I'll get you seen to and eat my tea but then I need you to give me a bit of peace because I've got work to do.'

He confined the cats to the sitting room once he'd eaten so he could spread his paperwork on the kitchen table without their well-meaning help, and at least make a start on it.

He jumped guiltily at the sound of his mobile when the screen told him two things: Trev was calling, and it was much later than he'd realised, because he'd planned on phoning him.

'Sorry, I was going to call you, honestly, but paperwork got the better of me. Did you go out for tea?'

He could tell as soon as Trev began to talk that he'd been

drinking much more than tea. At least he knew his partner would never drive if he was planning on drinking.

'I took Annie out to dinner to celebrate. And yes, Mr Policeman, I did get a taxi because I had a rather nice bottle of red. I even persuaded her to have a glass. She's gone to bed now. I think she's worn out by the relief that her ordeal is over and with a good result.'

'Good, I'm glad you both had a good time. I will try to call tomorrow but it's honestly a bit full on at the moment. Can you please make sure mam understands that nothing is going to happen quickly, with Gemma. Even when they've arrested her, it could all take months. And she might still get off.

'Tell her if she's worried about Gemma coming bothering her, trying to get her to change her statement, let me know and I'll arrange with DS Morgan to get a restraining order put on her.

'I'll see you on Sunday evening some time. I can't promise to be here when you get back, though. Sorry. I've got a lot to do before Monday.'

'That's fine. I'll be there waiting, whatever time you get back.'

The rest of his conversation had Ted laughing fondly, shaking his head and telling him, 'You're impossible? D'you know that?' as he ended the call.

* * *

Once the DCS had signed off on the cost of the aerial survey, there was no problem getting it arranged. The Big Man's house was conveniently near to Manchester Airport, in flying terms, without being too close to any flight paths. It meant that air traffic close by was not an unusual sight. Even a police helicopter, which could often be seen scouting around whenever there was the mere hint of a security alert.

Ted needed that aerial footage before he could finalise his

plans. That and his afternoon walk with Luca the Iggy, if that went to plan and brought him any new information.

Ted started Saturday by meeting Jo in his office to go over the next stages.

'It's gaining entry to the property which I think is going to be the hardest thing for us. I need to talk to Firearms at Long-sight, see if they have a good SFO there who can get us in through those remote controlled gates.

'There's no realistic way we could get anyone close enough to use a device to lift the code when someone was going in or out. Not without them doing a lot of lurking about and being spotted in an instant. The gates might need to be blown and that would need a Specialist. I might go over to Longsight later if I get time. Hopefully once I have the aerial footage and I've been to do my little walk around.'

Ted's own role in Firearms had been as an SFO, specifi-cally trained in points of entry. But those days were long be-hind him. His training was now well out of date.

'Be careful,' Jo warned him. 'I know you can usually look after yourself, but this lot are something else entirely.

'Ted, this is probably just the eternal optimist in me, but is there any chance that if we haul Usher in and confront him with the evidence that we know what he's been up to, we might be able to turn him and get him to help?'

Ted shook his head at the mere suggestion.

'I think that ship has long since sailed, Jo. He knows as well as we do that we can't offer him any deal or leniency. Not with what he's helped the gang to do. I appreciate the pressure he's been under but nothing can excuse helping people who kill kids who get in their way. He's going down for a long time and he must know that.

'And speaking of which, we need to be in a position to bring in the wife and daughter as soon as we make the slightest move to arrest Usher. Because of the sensitivity of this whole op, I think you should stick to using only those who have been in the know, or at least partly so, up to now. So we could perhaps put either Gina or Jezza on to finding out where the wife is likely to be, where she works if she does, plus where the daughter goes to college. We need to be able to bring them in at the exact moment we get Usher, or he's going to tell us nothing at all.'

* * *

Monday morning saw an early pre-op briefing at Central Park, with the DCS and various other officers, including the current Firearms Commander from Longsight. Ted and Sammy were being driven there once more by 'Eck, taking Jo Rodriguez with them. Ted insisted on being on site for the raid on the Big Man's house the following morning, so Jo would need to deputise for him, liaising where necessary.

Ted found himself sitting in the front seat, with Jo in the back next to Sammy. Even on a serious mission Ted noticed that Jo was quickly into charm offensive with the Superintendent. Jo admitted himself that flirtation was his default setting, despite being happily married and seemingly well under the thumb of his wife. Sammy didn't seem to mind. In fact she appeared to be enjoying it.

Both instantly switched back to professional mode as the three of them took their seats in the conference room at Headquarters. The Assistant Chief Constable (Crime), Russell Evans, was in attendance to oversee such a big operation.

'We're going to need distractions while that front gate is blown, or forced or whatever's going to be the best solution,' Ted said, looking at the Firearms officer as he spoke.

They had the aerial footage and all the available shots from dash cams and helmet cams in front of them. It showed the difficulties in getting anywhere near to the entrance to the property without being seen. There was no cover at all and not many dead angles from the CCTV cameras.

'We could try blocking their camera signal from the gate to the house, but if they're as efficient as you say, Ted, they'll have back-up to kick in immediately as soon as anything like that happens,' the Firearms officer, Inspector Bridger, told him.

'And no offence, Ted, but I would really have liked to do my own recce for something like this. But I accept you know what you're doing, and that the fewer of us who are hanging round the scene, the less they're going to be expecting us.'

'I was wondering about some distraction. Maybe get the chopper up again,' as Ted spoke he could see the expressions on the faces of both the DCS and the ACC at the thought of the cost of it all. 'I know, it will blow the budget, but the alternative is a serious risk to officers if they're going in and are expected. And it needs to keep a safe distance. I don't want to sound melodramatic, but there's no telling what weaponry these people will have at their disposal. They could well have something capable of bringing down a chopper.

'There's also a bit of a path that runs behind the target property and the others near to it. I found it when I was walking the dog. It's not an official footpath. A gang as experienced as this wouldn't want a property anywhere near a public right of way, for sure. I only found it by chance when I was walking the dog. I met a woman out for a walk and she told me about it. It's just the edge of a field, but it runs past close to the boundary fence of the property.

'Our Mr Big - Stefan Dervishi is the name we now have for him - lives there as a seemingly law-abiding, rates-paying individual. I wouldn't mind betting the local authority have had letters from him complaining of the intrusion on his privacy from the use of that path.

'Not that it gives anyone passing any glimpse into the properties there. The one we're hitting has a fence far too high to see over, plus it's screened. I thought we could perhaps send the bikers round that way, to make a bit of noise and hopefully draw attention to themselves, without taking any risks. They

can, at least, get away fairly quickly on two wheels. If they and
the helicopter are making some noise as we're trying to gain
entry, it might provide something of a distraction.'

'When are you going in?' Russell Evans asked.

'Tomorrow morning at nine. I would have liked to make it
much earlier but there are valid reasons not to. It's essential that
Usher is arrested at the precise moment we make a move, before he risks getting wind of anything. As a courtesy, I don't
want to do that at his home in front of his family. And it's vital
that his wife and daughter are also brought in at exactly the
same time. For their own safety, but also because he's not going to tell us a thing until he knows they're safe. Plus we know
where they should all be at that time.

'I'm planning on sending DCs Jezza Vine and Gina Shaw to
get the wife and daughter. I don't think it should be anyone in
uniform as that might press alarm bells and start things spiral-
ling out of control. But I don't think the same constraint applies
to DI Usher. I'd like him taken straight to Stockport for questioning. Get him off his own patch quickly and discreetly.'

'You need to send someone of at least equivalent rank to
bring Usher in,' the ACC reminded him. 'If nothing else, again
as a courtesy. He's not yet convicted.'

'I thought I could leave that to DI Rodriguez, with our Sergeant Eric Morgan. Eric can do diplomatic when he needs to.
The fewer people who know what's going on, the better for all
concerned.'

'And what about this lad Data? Where is he now? Do we
know? Is he a loose cannon that needs disarming before we can
do much else?' the ACC asked.

'We don't know, boss,' Ted told him frankly. 'He might still
be at the house. Alive or dead. I took the decision that keeping
any of the followers in the area to try to see if he emerged or
where DI Usher took him could potentially jeopardise the
whole operation. So if we've lost him, that one's entirely down
to me.'

'And what about DS Bradley in all of this?' the DCS asked. 'Is he still being kept in the dark?'

'He is, still snugly tucked up in the safe house with two armed babysitters.'

'Does he really still need two of them, Ted?' the Firearms Commander asked him. 'Because with the amount of officers you want me to field tomorrow I could really do with freeing one of them up. One of my best marksmen is off sick. Silly pillock was taking his waterproof trousers off, fell over, and cracked some ribs on the corner of a table.'

That brought a few smiles, despite the serious situation.

'Seriously, though, do you still rate the potential threat to the DS as highly as that?'

Ted hesitated. Logic suggested that if no one had found DS Bradley's safe house by now, they were unlikely to. He didn't seriously think the DS was desperate or stupid enough to try jumping an AFO to get away, but he'd been opting for caution all along.

'Take it down to one officer from this evening, then, until further notice. But can you please make it someone who's really on the ball and has some miles on the clock. It's not just the risk from outside, it's also the possibility that the DS might want to do a runner. He's not happy being kept in the dark.'

'So, we're all happy we have everything in place for tomorrow?' the DCS asked in summing up. 'High time we got these drugs types off the streets and behind bars where they belong.

'I know it's not easy when we're having to bring in one of our own. A good officer who's gone bad for reasons none of us yet understand. So let's all please keep it as professional as possible. Make sure everyone involved knows to leave emotions out of it. It's a job, like any other.

'Good luck, everyone.'

Chapter Thirty-two

Yet another anonymous van. This time parked in the quiet hamlet up the road from the Big Man's house. Ted was in the back, ready to follow everything which was said and done. His service vehicle was parked close by, already facing back towards the house. He intended to be in on the action as soon as the Firearms Commander allowed access to anyone other than his armed officers in their full tactical gear.

DC Virgil Tibbs was with Ted. One of the only other members of his own team who had been fully briefed all along on the intricate ins and outs of the case. He'd be going in with Ted at the spearhead of the officers who would be making arrests once the Commander had declared it safe.

The tension was palpable; the waiting almost unbearable. Ted would have preferred to be up there in the vanguard, going in first. It was all now down to split-second timing, plus a large dollop of good luck on their side.

He heard the noise of the helicopter first, circling overhead. Then a muffled 'whoomp' which could have been almost anything, but Ted recognised it immediately. The detonation to open the gates. Once that was done, it meant the Firearms officers could go in inside their vehicles which would get them nearer to the action under vital cover.

Ted and Virgil were already leaping from the van and jumping into the black Ford, to go screeching down the road, not yet going through the gates until Ted got the permission he needed to enter. All they could do was to watch and wait.

Ted was listening to the rapid exchange of gunfire, all the time following the exchanges through his earpiece. Then he heard the words no policeman likes to hear: 'Officer down.'

Everything now hung on a simple numbers game. All depended on how many of his men the Big Man had surrounding his fortress home. It sounded hopeful. They seemed to be outnumbered. But they were well dug in and clearly not about to give up without a fight. To the death, if necessary.

Ted could now see straight up the drive to the impressive house. He was quick to pick out a sniper on the roof, using a chimney stack as cover. At least until a skilled shot from an AFO caught him at the moment he exposed himself too far in order to fire again. He simply crumpled and folded, dropping his weapon and sliding slowly down the pitched roof to fall over the edge and land in a heap on the gravel driveway where it curved gracefully round the front of the house. He was certainly not going to move any time soon, if ever again.

The agreed plan had been to try to get close enough to the house to deploy grenades or gas if necessary, to draw the inhabitants out into the open without risk to officers. The likelihood of their opponents voluntarily surrendering had been considered too unlikely even to contemplate.

Ted had initially identified three shooters, as he waited with increasing impatience to be allowed in. Only two now, with the one from the roof out of the equation. The odds were looking favourable but he didn't allow himself to get his hopes up too high. He was fairly certain mercenaries of the calibre they were clearly dealing with would not run out of ammunition any time soon. But the numbers were lower than he'd feared they might be, so they clearly had the element of surprise.

Bridger was trying to create enough covering fire to get some of his officers round the back of the property to try to gain entry that way. They hadn't been able to get much of a sighting of the rear, apart from the aerial shots, but it was worth a try.

Like so many such operations, everything suddenly went from high drama to a state of calm finality. Through his ear-piece, Ted heard the shouts of officers who'd accessed the rear entrance announcing they were in, had disarmed and restrained one gunman and were on their way to do the same with the second one, now seemingly the last armed resistance.

Ted could contain himself no longer. He put the Ford into gear, let it creep into the driveway and start to inch closer to the house, still waiting for the all-important 'All Clear' from the officer in charge.

Other vehicles, containing officers from Uniform, fell into place behind them. All kept to the side of the wide track to the house, leaving room for an ambulance, which had been summoned, to get through when it arrived.

Ted's eyes were glued to the front of the house as he let the car crawl forward, still waiting for the vital permission to approach further.

Suddenly a diminutive figure appeared in the doorway and stepped out onto the top of the stone steps which led down from the house. Impossible to gauge his height from a distance but Ted would have put him at not much more than four feet. He was wearing dark glasses, one hand was held aloft in a gesture of surrender, the other gripping firmly to a white stick which he carried in front of him, swinging it from side to side to detect any obstacles in his path.

There was a woman just behind him, wearing a simple black dress with a white apron over it. She had a supportive hand under the back of the stick-swinging arm. Even from a distance, it was possible to read the terror in her posture.

Ted was subconsciously revving the engine in his impatience to get moving. His sudden loud shout through his mouthpiece risked piercing a few eardrums as realisation dawned.

'Watch that stick!' he shouted. 'Suspect is armed. Repeat,

armed. The stick has a concealed blade. I'm coming in.'

He didn't wait for a reply. He let the car leap forward with a sudden surge which had Virgil gripping the sides of the front passenger seat.

'Bloody hell, boss, how did you know that?' Virgil asked.

'Training,' Ted told him shortly, but with a grin.

This was what he was trained for. Endless sessions with Mr Green, learning that anything and everything could be a weapon, even something as seemingly inoffensive as a blind person's white stick. It was the height at which Dervishi, the Big Man, was swinging it which had triggered Ted's suspicions. Too high to alert him to anything on the ground. The perfect height to allow a lethal blade to appear from the end of it at the touch of the button. He'd seen one at close quarters. Been at the business end of it with Mr Green wielding it. He wasn't about to forget that experience in a hurry.

Ted brought the Ford to a smooth halt in front of the house, ignoring the tirade he was getting through the earpiece from Bridger. He got carefully and calmly out of the car, ordering Virgil as he did so, 'Stay in the vehicle.'

Virgil's muttered reference to a previous case, 'Yes, like you stayed on the church tower, boss,' was ignored by Ted, if he heard it at all.

He could hear shouts now from both the front of the house and its interior, ordering the small man to put down his weapon. Dervishi currently had all his attention focused on Ted who stepped slowly nearer, opening his jacket and lifting the sides up.

'Mr Dervishi? I'm Detective Chief Inspector Darling, from Stockport, and I'm here to arrest you. I'm showing you that I'm unarmed because I'm not sure that I believe you're unable to see me. For the same reason, I'm showing you my photo ID.'

Bridger's language grew stronger now, totally inappropriate radio procedure.

'Ted, get the fuck out of my officers' line of sight before

you get yourself shot!'

Dervishi cocked his head now. From close up Ted could see that the glasses were mirror shades, so he had no way of seeing the eyes behind them. Yet he felt them riveted on him.

There was an ominous click and a blade appeared from the end of the white stick. Exactly as Ted had anticipated. In a quick, fluid movement, Dervishi dropped his upraised hand and grabbed the woman's spare arm in a grip tight enough to cause her to cry out in pain and fear.

'Your problem, Chief Inspector,' the man's voice was surprisingly calm, given the circumstances, 'is that the minute anyone takes another step towards me, this lady will die, with my knife through her throat. She is my housekeeper. I call her Mrs Igor, and she doesn't deserve to die. She's too good a cook, for one thing.

'You and I both know that your officers cannot shoot me, either from in front or behind, because the bullet would pass straight through me and kill Mrs Igor as well. And you can't tell her to move out of the way because she doesn't speak a word of English. So unless you happen to have someone on site who speaks fluent Albanian ...'

'The thing is, Mr Dervishi, there's not really anything to stop me from coming close enough to arrest you. Because if you did carry out your threat to kill the lady, then the order would immediately be given to shoot you. And believe me, I could dive out of the way very quickly indeed, if necessary.'

Ted had stepped quietly one tread higher as he spoke. It was obvious that Dervishi was watching him from behind the shades. In the same way that Ted was watching his every movement, trying to assess his speed and mobility. He was gambling everything on it not matching his own.

Bridger's contribution had been reduced to random swearwords now but not much else.

'So really, your best, if not your only option, is to let the lady go and give yourself up to me.'

Ted could move as quietly and stealthily as one of his own cats when he needed to. He was now only one stone step below where the dwarf was standing, desperately seeking an escape route. The knife was not yet pointing at the woman, which meant that as soon as Ted made his move, it would be brought into play directly facing him.

Were his calculations right? The slightest error would put him in serious danger, as well as the housekeeper. Even Bridger was quiet now, joining the collective holding of breath.

Then Ted's foot flew up fast and deadly, connecting with complete accuracy with the man's hand, sending the white stick flying and making a sickening cracking noise as it came into contact with wrist bones.

Dervishi dropped the woman's arm with a howl to grab at his own hand, now agonisingly painful and totally disarmed.

Almost instantaneously, armed officers appeared from in front and behind, snapping out orders, pulling the woman to safety, and Bridger's voice in Ted's ear said, 'Ted, you bastard, I just aged ten years, and I think I need to change my kecks.'

Ted was ignoring everyone, busily cautioning his prisoner and issuing his instructions, in his usual polite and measured tone.

'I'll be taking Mr Dervishi to Stockport but I'd like to borrow an armed escort for him, and we'll need to call ahead and arrange for medical treatment for him. Anyone else on site needs arresting and taking to different stations for interview. Uniform officers will do that, they've all been briefed on holding charges and locations, and again, I'd like armed escorts, please. These people are dangerous. The housekeeper too is to be arrested at this stage, and can someone please arrange an Albanian interpreter for her.

'Thank you, everyone. I'm sorry if I gave anyone a scare.'

Then he went off to find Bridger. He had some serious grovelling to do, especially if he didn't want a ton of shit to descend on his head as a result of his actions. He knew Bridger would have to report exactly what had happened. He hoped he could persuade him to tone it down as much as possible.

* * *

'Mrs Usher? I'm DC Gina Shaw. Here's my ID. I'm sorry to bother you at work like this and I'll try to make this discreet. First of all, please don't panic. There's nothing to be worried about. Because of an operation currently taking place, I need to take you into protective custody for the time being. It would be best if you came quietly, without a fuss. But I must warn you that should it be necessary, I would have to arrest you for obstruction.

'My car is just outside, so would you please collect up your things and come with me? And no, I'm sorry, in these circumstances you do not have the right to call anyone at this moment.'

'Please come with me.'

* * *

Ted had just about finished smoothing things over with Inspector Bridger when his mobile rang. Jezza. He hadn't been expecting a call from her so soon. He hoped it wasn't going to be bad news, after things had gone better than expected on the op so far.

There had been only the one police casualty and, although the officer was seriously injured, their condition was not thought to be critical. They'd be on their way to hospital as soon as they'd been stabilised for travelling.

Ted excused himself to take the call.

'Yes, Jezza?'

'Boss,' she began.

Ted could tell immediately from her tone that things were not going according to plan for her. She sounded worried.

'I'm at the college. Only Poppy Usher isn't here. After a lot of faffing about and checking, they confirmed her absence and let me talk to her best friend.

'Apparently it's not all that unusual for her to nick off, especially lately. She has a new boyfriend and her friend told me she was going off somewhere with him today.'

'Boss, her new boyfriend's name is Data.'

Chapter Thirty-three

'Inspector Usher? I'm DI Jo Rodriguez, from Stockport, this is PS Morgan. I'm here with a warrant for your arrest on charges of perverting the course of justice.'

Jo and Eric Morgan had walked into the DI's office after the briefest of knocks. They knew he'd be at his desk. The DCS had arranged with his secretary to phone Usher and check his whereabouts.

Usher's face drained instantly of colour and he shot to his feet. A kaleidoscope of differing emotions passed over his face. There was no mistaking that the dominant one was raw fear.

'You'll be allowed to contact someone as soon as we get back to Stockport but I'm afraid I can't allow you to make any calls until then.'

He recited the words of the caution then said, 'I'd really like to keep this as low key as possible, for the benefit of all concerned. My preference would be if you'd just walk quietly out to the car with us so no one need know what's actually going on. But be in no doubt. If we have to handcuff you and do it the hard way, we will.'

Usher was clearly starting to panic now. The fear was taking the upper hand.

'My family ...' he gabbled. 'Poppy, my wife ... you're putting them at risk. You don't know what you're doing, what these people are capable of.'

'I would really strongly advise you not to say anything further at this time. Not until we're at Stockport and you've had time to talk to a legal advisor. It's up to you how we do this. My advice would be simply to come quietly with us.

'We've sent other officers to bring your wife and daughter into protective custody. As soon as we're in the car and on the road, I'll get a sit rep for you of where they are. So shall we go?'

For a brief moment, Jo thought that Usher was about to lose it and they would end up having to overpower and hand-cuff him. He sincerely hoped it wouldn't come to that. He knew he could rely on Eric Morgan if things got lively, but as he was always fond of saying, and not entirely in jest, he considered himself a lover, not a fighter.

A long, shaky sigh signalled Usher's reluctance but also his acceptance of the situation.

PS Morgan placed his considerable bulk in front of him as they headed for the stairs to deter flight, Jo bringing up the rear.

Once Usher was safely installed in the back seat, with Jo in the front, Eric Morgan pulled the car smoothly out of the car park and into the traffic, heading south for Stockport.

Jo had his phone's earpiece in while he caught up on what was happening. The last thing they needed now was for Usher to get any inkling if things hadn't so far gone to plan. He'd asked for voicemail updates, anticipating problems if Usher were to hear what was going on rather than the edited high-lights which Jo planned on giving him.

It was the boss's voice which had left him a detailed but concise message on the progress, or lack of it. Mrs Usher was safely on her way with Gina Shaw. Poppy Usher was as yet unaccounted for and reinforcements were being sent to help Jezza to find her and bring her in.

The one glimmer of hope on that score was that Poppy had told her best friend quite a bit about Data, her new boyfriend, and that had included the name of the road in which he was living. Officers were on their way there.

'What's the news? Where are they? Where's Poppy? Is she safe?'

Usher began speaking as soon as he saw that Jo had listened to the messages. He was leaning forward in the back seat, his tension palpable.

Jo half turned to face him, trying to keep his expression neutral.

'DC Shaw has collected your wife and is bringing her in. DC Vine is just collecting Poppy.'

He hoped he'd made it convincing. Another of his favourite sayings was that as a good catholic, he found it hard to lie. He wasn't entirely joking when he said that, either.

Bent copper or not, Usher's senses were still working. He spotted the slight hesitation in Jo's voice and it quickly tipped the balance towards panic mode.

'What's happened? Where is she? What the fuck are you not telling me? She should be at college. Have they checked there? Where the fuck is Poppy?'

'They're at the college now,' Jo told him, hoping it was at least partly true.

'Look, Dave,' he decided to try a softer, more personal approach. He was getting seriously concerned about the state of Usher's mental health, which was clearly deteriorating. As soon as he could he'd put in a request for him to be seen by a medic. Another reason Jo thought dragging him in handcuffed and kicking and screaming was not going to improve his condition. 'You know her safety and welfare is our top priority. We don't want anything to happen to Poppy, any more than you do.'

Usher was openly crying now. Tears rolling down his face unchecked. Rocking his body within the confines of the seatbelt. A man clearly in meltdown.

Jo and Eric Morgan exchanged worried looks, both feeling uncomfortable and inadequate in the face of it. All Jo could think of was what state he would be in if one of his own six children was missing in similar circumstances. In between the dark thoughts, he offered up prayers to any of the saints he thought might be of some use to him.

At least Usher was quieter now. He still asked for news, about every two minutes, but with each successive shake of the head from Jo, he seemed to get quieter, more despondent.

Jo had never been more relieved in his life to reach the sanctuary of the nick's car park. Eric Morgan pulled up close to the rear entrance while Jo got out and went to the back door to start extricating Usher. The man had slipped into silence and looked like someone on the brink of mental collapse. The sooner Jo could get him inside and seen to, the better he would like it.

Jo even had to help him off with his seat belt. Usher seemed to be now beyond even the simplest task. Numb, his expression blank. A broken man.

Jo reached out an arm to help him to his feet. In the next instant, the top of Usher's head connected violently with the bridge of Jo's nose, making a sickening crunch. He instantly saw stars and tasted blood, stumbling back against the side of the vehicle, the world spinning around him.

Usher was suddenly galvanised, sprinting at full pelt for the entrance to the car park. Eric Morgan, slower out of the vehicle and not much of a runner, on his own admission, made a valiant effort in pursuit.

* * *

David Bates hated being a white Tranny van man. Always under pressure. Hardly enough time to have a pee between deliveries, never mind to eat anything much. He couldn't risk speeding fines to make up lost time, which would cost him his licence and stop him from doing the job which he hated, but which at least put basic food on the table for himself and his family.

That's why whenever there was the slightest bit of clear road in front of him, he risked pushing the van a bit, even in short spurts. Anything to help him catch up valuable time.

Mornings were the worst, too. People hurrying, late for work. Racing to make appointments. He was trying now to recover those precious minutes lost getting caught up in it all, putting his foot down a bit.

He barely saw the blur of movement at the passenger side of the van. Didn't realise what was going on until he heard the sickening thump and felt the steering veer about as he fought to bring more than a ton of vehicle to a controlled halt, praying to a god he didn't believe in that what he feared had just happened wasn't true.

Jo had overtaken Eric Morgan, despite his own injury and his still-spinning head, and arrived just in time to see Usher bounce backwards off the left side of the van, fly through the air and hit the tarmac. His head snapped back to connect with a sickening thud, with enough force to whiplash it back up only to crack down a second time.

Jo was shouting into his phone, summoning reinforcements, an ambulance, the boss, anyone he could think of, at the same time starting triage on the crumpled and bloodied form which was DI Dave Usher.

* * *

'Marina, please, concentrate very hard. It's important.'

DC Jezza Vine was on the phone to Poppy Usher's best friend from college. She and the officers who'd been sent to help her had been up and down the mercifully short road repeatedly, trying to pinpoint the house in which Data was supposedly currently living, and where Poppy might possibly be. At least Jezza fervently hoped they were going to find her there. The alternative didn't bear thinking about.

'Was there anything, anything at all, which Poppy ever

mentioned to you which might give us a clue to which house it was? Think, please.'

'The front door's black and glossy,' she said. 'She likes that. Classy, she calls it, and a bit Goth.'

'Yes, thanks, but there's a lot of glossy black doors. There must be something else you can remember.'

'She was more interested in boasting about what she and Data get up to inside. We're bezzy mates. We tell each other stuff like that.'

'Marina, please,' Jezza told her, through gritted teeth. 'Poppy could be in danger and we're trying to keep her safe. Anything else at all you can remember. Anything.'

'Oh, I know. One of them trees, she said. I don't know what you call them, she didn't know either. But they have like spiky stuff instead of leaves. No way you could climb them. They'd cut you to pieces.'

Jezza couldn't resist a jubilant air punch as she said, 'Yes! Fabulous, thanks, Marina. It's a monkey puzzle tree, and I'm looking at one right now.'

She called up all the officers helping in the search and steered them towards a house they'd passed several times already, with no sign of life inside.

'We don't have a warrant so I'll have to wing it a bit,' she told them. 'I need some of you round the back, in case anyone tries to leg it, and a couple of you at the front door with me. We'll just keep knocking until we get an answer. If we don't, I'll have to come up with a Plan B.

'Just please be careful, everyone. I'm hoping it will be just Data and Poppy in there, but Data has some pretty nasty friends, so let's not take any risks.'

There was no knocker nor functioning bell on the door and Jezza nearly skinned her knuckles with her repeated knocking. She also kept shouting through the letterbox.

'Poppy? Poppy Usher? This is the police, Poppy. Don't be afraid, I'm not here to arrest you. I just need to make sure that you're safe. Can you at least come downstairs and talk to me, please?

'Poppy, we have your mum, and your dad, in safekeeping but we're all worried about your safety. Can you please come down and show yourself? I promise you I won't arrest you for anything, but I do need to make sure you're safe. And I'm not going away until I see you. If necessary, I'll get the door broken down. It's up to you.'

She spoke quietly to the officers from Uniform while she waited for a reaction.

'The minute she appears, if she does, you shove that door open and you get in there to look for Data. IC4 male, early twenties, wanted for supplying Class A drugs, for one thing.'

She was just about to start thumping on the door once more when it opened a crack and a young girl's face peered out at them from a cloud of bed hair. She looked younger than her actual age, fragile, and very scared.

'I'm Poppy Usher. What's happened? Why have you got my mum and dad?'

* * *

Ted had followed the route taken by the ambulance carrying Usher straight to Stepping Hill Hospital. He'd come back on blues and twos in his service vehicle as soon as he'd heard the news about him. The traffic chaos following the incident had delayed the ambulance's arrival and it had taken the paramedics some time to get Usher stabilised at the scene before transferring him.

Ted had been torn between wanting to get Jo's injury seen to as soon as possible, and needing to know Usher's condition.

He took Jo with him in the car as soon as Usher was loaded and the ambulance was on its way, blue lights flashing, the odd blast of the sirens when needed.

Jo, in the car with Ted, was showing increasing signs of

confusion from his injury, in between remorse and anxiety about what had happened.

'I honestly didn't consider him a flight risk, Ted. Quite the opposite. He was getting more withdrawn by the minute. I was going to arrange for psych evaluation as soon as we'd got him booked in.

'I certainly didn't consider him a suicide risk, or I would have requested back-up to transfer him inside from the car.'

'Is that what you think it was? An attempt to kill himself? Not just panic to run away, and not seeing the vehicle coming.'

'I genuinely don't know. I couldn't swear to it. Everything was a blur and it's all a bit mixed up in my memory. I was groggy from where he nutted me. Eyes running, nose streaming. I honestly don't know if he was trying to kill himself, or if he was just running blind, trying to go off and find Poppy himself because I hadn't been able to tell him that she was in safe custody.

'I should have forgotten my beliefs and lied to him that she was safe. Him not knowing was probably what made him run like that. I'm sorry I let it happen, Ted. I should have been more on the ball.'

'Don't worry about it, Jo. Time for an inquest into what went wrong when you've got yourself sorted out, and we've found out what's going to happen with Usher. But bear in mind that if he was determined to do away with himself, you'd have been hard-pressed to stop him. Anyone would.'

There was the usual seemingly interminable wait to be seen in the hospital's busy A&E department. Eventually Jo was checked over, pronounced fit for discharge, but told to take a couple of days off work and given a list of concussion symptoms to watch out for. Ted put him in a taxi, reassuring him once more, then headed back to wait for news.

He got a call from Jezza as he was walking back inside and paused by the entrance to listen to her tell him that Poppy had been found safe and was being taken to be with her mother, while Data, who had been found inside the same property with Class A drugs on him, had been arrested and taken to Stockport.

Finally, after seemingly endless hanging about, Ted was allowed to see Dave Usher. He'd been told he was on life support and the prognosis was not good. He'd explained that he wanted to tell him personally that his daughter was safe.

'I can't guarantee he will hear or understand anything of what you say to him,' the consultant dealing with the case had told him. 'However, there is always a chance that he might, on some level, and I'm sure news like that would be important to him.'

Dave Usher certainly didn't look like a man who was about to sit up in bed and engage in conversation with him any time soon. He was surrounded by machines which seemed to be doing everything for him, including breathing.

Ted stood as close as he dared to the bed, and put out a tentative hand towards one of Usher's. A nurse saw his gesture and nodded to him that it was all right to touch him.

'Dave, it's Ted Darling. I don't know if you can hear me but I wanted to tell you myself. Poppy's been found, safe. She's with your wife now. No one can get at her again. And we've got the rest of the gang too. It's all over, Dave.'

There was a brief blip on the monitor. Then it flat-lined.

Medical staff were hurrying to the bedside, waving Ted away.

He knew, though, instinctively. Dave Usher was dead. He'd been hanging on to make sure his daughter was safe, but he had no desire to linger after that. He knew exactly what would happen to a bent copper like himself in prison.

He simply had nothing left to live for.

Chapter Thirty-four

DS Ian Bradley had been brought from the safe house to the Stockport station for a further debrief from Ted and Sammy. Ted kept the armed officer with him until Bradley was safe inside the nick then stood him down. They were using one of the interview rooms so that once again everything could be recorded.

Ted began with the news of DI Usher's death. Bradley looked genuinely shocked.

'I'm sorry to hear that. I really am. Dave was a good officer, until he went rogue. A bloody good one. We had our moments of disagreeing, of course, and he could be a bit of a tw..,' he stopped himself just in time, looking at the superintendent '... a bit of a pain in the backside. That's bosses for you. That's their job. But he didn't deserve to end up like this.'

He looked from one to the other as he went on, 'I hope this is enough to convince you that I'm not, and never was, the mole. So when can I go back to work?'

'If your ears have been burning, DS Bradley, that's because I've been discussing you at length with the powers that be. We now accept that you weren't the informant, and that it was your preliminary work which pointed us in the right direction. That's a feather in your cap.'

Bradley was looking at her, his expression shrewd.

'First the carrot. So now you're going to hit me with the stick. And I'm not going to like it. Am I right?'

Ted left Sammy to deliver the news. She was the senior officer, and although Bradley might not like it, it meant he kept his job and stayed with his old team.

'You probably can't continue undercover in the same area, certainly not for the time being. Your appearance has changed too much, for one thing. You'd have to build up a whole new cover and that could take time.'

Bradley was already making a face. 'I'm not really the pen-pusher type.'

'But you do have valuable skills in the field. Which is why the DCS has suggested that for now you're put on to training potential undercover officers, as well as handling those already in that role, including those from DI Usher's list.

'The team is going to need a new DI, of course, but I've not yet heard who it's likely to be. So what do you say?'

Bradley was astute. He'd been in the job long enough to know when he had no real choice. He nodded his head in slow agreement.

'Do you need a lift somewhere?' Ted asked him as he showed him out. He'd filled him in briefly on where the case was up to as they walked to the doors together.

'My car is hopefully still in the lay-by where you kid-napped me,' Bradley told him with a grin. 'As long as it's not been robbed, although it wasn't much of a car. I'll go and see if I can find it.'

He held out a hand to shake Ted's.

'It's been interesting working with you, Ted. You can be a devious bastard when you need to, d'you know that? But I'm glad you got the Big Man. Have you enough to hold him?'

'The search of the property has barely begun and we have plenty already. Drugs, weapons, dodgy-looking accounting, illegal immigrant employees, you name it. He's not going any-where in a hurry. We'll need specialists to go through all of his affairs. It looks initially as if he's been hiding the drugs busi-ness behind legitimate ones. One of my former officers, Sal Ahmed, is now with Fraud so he'll be coming on board to help with all of that.

'I'm waiting on fingerprints and DNA from the two gunman who were arrested on site, and from the one shot dead, to see if there's any proven link between any of them and our dead boy, Noah Brooks. I hope so. I'd like to get someone for that. And one of the bodyguards arrested at the house is left-handed, so there's just a chance, albeit a slim one, that he could have been one of those involved in the killing of Noah Brooks.'

'And will you be able to track down the rest of the vermin in the gang? What about that little shit Data? Will he give up any useful information, assuming he knows any?'

'Not easily, I don't imagine. But I'm hoping that Sal will dig out other addresses for us. Properties the Big Man bought and put through his legitimate company books, so we might find some of his men still living in them, not yet fled the country.

'As well as that, another of my officers, DC Ellis, has found us a supplier who may well be connected to the same gang, so we're setting up another operation to reel him in to see where that leads us. We needed to get the raid done first, but that op is underway now and it might lead us somewhere.

'As far as Data is concerned, I honestly have no idea. He appears to display traits of antisocial personality disorder. He seems to show no understanding that what he does is wrong on so many levels. He's shown no signs of any guilt for any of his actions at all. And as one of my officers has already pointed out, the prospect of what lies in store for a good looking young man like him in prison doesn't seem to bother him in the least. I wouldn't be surprised if he's already thinking about how he can profit from his looks when he's inside.'

'A right charmer then, eh?' Bradley said dryly. 'Well, good luck with it all, and keep me posted, if you'd be so kind.'

Then he turned and was gone. Ted went back upstairs. Sammy had told him to go and find her in her office when he'd seen Bradley on his way. He was certain this could be the moment of reckoning, when he had to explain himself for his actions and for going in before he'd had the All Clear from the Firearms Commander.

She looked serious, for once, and didn't offer or request a brew. She did, at least, invite him to sit down.

'I expect your ears have been burning too, Ted, because your name also came up in discussions.'

'Ahh,' Ted said. He'd thought as much.

'Like I've told you, your admin is exemplary. I genuinely can't fault it. I'd heard on the grapevine that you could occasionally play the caped superhero and go wading in where others fear to tread. I confess I hadn't believed it. Until I had the Firearms Commander bending my ear about what happened. Although why he thinks I would have any control over you I don't know.

'So, explain yourself. What the hell happened and where was the risk assessment?'

'It was a split-second decision. I judged that I had the necessary weapons skills and training to disarm a suspect with minimal risk. Far less than would have been the case with Firearms, because of the close proximity of a civilian who was not, at that moment, a suspect.'

She studied him in fascination. Then she shook her head in apparent disbelief.

'Well, now I know why you write such good reports. You seem to have an answer for everything. So write me a detailed report on your actions, Chief Inspector,' she said, with heavy emphasis on his rank, 'and let me have it by end of play today without fail.'

'Ma'am,' Ted took his cue on formality from her.

'Right, that's your hand smacked, so now let's come on to the important stuff. You're being demoted.'

She saw the surprise on his face and laughed. A wicked sound.

'Sorry, that was my little joke. What we've actually been talking about is a radical reshuffle, and it is, of course, entirely dependent on your agreement. Starting with Ashton.

'We both know that team needs a strong hand on the tiller and hasn't currently got one. The latest update on Judy Collier is not good news. It's looking less likely than ever that she'll be able to return at all. So they need a DI.

'Now, I'm very taken with your Jo Rodriguez. And not just because he tried to chat me up. He's quietly efficient. A steady influence. So here's the plan. And the rest of it means he won't need to be based here, just to come back as needed.

'Firstly, DI Rodriguez moves to Ashton to be in charge there and knock them all into some sort of shape. Meanwhile you resume your old active role here.

'You're good behind a desk. There's no denying that. But you're better in the thick of it as an SIO. You step down as Head of Serious Crime and become Deputy. To me. We both know there's no change to salary or anything, and we can easily get the smart sign on your door changed to reflect the different status. Because yes, you can have your old office back. I'm moving downstairs into Deb Caldwell's former domain while she moves up to the top floor as befits the Deputy Divisional Commander.

'What do you say, Ted? Some might see it as a backward step, career-wise. But I somehow don't think you're that type. You do the exciting stuff - but no more pissing off Firearms Commanders, or anyone else - and leave me to balance the books.

'Which means, of course, you stick with this case right through to the end, and make sure you get us some good convictions on it.

'And while I think about it, what's the situation with the supposedly blind dwarf? Have you checked and is he really blind? We don't want a case to go tits up because we've not made proper provision for a disabled suspect.'

'One of the first things we did when he was brought in. He's been seen by the doctor who can find no evidence of any visual impairment at all. We've asked for his medical records, for belt and braces. I'm trying to anticipate defence objections and head them off at the pass.'

'So what d'you say? Are you happy to go back to the sharp end? If you do, that would nicely free up Jo to go to Ashton, ready to rush back here any time you need his services.'

'It sounds good to me,' Ted told her, raising another chuckle from her.

'That's the first time I've known anyone happy to step back from a promotion,' she told him.

'We haven't started shuffling offices yet, pending your decision. But I'll let Debs know you said yes and she can deploy her minions to make it all happen in short order.

'That leaves an empty seat in with your DS Hallam. It's entirely up to you, but you might like to think of putting your other DS in there, make it a sergeants' office.

'Oh, and I take it you want to hang on to Gina Shaw? She really can't go back to Drugs for the foreseeable and she seems to have settled in well here.

'Right, for now, I'll let you get on with your current case.'

That was clearly the signal to give him his marching orders. Ted felt his head spinning with it all as he went back downstairs to the MIR for an update.

He paused before going in to take out his phone and call Trev.

'I'm hoping to get to judo, at least, tonight, if not self-defence. D'you fancy going for a bite to eat afterwards? Just the two of us? Nothing fancy, maybe just a pub.'

'That sounds good. Are we celebrating something? All the baddies are going to plead guilty, saving you all a load of work?'

'We are celebrating, in a sense,' he told him. 'I've been demoted.'

Trev laughed. 'Ted, you strange person, it's customary to celebrate a promotion and be gutted about being reduced in rank. D'you mean you're not a DCI any more, for some reason?'

'Oh, I'm keeping my rank. I've just had a sideways step to Deputy Head of Serious Crime and Sammy is taking over as Head. It suits me better, but you might not like it. It means I'm escaping from behind a desk and going back to the sharp end a bit more. Do you mind?'

Trev's hesitation was only for a fraction of a second, but Ted heard it.

'If it's what you want, and if you promise to take care then it's fine by me.'

'Thank you. I'll try not to be late back. Oh, and I intend to take the weekend off. We should be at a stage where I can do that. So think of somewhere you'd like to go. Only not too far away, in case I get called back. I'm afraid I'm going back to that being a distinct possibility.'

* * *

'Well, of course I'd love to come and watch you compete. Ted's off this weekend, so I don't expect he can get another weekend off on the trot. But if it's possible, I'll be there. Then I can bore you rigid with all the photos I took of my baby god-daughter, who is simply the cutest thing you have ever seen.'

Trev was on the phone to his sister, Siobhan Eirian, as Ted drove. They were heading down to Wales to see Annie and to find out how the house purchase was progressing. Trev was looking forward to planning interior decorating and choosing curtain fabric. Ted found himself, surprisingly, thinking of quiet walks with Cariad, while Trev and Annie were deciding on colour schemes.

'I don't think I'm quite ready for cosy chats in public with Sir Gethin just yet, but I promise to behave myself if I happen to run into him. I take it Her Ladyship won't be there, as it's not Badminton or Chatsworth?' Trev continued.

Their mother, Lady Armstrong, did not share the family

love of horses. She attended few events to watch her daughter compete, and then only in the right places in which to be seen.

'Right, well, we're on our way down to Wales to see Annie, so I'll give you a call sometime over the weekend. And behave yourself!'

'Is she all right?' Ted asked him. 'And has she decided on her sexuality yet?'

'She's as fickle as I am. It's in the genes, clearly. She currently thinks she might be bi. But enough of my kid sister. Let's forget about everyone and everything else, except Annie, of course, and have a nice break and a bit of fun.

'I hope you've made it clear that you're off duty this weekend? Out of contact? Not to be bothered, no matter what? Definitely no policing allowed for you until Monday morning.'

Ted was, as ever, obeying the speed limits. As they rounded a bend in a quiet part of mid-Wales, he took his foot off the accelerator and changed down through the gears to slow the car's progress.

There was a police vehicle parked at the side of the road, a Traffic car, with blue lights going and an officer standing near it, one hand raised in a halting gesture.

Trev was laughing hysterically as Ted lowered the driver's window and the officer leaned closer to speak to him.

'Good evening, sir. This is just a routine check. Would you mind showing me your licence and documentation, and telling me your destination and the reason for your journey?'

The End

Made in the USA
Coppell, TX
10 March 2021